Journey to a Woman

Journey to
a Woman

Ann Bannon

CLEIS
PRESS

Published in the United States by Cleis Press Inc.,
P.O. Box 14684, San Francisco, California 94114.
Printed in the United States.
Cover design: Scott Idleman
Text design: Karen Quigg
Cleis Press logo art: Juana Alicia
10 9 8 7 6 5 4 3 2 1

ISBN: 0-930044-37-1

Introduction

I. Foreword/Forward

When these stories of lesbian love were forged nearly half a century ago, I thought—I *knew*—that I was writing ephemeral literature for a casual audience. That was what was being asked of me, and what I tried to do. I had no fine ideas of recording the saga of a community, nor that these stories would come to have real sociological or historical value. Quite truly, I had no thought that I was preserving a slice of GLBT history that would help to form the perceptions of the era for succeeding generations. I thought I had been given the opportunity to write popular throwaway tales for an avid, if fleeting audience, and that was quite enough. I would write them the very best I could, understanding from the beginning that the first one would be forgotten even as the second was being written. I had not the slimmest sliver of recognition that what I was really given was the opportunity to speak for my generation of young gay and lesbian people.

It is interesting to speculate as to whether or not such knowledge would have destroyed these books. It would have made them more carefully crafted, but also immeasurably more cautious. It very likely would have made them self-conscious and defensive, as well. Instead, they are fully flawed and full of life. It's a trade off, and on the whole, perhaps for the best. All I can say now to the wonderful young people who power our amazing community is, "Thank you for caring about these stories. Take what you can, learn what you can, and know that they flowed uncensored from the imagination of a girl in her twenties, sitting alone by a type-writer and dreaming up a life she wanted to share with you. Bless you for being there to read about it."

When it was suggested to me that I write introductions to most of the new Cleis Press editions of my books, it sent me back to reread the original stories. It also propelled me back in time. It had been over twenty years, dating to the Naiad editions of the early 1980s, since I had immersed myself in them. And twenty-five years before *that* when the actual writing had been accomplished.

Perusing my novels again was a trip in a time machine, an exercise both embarrassing and exhilarating. How very young I was! How deep those feelings ran! And how startlingly sparse was my worldly knowledge. All of the books were completed and in print before I was thirty years old. And now in my sixties, I resisted going back to visit them again. But the rereading was essential. As George Santayana is supposed to have said, "How do I know what I think till I see what I said?"

As I reacquainted myself with my authorial life and times, several themes seemed to emerge and to run like threads through all of the books. There is not room to analyze all of them here, but one or two stand out. The first is the emotional development and personality portraits of the characters themselves; the sheer punch of the interior drama, that so fascinated me. I wanted to follow them and discover how the characters connected to one another, why they chose the partners they did. The other was the symbolic use of liquor and cigarettes as the banners of libera-tion. I'd like to look at these themes as they apply to *Journey to a Woman*.

II. Personality Portraits

Not everybody likes to travel, but almost everybody loves a jour-ney of self-discovery, especially if it leads to the uplands of love. This book is an odyssey from sorrow to sunshine; from the drama and heartache of breakup to the astonishment of passion. If the preceding book, *Women in the Shadows*, was a story of breaking away from smothering relationships and claiming the right to define yourself (even if you got it wrong, be it said!), *Journey to a Woman* is more about achieving youthful maturity, coming to terms with who you really are. It's about what happens to three strong, beautiful women when one of them—Beth—rediscovers her passion for another—Laura—only to fall headlong into the arms of the third—Beebo Brinker herself.

When I first started writing these books, I was a woman in love—not just with a few individuals, but with a whole community, the entire world full of wonderful women and endearing gay men. I idealized them all. I was in love with being in love with them. They could do no wrong in my eyes. But time went by. I listened, I watched and learned. I was also doing my own growing up and having to accept, book by book, that people aren't perfect—fascinating and lovable but not flawless. I had to include myself in that "not-flawless" category, too.

People have asked if I am the Beth in these stories. I am reminded of the response Gustave Flaubert gave when he was asked the identity of Madame Bovary. "Madame Bovary," he replied calmly, "is me. *Madame Bovary, c'est moi.*" The French have been scratching their heads and repeating the phrase ever since. But Flaubert had hit on something. For any writer, all of our various characters are "us" when we create them. I have always responded that Beth was based, physically and socially at least, on a former sorority roommate who inspired lust in many hearts, more than one of them womanly. That said, however, perhaps it is fair to allow that there is a lot of me in Beth, and a lot of her problems are the ones I was wrestling with in my twenties, especially the awkward relationships, skewed by chaotic, unsorted emotions. Beth was a woman who needed women, heart and soul, and didn't know how to give herself permission to reach out to them. We differed most in two ways: she spoke out to her husband about her fears and misgivings while I swallowed mine. And she was dubious about her feelings for her children while I was passionately attached to mine.

So Beth was vulnerable when the lovely but dangerous and fatally wounded Vega crossed her path. We have all had the experience she had: a first breathtaking glimpse of a bewitchingly beautiful human being, and perhaps even the pleasant shock of seeing a responsive spark in that person's eyes. But after you bring them home you find something scary under the irreproachable veneer. They are hurt and want to hurt someone back; they need you to fix them, while you need them for love. They don't have it to give, and you can't supply the fix. It's a match made in purgatory. What to do? This is where you learn fast how rocky saying goodbye can be.

There was a woman living near me in Southern California who served as the original of Vega Purvis. She was handsome, sleek and chic, witty, and, in Edward Arlington Robinson's apposite phrase, "imperially slim." She could be endearingly funny about her physical ills, in a way that made you want to cuddle and comfort her. It was Vega herself who described her abdominal scars as resembling a ball of yarn tangled up by a kitten. But she carried a freight load of psychological damage everywhere with her, and it gave her a mercurial temperament. I could never wait to spend time with her, and never wait to get away home.

My fictional Vega was also a woman whose prejudices reflected almost perfectly those of her homophobic family, and yet who broke out of that box from time to time. Her forays were thrilling, risky, and ultimately disastrous, as Beth discovered. But they do bespeak the strength of that drive to find and possess and yes, love, one of your own. And always, in that era and even now, there were perplexed and resistant men hovering in the background—impatient husbands or brothers or uncles, wondering why their influence doesn't sweep away such treacherous notions from their women's heads.

Some women take refuge behind a man, as Laura did, and some men behind a woman, as did Jack Mann in this tale. Laura never gave up her delight in women, and they remained the romantic joy of her life. But she wanted children and so did her supportive and affectionate best gay friend, Jack. They made common cause to provide a home for their child and a facade of respectability each for the other, a sort of honorable camouflage to shield them from the ostracism of their social circle.

Knowing none of this, and running almost as much from Vega as Charlie, Beth arrives in New York obsessed with tracking Laura to earth and virtually devouring her with the resurgent sexual excitement she thought she had forever abandoned with her marriage. And when, in her search, she runs into the provocative and manipulative writer, Nina Spicer, who leads her to Beebo Brinker, the stage is set for a fiery intersection of different personalities, conflicts, and clashing needs. And ultimately, of course, for resolution in love. (These *were* the pulps, after all!)

III. The Partying

So many of us in that tough age, whatever our social class, grew up thinking we had to be what our parents and society told us to be: "nice girls," "good girls." We had no notion that we could give ourselves permission to "transgress." Yes, there was too much booze and too much angst. But you know what? We romanticized it all. We really thought that since we couldn't give ourselves permission to be who we were, the liquor could. At the very least, it relaxed the strictures against marginalized social roles. It let us look at and think about the women we suspected we might truly be with affection, not socially mandated contempt. It was a conspiratorial act when a bunch of handsome, adventurous young women sat down to share a beer and cigarettes. But more than that, we were carrying a flag handed off from our mothers, both straight and gay, claiming autonomy and equality for women. That's what made the brew and the smokes so appealing. They had a significance for us beyond the mere conviviality they fostered.

Those of us who were young in the 1950s and 1960s have bright memories of mothers who, in their turn, were the "flappers" of the 1920s: the pert girls in the cloche hats, growing up in a prosperous era, flattening their breasts, wearing their hair in "boyish bobs," and raising their skirts above their knees. The Great War to end all wars was over and the world was throwing a decade-long party. For the first time, women were starting to claim the theretofore masculine privileges of smoking and drinking. It was a way of demanding parity with men, of trying to be taken seriously by donning the trappings of the ruling class. Many of them were playing at this game, but a significant few took it seriously.

And the new advertisements were seductive. A man lights a Chesterfield and his woman companion gazes into the curling smoke. "Blow some my way," she says. Murad brand, with a not very subtle nod to the ladies, adopts the slogan, "Be Nonchalant— light a Murad." And here's the one that got so many women: "Reach for a Lucky instead of a sweet."

But shockingly, the Great War and the Great Prosperity were followed by the Great Depression. Women were thrust back into their traditional routines of *kinder, küche, kirche.* In their millions, they broke out the white ruffled aprons and little wash dresses and rediscovered the joys of floor wax and tuna casseroles. Still, they could not forget the brief, exhilarating fling with freedom of a sort. When Prohibition ended in the early 1930s, many young women participated enthusiastically in the afternoon "cocktail hour," which seems to have entirely replaced the hour for high tea. One expanded one's wardrobe to include a semi-formal outfit for late afternoons that became known as a "cocktail dress." That useful article of furniture, the once-and-future "coffee table," became the "cocktail table." Fashionable young women drank highballs or bourbon on the rocks, right alongside their mates.

If the men bought the booze, women could share a "wee drop of the creature," too. My own mother, preparing for her second wedding in 1934, was given that trendiest of bridal parties, a "liquor shower," including highball glasses, engraved pewter liquor labels on little chains, glass swizzle sticks, and her own personal hammered silver flask, in case she got chilly at a football game. It was the height of young, trendy 1930s urbanity, in the grand style of the charmingly bibulous Nick and Nora Charles— "The Thin Man" and his delectable mate.

When World War II intruded on our lives, for many women, and aside from genuine hardships and losses, it truly was a glimpse of a brave new world. They came out of that experience more changed than the surface serenity and convention of the 1950s would suggest. Cigarettes and liquor had been offered everywhere and to everyone during the war; they were blended in the memory with recreation, rest, relief from stress and fatigue, and just plain fun. Freedom to smoke and drink without the intermediary of a protective male became associated at last, for better or for worse, with a defiance of past constraints on women's lives. It became, in short, an outward show of independence.

When I arrived in Greenwich Village in the late 1950s, this perception was firmly entrenched and I did not think to question it. There were wonderful women everywhere I looked, and many intriguing gay men. When they gathered to socialize at a Village pub, they enjoyed a smoke, they took a drink, they created a charmed circle. If you wanted to join them, to fit in, you did as they did. If you went a little over the top, they picked you up, dusted you off, spared you the sermons, and took you home to sleep it off on their sofas. You, in time, returned the favor as needed. It was another form of bonding, of "us against the world."

But a time does come in one's life when it is prudent to step back from all that seemed fully pellucid in the first enchantment of one's twenties; a time to take stock and a time to question. I am reminded of Max Ehrmann's wise and compelling advice: "Take kindly the counsel of the years, gracefully surrendering the things of youth." ("Desiderata," 1927). I did, as in good time and with luck, we all must. Finally, for all those who press reproach without understanding, this is just to say how it was for so many of us back then.

IV. Afterword/Afterward

No, I didn't become an alcoholic. I even stopped smoking in my early twenties and today drink only the occasional, if welcome, glass of wine. And I can reassure you that Beebo and Beth, at the end of *Journey to a Woman*, made it out happy and intact. How do I know this? Because I know where they are now: sitting on the pages of a manuscript written some years ago and awaiting resurrection and revision. Beth went through a sort of fever dream in extricating herself from her marriage and fashioning a life for herself that differed greatly from the one imagined by a younger Beth in her undergraduate days. It's often in such a fire that we forge and purify our true identities, and that's what her journey was all about. Parts of the personal odyssey are daunting and parts of it are brilliantly beautiful, and both reveal us to ourselves as no other experience could. Not everyone has the stomach to take this sort of interior trip. If it were easy, wouldn't everyone do it? But for survivors, it brings the gift of deeper self-knowledge and a capacity for sweeter and more selfless love of others.

And so, we come to the endpoint in this story. Beth at last meets Beebo, and all sorts of good things start to happen. She has fought her way through the tough stuff and earned the joy, and so, in the earlier tales, had Beebo. I should have written a novel then that pursued them into their life together. Now, I will.

Ann Bannon
Sacramento, California
September 2002

Chapter One

SHE LAY IN THE DARK AND CRIED. SHE LAY CLOSE AND WARM IN her husband's arms while their breath slowed to normal and their hearts quieted together and she wept silently at his sigh of relief. She had learned to cry without making a sound. It had taken a while but she had had plenty of opportunities to learn. If he caught her crying there was always a terrible scene. He started out by questioning her love and ended by questioning his own manhood.

"Goddamn it, Beth!" he had cried to her once, when they had been married only two months, "If I'm doing it wrong, *tell* me! How do I know what you want me to do if you don't tell me? A woman isn't like a man. I can't tell if it's any good for you or not."

He was blaming her for his own faults of love she thought, and, stung, she snapped back, "What am I supposed to do, give you a play-by-play analysis? Can't you figure it out for yourself, Charlie? You did well enough before we were married."

"So did you, before we were married," he flung at her. He got out of bed, lighted a cigarette in the dark, and sat down on the floor. They could not afford chairs yet, and he didn't want to share the bed with her for a few minutes. Not until the anger wore off.

"Beth, you've got it just backwards," he said. "Most girls can't enjoy it until they're married. Their consciences hurt, or something. They're afraid they'll get pregnant. But not you. Not Backwards Beth. The minute we get married it's no fun anymore. Does love have to be immoral or illegal before you can enjoy it, honey?"

Insulted, she turned her back to him and pulled the covers over her disappointed body. She was afraid to think of what he had

1

just said. It had too much the shape of truth and she had had to work very hard to forget it completely. Charlie finished his cigarette and climbed gingerly back into his place in bed, more chilled by his wife's behavior than the night vapors.

It had been nine years since the first such quarrel. There had been others, but Beth had learned fast to hide the tears of frustration. True to her contrary nature, there were times when she loved Charlie—if love can be an on-again, off-again affair. And sometimes, when she didn't expect it, desire sneaked up on her and made the moments in his arms unbearably lovely, the way they had been in college. But that was only sometimes, and sometimes was not enough.

On this night, like so many others, she got up after he had fallen back to sleep and went into the bathroom and washed herself. It comforted her obscurely to tidy herself up this way. And when she went back to bed, she dreamed. Beth dreamed often and vividly.

But tonight it wasn't a dream like any other. She dreamed of Laura. Just Laura, sitting on the studio couch of the room they had shared in college, looking at Beth and smiling. Laura with her long light hair and periwinkle eyes. Laura, who didn't know herself until Beth discovered her. Laura, who loved her and who had disappeared from her life like frost from a spring lawn, and who never came back.

That was all. Beth spoke her name, trying to make her answer and explain herself, but Laura only sat and smiled. Beth repeated the name until suddenly she wakened and pressed a hand over her mouth. Had she spoken aloud? But Charlie slumbered undisturbed and she relaxed again, leaning back on her pillow and staring at the dark ceiling.

I haven't even thought of her for months, she pondered. *How strange. It's been years since I dreamed of her. I'd half forgotten. I wonder how she is...where she is. In Chicago with her father, I suppose. He always ruled her life like a tyrant. She wouldn't have married, of course.*

In the morning she told Charlie, "I dreamed of Laura last night."

2

"Oh?" He looked up from the financial page of the paper. He spoke casually enough, although he stiffened inwardly. Charlie remembered Laura, too. A man does not easily forget a rival and for a few months, many years ago, when they were all in college, that was what Laura had been. A strange cool girl she was, with a capacity for violent love that Beth had almost accidentally roused. It had only lasted a short while—the space of a semester—and for Beth it had not seemed serious, for she was falling in love with Charlie at the time, and Charlie won her handily. That was when Laura had disappeared.

Beth and Charlie had talked it over, had even tried to help Laura. There was little about the curious affair that Charlie didn't know; little that he couldn't forgive. And, it should be added, little about it that he understood.

When he and Beth married he was confident that she would forget it, and to a large extent she had. At first, anyway. She liked men, she was married to one. She had children now and a stable home. Most important in Charlie's eyes, she had him. And besides, she was a sensible girl. When Laura dropped out of Beth's life physically, Charlie had faith that she would drop out emotionally as well.

Beth had rarely mentioned Laura over the years, and now, when she spoke of her dream at the breakfast table, it was the first time Charlie had even thought of Laura in over two years. So he was startled, but he didn't want it to show.

"What was the dream?" he asked.

"Not much. Just Laura, sitting there."

"Where?"

"That room we had on the third floor at the Alpha Beta house."

"That's all?"

"That's all. Polly, damn it, don't wipe your fingers on your dress!" Her four-year-old daughter grabbed a paper napkin guiltily.

"Don't swear at the kids, honey," Charlie said mildly.

"Don't scold me in front of them," she said.

3

He sighed, feeling a quick hot frustration, a sensation that was much too common for comfort these days, and picked up the paper again. "What else about Laura?" he said.

"Nothing else. Silly dream."

But it haunted her. And Charlie had a feeling there was more to it than she told him. He kept his eyes on the paper another five minutes and then rose from the table. "Got to get going," he said. He kissed his two children goodbye and then came around the table behind Beth.

" 'Bye, honey," he said into her ear, and blew into it gently.

"Have a good day," she said absently.

He wished gloomily that she would see him to the door.

"Daddy, when you get home will you make me a kite?" Skipper said suddenly. He was five, just a year older than his sister, and he looked very much like Beth.

"Sure," Charlie said, still looking at the short dark curls on the back of his wife's head. He stroked her neck with his finger.

"Yay!" Skipper cried.

Beth squirmed slightly, irritated by Charlie's wordless loneliness and a little ashamed of herself. Charlie left her finally and went toward the front door, slipping into his suit coat as he went. Beth felt his gaze on her and glanced up suddenly with a little line of annoyance between her eyes.

"Something wrong?" she said.

"No. What are you doing today?"

"I'm flying to Paris," she said sarcastically. "What else? Want to come?"

"Sure." He grinned and she softened a little. He was handsome, in a lopsided way, with his big grin and his fine eyes. The kids set up a clamor. "Can I come too? Can I come too, Mommy?"

And when Charlie went out the door he heard her shout at them in that voice that scared him, that voice with the edge of hysteria in it, "Oh, for God's sake! Oh, shut up! Honest to God, you kids are driving me insane!"

4

And he knew she would slam something down on the table to underline her words—a jam jar or a piece of tableware, anything handy.

He drove off to work with a worried face.

Chapter Two

BETH LOVED HER KIDS THE WAY SHE LOVED CHARLIE: AT A distance. It was a real love but it couldn't be crowded. She had no patience with intimacy. The hardest years of her life had been when the two babies arrived within eleven months of each other. One was bad enough, but two! Both in diapers, both screaming and streaming at both ends. Both colicky, both finicky eaters.

Beth was completely unprepared, almost helpless with a screaming nervousness that put both Charlie and the kids on edge. She never quite recovered from her resentment. A few years later, when the worst was over, she began to wonder if her quick awful temper and desperation had made the children as nervous as they were. She blamed herself bitterly sometimes. But then she wondered how it could have happened any other way.

But when Polly shut herself in a closet and cried all afternoon, or Skipper threw a tantrum and swore at her in her own words, or when Charlie sulked in angry silence for days on end after a quarrel, she began to wonder again, to accuse herself, to look wildly around her for excuses, for escape.

Beth had just one friend that she saw with any regularity, and that was the wife of Charlie's business partner. Her name was Jean Purvis, and she and Beth bowled together on a team. Beth had been searching for ways to get out of it since she had started it. Bowling bored her and so did Jean. But you couldn't help liking the girl.

Jean Purvis was a good-hearted person, a natural blonde with a tendency to plumpness against which she pitted a wavering will power. She had two expressions: a little smile and a big smile. At first Beth envied her sunny nature, but after a while it got on her nerves.

She must have had days like other people, Beth thought. *She must get mad at her husband once in a while.*

But if Jean ever did it never showed and her eternal smile made Beth feel guilty. It was like an unspoken reproach of Beth's sudden wild explosions and cloudy moods, and it made her resent Jean; it made her jealous and contemptuous all at once.

Jean Purvis and her husband Cleve were the only people that Beth and Charlie knew when they first moved to California. Cleve and Charlie were business partners now, manufacturing toys, and it had been Cleve's drum-beating letters that encouraged Charlie to give up his law apprenticeship and move to the West Coast.

Beth reacted angrily at first. "I like the East!" she had exclaimed. "What do I know about California? Everybody in the country is headed for California. It'll be so crowded out there pretty soon they won't have room for the damn palm trees."

"Cleve has a good start in business," Charlie said.

"Charlie, what in God's name do you know about making toys? I'd be glad if you'd make one decent slingshot for Skipper and call it quits," she told him.

But his stubborn head was already full of ideas. "One craze, one big hit—we'd strike it rich," he said. "One Hula Hoop, one coonskin cap, something like that."

"You sit there like a grinning happy idiot ready to throw your whole career, your whole education, out the window, because your old fraternity buddy is making plastic popguns out in Pasadena and he says to come on out," Beth cried, furious. "I don't trust that Cleve Purvis anyway, from what I've heard about him. You always said he was a heavy drinker."

But he had made his mind up, and with Charlie that was the same as doing a thing. He could not be moved.

Charlie left Beth and the two babies in Chicago with her uncle and aunt while he went out to Pasadena to join Cleve and find a place to live.

Beth loved it. Her Uncle John was fond of spoiling her. Beth was his daughter by proxy; he had no children of his own. She had been dumped in his lap, sobbing and runny nosed and skinny at eight years, when her parents were killed. Miraculously, she had learned to love him and he returned her love. With Aunt Elsa it was all a matter of keeping up good manners, and she was automatically friendly.

For four months Beth slept and ate and lazed around the house. It was delicious to be waited on, to have civilized cocktails in the afternoon, to let somebody else pick Polly up when the colic got her. To go out for whole evenings of food and glittering entertainment and know there were a dozen capable baby-sitters at home. Beth refused to join her husband in California until she threw him into a rage.

She realized with something like a shock that she didn't miss Charlie's love-making at all. She missed *Charlie,* in a sort of pleasant blurry way, and she loved to talk about him over a cold whiskey and water, laughing gently at the faults that drove her frantic when they were together. But when she heard his anger and hurt on the telephone it came to her as a surprise, as if she would never learn it once and for all, that a man's feelings are urgent, even painful. She remembered feeling it like that once, long ago, in college. Was it Charlie, was it really Charlie that did it to her? Or was it somebody else, somebody tall and slight and blonde with soft blue eyes, who used to sit on the studio couch in their room at the sorority house and gaze at her?

Charlie was in a sweat of bad-tempered impatience when she finally, reluctantly, agreed to come out and resume their marriage.

8

Marriages would all be perfect if the husband and wife could live two thousand miles apart, she thought. *For the wife, anyway.*

And Charlie missed the kids. "He misses them!" she cried aloud, sardonically. But she knew if they were far away she would miss them too. She would love them at her leisure. They would begin to seem beautiful and perfect and she would forgive them their dirty diapers and midnight squalling sessions.

It scared her sometimes to think of this streak in herself; this quirk that made her want to love at a distance. The only person she had ever loved up close, with an abandoned delight in the contact, was...Laura. Laura Landon. A girl.

Charlie drove her home from the International Airport in Los Angeles. He was bursting with excitement, with things to say, with kisses and relief and swallowed resentments.

"How's business?" she asked him when they were all safely in the car.

"Honey, it's great. It's everything I told you on the phone, only better. We did the right thing. You'll love California. And I have a great idea, it'll sell in the millions, it's—oh, Beth, Jesus, you're so beautiful I can't stand it." And he pulled over to the side of the road, to the noisy alarm of the car behind him, and kissed her while Skipper punched him in the stomach. He laughed and kept on kissing her and they were both suddenly filled with a hot need for each other that left them breathless. Beth felt a whole year's worth of little defeats and frustrations fade and she wished powerfully that the children would both fall providentially asleep for five minutes. She was amazed at herself.

They got home after an hour's driving on and off the freeways. It was a small town just east of Pasadena: Sierra Bella. It was cozy and old and very pretty, skidding down from the mountains, with props and stilts under the oldest houses.

It was quite dark when they drove into their own garage and Beth couldn't see the house very well. But the great purple presence behind them was a mountain and it awed and pleased her.

She was used to the flat plains and cornfields of the Midwest. Below them were visible the lights of the San Gabriel Valley: a whole carpet of sparklers winking through the night from San Bernardino to the shores of the Pacific.

"Like it?" Charlie said, putting an arm around her.

"It's gorgeous. Is it this pretty in the daytime?"

"Depends on the smog." He grinned.

Inside the house she was less impressed. It was clean. But so small, so cramped! He sensed her feelings.

"Well, it's not like Lake Shore Drive. Uncle John could have done better, no doubt," he said.

"It's—lovely," she managed, with a smile.

"It's just till we get a little ahead, honey," he said quickly.

Beth fed the children and put them to bed with Charlie's help. And then he pulled her down on their own bed, without even giving her time to take her clothes off. For fifteen minutes, in their quiet room, they talked intimately and Charlie stroked her and began to kiss her, sighing with relief and pleasure.

Suddenly Skipper yelled. Bellyache. Too much excitement on the plane. Beth jumped up in a spitting anger and Charlie had to calm the little boy as best he could.

Beth was surprised at herself. She was tired and she had had an overdose of children that day. And still she responded to Charlie with a sort of wondering happiness. She didn't want anything to intrude on it or spoil it. Maybe this was the beginning of a new understanding between them, a better life, even a really happy one.

A half hour later Skipper woke again. Scared. New room, new bed, new house. And when Beth, nervous and impatient, finally got him down again, Polly woke up.

Beth's temper broke, hard. "Damn them!" she cried. "Oh, damn them! They've practically ruined my life. They're driving me nuts, Charlie, they'll end up killing me. The one night we get back together after all these months—" she began to cry, choking on her self-pity and outrage—"those miserable kids have to spoil it."

"Beth," Charlie said, grasping her shoulders. His voice was stern and calm. "Nothing can spoil it, darling. Get a grip on yourself."

Polly's angry little voice rose over Charlie's and Beth screamed, "One of these days I'll croak her! I will! I will!"

And suddenly Charlie, who adored his children, got mad himself. "Beth, can't you go for a whole hour without losing your temper at those kids!" he demanded. "What do you expect of them? Skipper isn't even two years old. Polly's a babe in arms. Good God, how do you want them to act? Like a pair of old ladies? Would that make you happy?"

"Now *you're* angry!" she screamed.

He clasped his arms against his sides in an expression of exasperation. "You were in love with me five minutes ago," he said.

Beth didn't know quite what had gotten into her. She was tired, worn out from the trip and the emotions, fed up with the kids. She had wanted him, coming home in the car. Now all she wanted was a hot bath and sleep.

She walked out of the bedroom and slammed the door behind her. But Charlie swung it open at once and followed her, turning her roughly around at the door to the bathroom.

"What's that little act supposed to mean?" he said.

She stared at him and the kids continued to chorus their sorrows in screechy little voices. Charlie's big hands hurt her tender arms and his eyes and voice had gone flat.

"I won't argue," she said, her voice high and shaky. "I won't argue with you. You don't understand anything about me. You never have understood me!"

He looked into her flushed face and answered coolly, "You never have understood yourself, Beth. If you knew who you really were it wouldn't be so hard for me to know you. Or anybody else."

That infuriated her. She hated to be told that she didn't know herself and it was one of the things Charlie always told her when he was mad at her. She hated it worse because it was true.

"You lie!" she cried. "You bastard!"

Charlie pushed her back against the wall, so hard that her head snapped and hit the plaster with a stuffy thump. He kissed her. He was not very nice about it.

"If you think you're going to make love to me, tonight, after the way you've just been acting—" she panted furiously at him, struggling to free herself— "if you think I've come two thousand miles just to let you *rape* me—"

"You shut up," he said harshly, and kissed her again. He nearly crushed her mouth and she would have screamed again if she had been able. When he released her she slashed at him with her nails and he pulled her by her wrists back into the bedroom.

Beth tried all the old favored tricks of crossed women. She kicked, and flailed with her dangerous nails; she tried to bite him; she whacked him with a knife-heeled pump, thrilled to see a slightly bloody scratch bloom on his shoulder.

But Charlie smothered her with his big body. He just rolled on top of her and told her, "Shut up. You're noisier than those poor kids you complain about all the time." The sheer weight of him overwhelmed her. Struggle was futile, arguments were useless.

While he fumbled with her underthings she said, "You're a brute. You bring me home to this miserable little cracker-box, you drag me all the way to California for this. *This!*" She tried to gesture at the four walls, to make him feel her disdain. "At least in Chicago I'm treated like a human being."

He kissed her angrily.

"I *am* a human being, in case you didn't know."

He kissed her again, and his hands found her breasts.

"If you touch me I'll be sick. I'll throw up every goddamn thing I ate on that plane. Including the biscuits."

But he touched her. He touched her all over, shivering all through his large frame and groaning. Beth began to sob with hurt and confusion and rebellion. And most dreadful of all, most humiliating, with desire. She wanted him. He was wonderful like this, the live weight of him on her yielding flesh, the thrust, the warmth, the

12

sweat, the sweet moaning. When he took her like this, like a master claiming a right, she submitted, and she experienced relief. She did not know who she was, but for a little while he made her think she knew. He made her feel her womanhood.

And when he had forced her to surrender once, she gave in again without fighting. He kept her busy for a long time. If the kids kept up the noise their parents didn't know it and didn't care. Charlie wouldn't let her out of his arms. He wanted her there where he could fill his nostrils with the scent of her, his arms with the smooth round feel of her. Four months is a damn long time for a husband in love with his wife to make love to a pillow.

It had not been quite like that between them since their college days and it was not like that again very often.

Chapter Three

THEY FELL INTO THE ROUTINE THEN WHICH BECAME SO DULL and empty to Beth over the next few years. At first she was too busy getting settled in her new home to be bored. She inspected the holly, the palms, the poppies, the bamboo that grew, rare and exotic, in her own backyard. She breathed in the mountains in back and the sparkling valley in front. But little by little she grew used to them. You can't live with the marvelous every day and keep your marvel quotient very high.

Charlie and Cleve worked hard on the toys, and Charlie loved it. He liked keeping his own hours, being the boss, running the show. Almost imperceptibly he began to take on the lion's share of the work and, with it, the lion's share of the decisions. He was willing to spend nights in the office working out new plans or briefing new men. It made Beth cranky with him. And the crankier she got the more he stayed away. It was the start of a vicious circle.

"It must be my fault. I must bore you to death!" she cried. "No, Beth, you don't bore me," he said, climbing into his pajamas while she watched him from her place in the bed. "You scare me a little, but you don't bore me."

"I *scare* you! Ha!" She said it acidly, but only to cover her chagrin. She didn't dare to ask exactly what he meant, and he didn't bother to tell her. But her fits with the children, her depressions, her lack of interest in the love that should have sparked between them, had something to do with it.

Charlie reached the point where he couldn't tell if Beth ever wanted him or not. She got him, because he didn't have the strength or the patience to turn monk. But there was none of the old smoldering response that had used to thrill his senses and reassure him of her answering passion. She was quiet and she made the minimum gestures mechanically. As he had blurted unintentionally, it scared him. Dismayed, he had tried once or twice to talk to her about it. Not knowing how to be subtle, he simply exclaimed that something was wrong and she had damn well better tell him what it was before it got worse. But Beth had given him a smirk of half amusement and half contempt that had withered his pride and driven him to silence.

So things rolled along. The business was never quite good enough to get them a bigger house or the flashy sports car Beth wanted. Cleve was never quite drunk enough to botch his job. Beth didn't have enough love and Charlie didn't have enough insight. And that was their life.

For Beth it was dismal. She yearned for a diversion, an escape hatch, *anything*. Travel, a new car, an affair even. But all she had were her boisterous children, her irate husband, and bowling twice a week with Jean Purvis. Her mood was desperate.

Things took an odd turn finally, one night when Jean and Cleve invited Beth and Charlie to a birthday party. It was for Cleve's sister, Vega Purvis. Beth remembered Vega very well. She had met her shortly after she arrived in California, and though she had never gotten to know Vega well, she was interested in her.

Vega was a model. She was a very tall girl, at least as tall as Beth herself, and excruciatingly thin. Throughout her twenties she had worked at modeling in Chicago and then suddenly came down deathly sick with tuberculosis, ulcers, and Beth had never known what else. Everything. It had meant the temporary finish to her working days and a long trip to the West Coast, where she went directly to the City of Hope for help. She was there for over two years.

Vega had sacrificed a lung to her tuberculosis, a part of her stomach to her ulcer, and perhaps more of herself to other plagues. And still she was stunningly beautiful. Still she smoked two or three packs of cigarettes a day—something that struck Beth as insane but rather wonderful, as if Vega had taken a bead on Death and spat in his eye. Nobody else would have gotten away with it. Vega brushed it off, laughing. "The first thing I asked for when I came out of the anesthetic," she said, "was a cigarette. The doctor gave me one of his. Tasted marvelous."

Vega had deep-set eyes, almost black, and fine handsome features, and she was witty and interesting. She was running her own model agency now on Pasadena's fashionable South Lake Street—mostly teenage girls, with one or two older women who took the course for "self-improvement." Or, perhaps, self-admiration.

Beth recalled the night she had first met Vega. They waited for her, Cleve and Jean and Beth and Charlie, in a small restaurant near her studio. Vega came late. It was necessary to her sense of well-being that she arrive late wherever she went. So Charlie and Beth and the Purvises waited for her in a small booth in the Everglades, where everything was chic and expensive.

Vega swept in at last, forty minutes late, wrapped in a red velvet cloak, and she was so striking that Beth had stared a little at her. She sat down and ordered a martini—double, dry, twist of lemon—before she greeted anybody.

She had a lovely face but it was, like the rest of her, painfully thin, with the fine bones sharply outlined. It soon became apparent why she didn't put on weight. Vega rarely ate anything. She drank her dinner, though they had ordered her a steak. She seemed to depend on booze for most of her calories. Cleve persuaded her to take one bite, which she did, promising to finish the rest later—but of course she never did. Charlie and Cleve finally split the meat and ate it, but the rest was wasted.

Charlie was interested in her too. Beautiful women interest almost any man without making much of an effort.

"What do you do here, Vega?" he asked her. "Cleve said something about modeling."

"I *teach* modeling," she said, accepting a fourth drink daintily from the waiter. "Women are my business. Men are my pleasure," she added, smiling languidly.

Charlie smiled back, unaware of the silly look on his face. Beth saw it, but it didn't alarm her. It struck her funny, and before she had time to think about it, she was laughing at him. And suddenly the fun and flavor went out of the game for him, and he turned his attention to his meal. Beth saw his embarrassment and rebuked herself.

I should have been quiet, damn it, she thought. *I should have let him have his fling. Such an innocent little fling. What's wrong with me?* But it was too late. Charlie was carefully casual with Vega the rest of the evening. It didn't console him much, when he got home that night, to check his muscles in front of the mirror or stretch to his full six feet two. He was baffled and shamed by his wife, who laughed at even his normal masculine reactions. He was almost defeated by his inability to make Beth's life mean something. On Vega's birthday night they waited, as before, at the Everglades for her entrance, drinking whiskey and waters, and talking. Beth felt warm and relaxed after the first two drinks and she squeezed Charlie's arm. It caused him some concern, instead of reassuring him, because it was unexpected.

"Good whiskey?" he asked, nodding at her glass. That must be the source of her pleasant mood.

"The best," she said and smiled. "Why aren't you nice like this all the time?" she teased clumsily.

"I'm only nice when you're a little tight," he said. "The rest of the time I'm a damn bore."

It was so short and sad and true that it almost knocked the breath out of her. She looked at her lap, despising herself for the moment, feeling the tears collect in the front of her eyes. When she had to reach for a piece of tissue to stem the flood he murmured, "I'm sorry. God, don't do that in here." He had a masculine horror of scenes, especially in front of Cleve and Jean. Jean had noticed the little exchange between them and her smile—her permanent smile—wavered, but Cleve was talking to her and didn't see.

"Come on, honey, this is a birthday party," Charlie whispered urgently in Beth's ear, exasperated and helpless like all men before a woman's public tears.

Beth pulled herself together. She would save her bad feeling for later. Now she wanted to enjoy herself, to let the liquor take over, and the muted lights and the piped music. She wanted to forget her kids, forget she was married. Charlie lighted a cigarette for her.

"Peace pipe," he said. And when he snapped out the match he saw Vega coming and added, relieved, "Here comes the guest of honor." He got up as she approached the table and took her coat for her.

"Thank you, Charlie Ayers," Vega said with a smile. She had a habit of calling a man by his whole name, as if it made him completely special, unique, valuable—and perhaps a little bit labeled. But the men loved it. It sounded foolish when you tried to explain it to somebody else, because it was impossible to imitate Vega's intonation, her peculiar lilting voice in its contralto register; but when she said your name, your whole name soft and low and very distinct, the whole company reacted. You were looked at, and the beautiful woman who had spoken to you was looked at, and it was a wonderful, slightly silly, but charming, ceremony.

Vega sat down between Cleve and Beth, and the waiter, who was an old buddy of hers, came up, as soon as she had adjusted herself, with her usual order: a martini, double, dry, with a twist of lemon. The waiter went up to the bar as soon as she had thanked him for it and began mixing the next. She always took the first three or four on the run. It amazed Beth to watch her. Oddly, Vega never seemed drunk.

Vega was all in black with a single small diamond clip at her throat and diamond earrings. On her they looked real, whether they were or not. Vega looked very very expensive, though she was quick to tell you the price of anything she was wearing. Her clothes were usually bargains picked up at sales in the better shops. Some of the shops gave her discounts, in return for which she told people she bought her clothes exclusively from them. She had this arrangement with at least five shops, all of them unaware of the others, and she lied to them all with charm and grace.

Beth watched her with an interest that intensified as the total of highballs went up. There were two gifts in the center of the table, one from the Ayerses and one from the Purvises. Vega ignored them.

"I've been teaching my girls how to walk," she told them, "to rock and roll records. Are you familiar with Elvis Presley?"

"Polly's got a crush on him," Beth said. "I think he's godawful myself."

"You're wrong," Vega said. "He's very useful. Especially with a gang of teenage girls. You put one of his records on and suddenly you've got—cooperation." She emphasized the word and smiled. "They walk around the studio like so many duchesses—just what I want. I used to play Bing Crosby for them but all it got me was a slouch and a lot of behind-the-hands giggling. Now I play crap and suddenly they're ladies." She turned to Cleve. "Explain that to me, brother," she said. "You know all about ladies."

Cleve ran a finger over his moustache in the wrong direction. "Simple," he said. "You have one rule: treat a bitch like a duchess and a duchess like a bitch. Never fails."

"What has that got to do with Elvis Presley?"

"You didn't *ask* me about Elvis Presley."

"Cleve, are you drunk?" Vega said. "It's against the family rules. You can't be. We never get drunk," she explained to Beth and Charlie. "Limber, but never drunk."

"You're right." Cleve ordered another round and when the drinks came he stood up and Beth saw that he really was pretty high. "A toast," he remarked, "to my charming sister, who is thirty-nine years old today. For the fifth time." He glanced down at her and Vega smiled seraphically at the ceiling. "Her company is charming," Cleve went on, while heads turned to grin at him from across the room, "her face is beautiful, her manners are perfect. Thank God I don't have to live with her. Vega, darling, stand up and take a bow."

Vega stood up with a lovely smile and told him tenderly, "Go to hell." They both sat down and drank to that while Jean laughed anxiously.

"They're always like that," Jean said, "It strikes me so funny."

Beth wanted to put a gag on her. Jean only wanted to make it seem friendly, teasing. Everybody in the Everglades had heard her husband and his sister. She wanted them all to know it wasn't serious.

But Beth liked to think they really hated each other, for some weird romantic reason. It gave an edge to the scene that excited her.

They ordered their meal and Vega, as always, ordered with them. Beth wondered why she bothered. Maybe it was just to give the men an extra helping. Maybe it was to ease her conscience about her drinking. At least if she had a plate of food in front of her she could always eat; she had a *choice.* If she didn't order anything her only choice would be to drink, and the people with her would take it for granted she was a lush. That would never do, even when she was with her own friends, her own family, who knew the truth anyway. It just didn't go well with her elegant exterior, her control.

So she ordered food, and ate one bite. It was a sort of ritual that comforted her and shut up the worriers in the party who tried to force French fries or buttered squash down her. When they had all finished she could divide her meal among the men unobtrusively.

Beth yearned to ask Vega how old she really was, but she didn't dare. She wondered at her own curiosity. Everything about Vega seemed valuable and interesting that evening. The glamorous clothes, the strange feud with Cleve, the dramatic entrance, the illnesses, the modeling.

I wonder how she'd like being a suburban housewife, she mused, and almost laughed aloud. Vega, with kids. Vega doing dishes. Vega, with—God forbid—a husband! On some women all the feminine ornaments and virtues only look out of place. Those women seem complete in themselves, and so it was with Vega. Beth couldn't imagine her, sleek and tall and with a hint of ferocity beneath her civilized veneer, being domesticated by any man. There was something icily virginal beneath her sophistication that made Beth doubt whether Vega had ever given herself to a man.

Vega opened Beth's birthday gift to her while the rest of them ate. "How did you know?" she said, so quietly that Beth almost missed it.

"It's only a book," Beth murmured.

"You picked it out yourself. I've been wanting to read it, too."

It was such a personal exchange, almost intimate, that Beth was taken aback. Vega treated the book like a private present from Beth—as if Charlie, who after all paid for it and wrote his name on the card with his wife's, had nothing whatever to do with it.

Beth found herself oddly drawn to this lovely, rather secretive woman; to the warmth of her voice and the way she spoke. Vega articulated carefully, conserving the small quota of air in her one remaining lung. And yet, her voice carried. She had turned the handicap into an asset, learning to develop and project her voice with the skill of a musician. It was pleasant to hear her talk, and she arranged her breathing so artfully that one was never aware that it was a chore, or that her very life's breath came to her in half doses.

At the end of the evening the three women went to the powder room together. Beth found herself impatient with Jean, wanting her out of the way.

What for? she thought, amused at herself. And still her impatience persisted. She stood next to Vega at the mirror while Jean leaned against the wall and waited for them to finish with their makeup. Beth wanted to say something, something memorable and witty and complimentary to Vega, but her mind was too busy admiring the woman. She only stared at Vega's large brown eyes and parted lips and puzzled over her.

21

"You know," said Vega, startling her, "you should model. You have a good figure for it."

Beth was nonplussed. When could Vega have studied her figure? But Vega was adept at observing people without seeming to. She had seen the restlessness in Beth, just as she had seen the ardent mouth and purple eyes and short brown curls, without apparently even looking at her. Now she turned to appraise her.

"I speak purely as a professional," she said, her mouth showing a humorous twist at the corners. She gazed frankly at Beth now, up and down, stem to stern. "Turn around," she said.

Beth said, "Vega, I could never model. I'm too old."

"Nobody's too old. Except my mother, and she was born fifty years B.C. You have nice hips, Beth."

The remark, so casual, sent an unwelcome tremor through Beth, who tried to shrug it off. "I'm thirty," she said. "Who wants to show their clothes on a thirty-year-old when they could show them on a teenager?"

"You'd be surprised," Vega said. "Me, for one." Beth stared at her. "Oh, not my own clothes. Only a scarecrow like me can squeak into those. I mean I like the way a woman your age wears her clothes, and so do the men who hire them. They have something no teenager has."

"A woman my age?" Beth repeated dolefully.

Vega laughed. "You still look like a college girl, Beth. You aren't, of course, let's face it. But you look it."

Beth gave her a wry grin. "I don't know the first thing about modeling, Vega," she said.

"I'll teach you."

Beth was secretly pleased, very pleased. But she wasn't thinking of the makeup tricks, or the poise she might acquire. She was thinking, in spite of herself, of the pleasure of spending some time in Vega's company. She had never been able to bring herself to form a lot of friendships with women. It was not possible for her to be friendly with them, curiously enough, just as it is rarely possible for a man to be friendly with women. Beth had known Jean Purvis for years now and knew her well, but they were still only acquaintances, not friends. And Jean, though she regretted it, understood this, and had given up long ago trying to pull Beth closer to her.

"I don't know if I could afford it—" Beth began, but Vega interrupted her.

"It's free, darling," she said, with an injured air, and Beth, transfixed, felt the "darling" echo through her head with a dangerous delight. She hardly heard Vega add, "Charlie won't mind. You have a housewife pallor, anyway. You need to get out. Come on down next week and we'll make you over. Not that you need much remodeling." Vega glanced again at Beth's trim torso and smiled. Beth smiled back and there was a single brief electric pause before Vega said quickly, "Everyone all set? Let's go." And turned to leave.

The three of them filed out, Beth so close behind Vega that she stumbled against her once.

Chapter Four

BETH, RIDING NEXT TO CHARLIE ON THE WAY UP TO SIERRA Bella, put her head back and pondered Vega's offer with a smile.

"What's up, honey?" Charlie said, seeing her expression in the red glow of a stoplight.

"Nothing."

She wouldn't tell me to save her own skin, he thought resentfully, and a wave of hatred for her secretiveness, her airs, came over him. He tried to swallow it down. He didn't want to ruin another evening, and this one held promises. Just a few, but still, a few. She had been receptive, pleasant with him, at the Everglades.

"Have fun?" he said, starting the car up again as the light changed.

"Um-hm." *How can I tell him so he won't say no?* she wondered. For she felt instinctively that he would object to her desire. It seemed to Beth that all the things she truly wanted to do, he didn't want her to do. Travel— "You can't leave me!" Work— "Your place is at home with the kids." Hire a nurse— *"You're* their mother!" Get a little tight— "Beth, you're turning into a damn souse."

She thought he was staid, stuffy; he thought she was wild, or would be if he didn't keep a tight rein on her.

They undressed quietly by the light of one dresser lamp, and Charlie, watching the clothes slip off her scented flesh, revealing the fluent curves of her back and breasts, felt his body flush all over. He was overcome with tenderness, with a desire for wordless communication.

Just be gentle with me, yield to me this one night, he thought, trying to press the idea into her head with the sheer force of wishing. He would never have spoken such a wish; it would have aroused her contempt, or worse, her amusement.

Beth pulled open the wardrobe door, reaching around the corner for her nightie. But he pulled her arm away. "You don't need it," he said. "Not tonight."

She let herself be held, submitting quietly to his kisses. When he seemed all warm and loving and tractable she whispered, "Charlie, I'm going to study modeling with Vega. Starting next week."

He only half heard. "Let's not talk. Let's not spoil it," he said.

But she felt that if he didn't acquiesce now, in the mood he was in, he never would. "If you don't say yes I'm going to do it anyway," she whispered into his ear.

"Do what?" he murmured, pulling her closer.

"And we'll have one hell of a fight over it."

"We're not going to fight, darling," he told her with the confidence of his passion. "Never again. We're just going make love twenty-four hours a day."

"Where? The toy factory? That's where you spend most your time." Her sarcasm cut through his euphoria and the words registered harshly in his ears. He shut his eyes tight, shifting his weight a little. "Not tonight, Beth," he begged her. "Please, not tonight."

The pleading in his voice irritated her. If she had been another kind of woman she might have responded with a wealth of sweet reassurance; she might have been *able* to respond that way. But instead she felt disdain for him, the sort of scorn most women reserve for a man who shows himself a weakling. Charlie was not a weakling and Beth knew it. And yet it seemed that over the years, as the ominous cracks developed in their marriage, he had made most of the concessions to keep them together, and that too aroused her scorn. It was true that she would have suffered fits of guilt and loneliness if he hadn't, and she was grateful to him for his "tact." But the very role she forced him to play and thanked him for in her secret conscience, lessened him in her eyes.

Dimly, Charlie realized this too. But he was caught in the squirrel cage and there was no way out.

Carefully Beth said, "I just want you to say it's okay."

With a weary sigh he loosened his embrace in order to look at her. "Say what's okay?"

"If I model with Vega a couple of days a week."

His eyes widened then as he heard and understood, and he turned away from her, picking up his pajamas and carrying them in front of him. His unwanted love was too obvious and it embarrassed him. "Vega Purvis is a Class-A bitch," he said.

Beth's cheeks went hot with indignation. She whipped her nightie out of the closet and slipped it over her simmering head. If she threw her anger in his face now he would never agree to it. But to call Vega a bitch, when he hardly even knew her!

"I think she's delightful," she said haughtily, when the covering of the nightie gave her some pretense to dignity.

"Sure. Delightful. What in hell do you want to learn *modeling* for? From that winesop?" He climbed under the covers and lighted a cigarette, and there was a flood of misery in him at the sight of her drawn up stiff and chilly in her resentment.

"You say modeling like you meant whoring!" she flashed.

"Well, what *does* it mean?" he asked with elaborate courtesy. "You tell me."

"I'd probably go down there once or twice a week," she said, suddenly softening in an effort to bring him around. "It would be just for fun, not for money. I'd never model professionally. But it would be something to get me out of the house, something really interesting for a change. Not that goddamn interminable *bowling* Jean dotes on."

"I can't see that walking around with a book on your head is so damn much more interesting than shoving a ball down an alley."

Her fleeting softness vanished. "I *knew* you'd be this way!" she cried. "Just because *I* want something, you *don't* want it! When in doubt, say no. That's your motto." She continued to berate him for a moment until it became clear that he wasn't listening. He was staring past her, beyond her, at nothing, thinking. And his eyes were dark and heavy. He held his cigarette in one hand, so close to his chest that she had a momentary fear the hair would catch fire and scorch him.

"Charlie?" she said, after a moment's silence.

"Beth, tell me something," he said seriously, and his eyes, still aimed at her, focused on her once again. "I want you explain to me what is the matter with our marriage."

For a long minute neither of them spoke. And then Beth sat down on the bed, at his feet, biting her lower lip. "You explain it to *me,*" she said.

"I'll gladly tell you all I know," he said. "I know we have two lovely children. I know we have a pleasant house to live in, even if it is small. I know *I* love *you.*" There was a significant pause, in which she should have said, *Of course I love you too.* But she didn't. He sighed. "I know we *should* be happy. There isn't anything specific you can put your finger on that's out-and-out wrong with us. So why do we argue all the time? Why, when we're still together, we still have each other, and things are going along the right way—*why* aren't we happy, Beth? Because we're not. We sure as hell are not."

Beth couldn't look at him, at his frowning face. "If you'd pick up after yourself once in a while," she said. "if you'd agree, just once, to let me do something I really want to do." The spite in her voice piqued him.

"Oh! Now I understand. This would be a gloriously happy household if it weren't for me, is that it? If the husband and father would just get the hell out, the family would be perfect. Right?"

"Cut the sarcasm, Charlie," she said. She tried to sound firm but her chin trembled.

"I get it from you, dear. It's catching," he said. "Besides, I'm not convinced that you'll swoon happily in my arms if I pick up my socks in the morning."

27

She made a helpless gesture with her hands. "All right, Charlie, I'm at fault too. Is that what you want me to say? I fly off the handle, I'm cross with the kids. I—I—"

"You kick me out of bed three or four times a week."

She turned a blazing face to him. "Charlie, goddamn it, I'm your wife. But that doesn't mean that any time you feel like having me, I feel like being *had*. Three or four times a week is *too much!*"

"It didn't used to be," he said, his voice as soft as hers was loud. "What happened?"

Tears started to her eyes for the second time that evening and she turned away. "Nothing," she exclaimed.

"Something must have happened, Beth. You just don't want it anymore. Ever. You give in now and then to shut me up—not because you really want me."

She covered her face with both hands and wept quickly with fear and confusion. "I don't *know* what happened," she admitted finally.

He leaned toward her, hating to hurt her. "Beth, I'd do anything for you," he said earnestly. "I'd let you go model in Timbuktu if that would make you happy. But it won't. All these things you think you want so badly—did you ever stop to examine them? What are they? So many escapes. You're running away. The one thing you can't stand, you can't bear to face or live with or understand, is your relationship with me. Your home. Your kids. But mostly me. Are you sorry we got married, Beth? Tell the truth?"

There was a terrible, painful pause. It took all of her courage to admit, "I don't know. That's the truth. I don't know."

He shut his eyes for a moment, as if to recover a little.

"Do you love me, then?"

She swallowed. "Yes," she said. Her courage would not stretch so far as to let her hedge on that one.

"Do you love the kids?"

She caught her breath and bit her lip. *I will be truthful, I'll be as truthful as I can,* she told herself sharply.

"Do you love the kids, honey?" he prompted her.

"When they're not around," she blurted, and gave an awful sob, covering her wicked mouth with one hand. When she could talk a little she said, "I love them, I love them terribly, but I just can't *stand* them. Does that make any sense?"

He lay back on the bed and gazed at the ceiling. The sight of Beth tore his heart. "Not to me, it doesn't," he said. And seeing her despair, he added, "But at least it's the truth, Beth, Thank you for that much, anyway." There was no sarcasm in his voice now.

Beth got up and walked back and forth at the foot of the bed. "I know I'm not the world's greatest mother, Charlie. Far from it." She wiped her eyes impatiently. "Or the best wife. I guess I hound you all the time because I'm ashamed of my own behavior. At least that's part of it. You're no dreamboat yourself sometimes." She turned to look at him and he nodded without answering.

"The trouble is, I just don't know what I *would* be good at," she said helplessly. "I don't know what I want to do. I wish I could want something, good and hard, and it would be the right thing. Sometimes I wish somebody would *tell* me what I want. Maybe my ideas about traveling and the rest of it are just daydreams. Escape, or whatever you said. But Charlie, that's not criminal. I *need* an escape. I really do." She felt a note of semi-hysteria pulling her voice higher and higher and she stopped talking for a minute to catch her breath.

"I wanted to go to Mexico last year. You said no. I want to get that MG we saw in Monrovia. You said no. I have a couple of cocktails by myself in the afternoon and you blow your top. You think I'm headed for Skid Row. I ask to go home and visit Uncle John. No again."

"The last time you visited Uncle John," Charlie pointed out with heat, "I didn't see you for four whole months."

"And those four months saved my sanity!" she cried, thrusting her angry chin toward him.

He lighted another cigarette in offended silence.

After a moment she resumed, trying to keep her voice level, "Now I want to model a couple of days a week. Is that so very awful? Am I really a case for the bughouse because I want to *escape* once in a while?" She tried, with her voice, to make it seem ridiculous.

"If it were only once in a while," he said sadly. They were silent again. Beth had stopped her pacing and he look at her lovely figure, shadowy beneath the nylon film of nightie. He wanted her so much...so much. At last he said, quietly, "Well, I guess it's better than losing you to Uncle John for half a year."

She turned around slowly and her face was grateful. "Thanks, Charlie," she said. "I would have done it anyway, but—" She was sorry she had said it. He looked so despondent, utterly stripped of his husbandly influence, almost a stranger to her. "But I wanted you to approve," she went on hastily. "I wanted to be able to tell you about it and everything." He refused to look at her. "She—she's doing it for nothing." Beth added, hoping to make it more acceptable to him.

He laughed unpleasantly. "She's doing it for *something,* Beth. Not money, maybe, but *something.* Vega's not the kind of girl who does things for nothing."

She went around the bed and sat down beside him. "Look at me, honey," she said. "I want to thank you."

"I know," he answered, but the thought of her kiss suddenly made him weak and a little sick. He sat up, turning to give her his back and was suddenly mortified to feel her lips on it in a brief shy salute. He froze.

"Beth," he said sternly. "Vega is a strange girl. You should know..."

"Know what?" she said eagerly.

"Cleve has told me," he said reluctantly. "She's been married a couple of times."

"To whom? Beth interrupted, astonished. Vega? *Married?*

"Well, I didn't know them. The first marriage was ideal, by your lights: she lived in Chicago and he lived in Boston. For eight years.

Cleve said she never let him in her bed. His name was Ray something. She calls him ex-Ray."

Beth had to grin at his back. It began to sound more like the elegant enigma she knew. "Who was the other one?" she asked.

"Some good-timer, backslapping sort of guy. A roommate of Cleve's once, before I knew him. Younger than Vega. It's only been two years since she divorced that one. I guess he didn't get past the bedroom door either, but he did get into her bank account. Spent all her money and then disappeared. Nobody knows where he is. She never talks about him."

"Well," Beth said cautiously, "that's not so strange. I mean, she obviously wasn't a good marriage risk, but lots of women have behaved that way. Maybe the men she picked weren't such prizes either."

He shrugged. "Maybe." He turned to look at her. "She lives alone with her mother and her grandfather. Cleve says they're a trio of cuckoo birds. You can't get him over there. Except Christmas and birthdays, and he only goes because he feels he has to."

"Do they really hate each other—Cleve and Vega?" Beth asked.

"Only on the bad days," he said. "Now and then they quit speaking to each other. But then their mother breaks a leg or Gramp poisons the stew and they get back together. Takes a family calamity, though. Right now they're as friendly as they ever are, according to Cleve. I don't know why it should be that way. Doesn't seem natural."

"They're both such nice people. It's a shame," she said.

Charlie couldn't stand to look at her any longer and not touch her. He put his arms around her and felt her nestle against him with a shattering relief. After a few minutes he heaved himself over her to turn out the dresser lamp, returning fearfully to her arms, only to find them open.

"Is this my thanks for giving in?" he said. It was flat and ironical. He couldn't help the dig. But she took it in stride by simply refusing to answer him. He made up for several weeks of involuntary virtue that night.

Before they slept, Charlie had to say one last thing. He saved it until he knew they were both too tired to stay awake and argue. He didn't want to ruin things. She lay very close to him, in his arms, too worn out for her usual tears of frustration, and he whispered to her, "Beth?"

"Hm?"

"Darling, I have to know this. Don't be angry with me, just tell the truth like you did earlier. Beth, I—" It was hard to say, so awkward. He was afraid of humiliating her, rousing her temper again. "I keep thinking of Laura," he said at last.

"Laura?" Beth woke up a little, opening her eyes.

"Yes. I mean, I can't help but wonder if you—you know how you felt about her—if it's the modeling that interests you or if it's—Vega."

In the blank dark he couldn't see her face and he waited, fearful, for her answer. *God, don't let her explode,* he prayed.

Beth turned away from him, her face dissolved in tears. "It's the modeling!" she said in a fierce whisper. And they said no more to each other that night.

Chapter Five

VEGA'S STUDIO WAS LOCATED ON THE SECOND FLOOR OF A building that housed an exclusive dress shop and a luggage and notions shop. It was an expensive place to rent and Beth was rather surprised to see how bare it was. There was a small reception room which was tastefully decorated, though there was space for more chairs in it. There was a door marked "office," which was closed, and there was a large, nearly empty studio room with eight or ten folding chairs, the kind you sit on at PTA meetings.

Beth peered into the studio hesitantly, and instantly Vega materialized from a small group of high school girls who had surrounded her while she spoke to them. There was silence while she walked, regally lovely in flowing velvet, both hands extended to Beth. The teens examined the newcomer with adolescent acuteness, and Beth took their silent appraisal uneasily.

Vega reached her. "Darling, how are you?" she said in her smooth controlled voice, and kissed Beth on the mouth. Beth was shocked speechless. She stared at Vega with big startled eyes.

"Oh, don't worry," Vega laughed, seeing her expression. "The doctor says I'm socially acceptable. The TB has been inactive for almost two years—really a record."

But it wasn't the infected lung, the possibility of catching TB, that upset Beth. That, in fact, never occurred to her. It was the sudden electric meeting of mouths, the impudence of it, the feel of it, the teen-aged audience taking it all in. Beth was piqued. Vega had no business treating her so familiarly. Still, it was impossible to make a fuss over it, as though she were guilty of some indecent complicity with Vega.

"How are you?" she said uncertainly.

The knot of girls began to talk and giggle again, and Vega turned to them. "Okay, darlings, you can go now," she said. "That's all for this afternoon."

She took Beth's arm and led her into the studio while the girls filed past them and out, still staring. Beth began to be seriously disturbed. Vega behaved as if they were sisters, at the very least, and at the worst...Beth turned to her abruptly.

"Vega, I hate to say anything, but really, I—I—" She paused, embarrassed. Vega would surely take it the wrong way. Who but a girl with a problem would take the kiss, the familiarity, so hard? What, after all, was so dreadful about a kiss between two women? Even if it was so unexpected, even if it was so direct that a trace of moisture from Vega's lips remained on Beth's own.

I'd only look like a fool to complain, Beth thought. *She'd think I was—queer—or something.* How she hated that word!

"Something wrong?" Vega said helpfully.

"I—well, I'm just not so sure I should do this, that's all," she said lamely. "Charlie said—"

"Charlie be damned. Charlie's as stuffy as Cleve. They make a beautiful couple," she shot at Beth, who was startled by the sharp emphasis. "However..." Vega turned away, walking to one of the folding chairs to pick up her purse and fish out a cigarette. "Maybe he's right. Maybe you shouldn't try to do this."

"What?" Beth exclaimed. "After all you said—"

"Oh, just for today, I mean," Vega laughed. "I don't feel much like giving another lesson. I get so sick of this damn place," she added plaintively, and her change of expression impressed Beth. Vega looked tired for a moment, and perhaps not as young as usual. But her face smoothed out quickly. "You don't really mind, do you?" she said.

"Well, I—I do a little," Beth admitted. After what she had gone through to get Charlie's approval she minded a lot. But Vega intimidated her somehow, and she hadn't the nerve to show her irritation. "But if you're tired..." She paused.

"I am," Vega said. "But I have no intention of abandoning you, my little housewife." She swung a plush coat over her shoulders. "I'm tired and fed up and sick to death—not really," she added with a brilliant smile that did not reassure Beth at all. The edge in Vega's usually soft and low voice made her words sound literally true. *Tired, fed up, sick.* And those eyes, so deep and dark and full, had turned lusterless again, as if Vega were defying her to look into them and see her secrets.

"Let's go slumming," she said, and the way she said it, the quick return of life to her face, the odd excitement so tightly controlled, was infectious.

"Where?" Beth said, intrigued.

"Well, you look so nifty we can't go too far astray," Vega said, looking at her professionally. And yet not quite professionally enough. "Do you have your car?"

"Yes."

"Good. I'll show you where my girls hang out. My teenagers." She spoke of them with visible affection. "It's a caffè espresso place—The Griffin. It's not far. Have you been there?"

"I've heard of it but I never thought I'd see it. It's the last place in Pasadena that would interest my adventurous husband."

"Let's go!" Vega spoke gaily and caught Beth's arm. They left the studio together, walking down the narrow flight of stairs to the street, and Beth thought, *My God, I never even got my coat off.*

"I like your studio, Vega," she said, because the silence between them was becoming too full.

"Do you?" It was almost a listless response. "I'm going to redecorate it. That's why it looks so bare."

Beth tried to look at Vega's face but they had reached the foot of the stairs and she had to pull the door open for her instead. Vega would not release her arm, even through the clumsy maneuver of getting out the door, and Beth was peeved to find her clinging to her still as they walked down the street toward the car.

She was grateful when they reached it for the semi-privacy it afforded.

"Where to?" she said, starting the motor.

The Griffin was dark and dank, jammed with very young, very convivial people very sure of themselves. In a corner an incredibly dirty minstrel twanged on a cracked guitar and sang what passed for old-English ballads. There were beards aplenty on the males and pants aplenty on the girls. Only a few females, Vega and Beth among them, wore skirts. And there was coffee of all kinds but no liquor. Not even beer.

"Coffee—that's all you can get in here," Vega said. So they ordered Turkish coffee and drank it while Vega told her about the place. "It's just an old private house," she said. "The kids have redone it all themselves."

"They did a godawful job," Beth commented and immediately sensed, without being told, that she had injured Vega, who seemed actually rather proud of the place.

"Yes, I guess they did," she admitted. Vega looked around, her eyes bright and probing, wafting smiles at the familiar faces and studying the strange ones. Beth saw her nervous pleasure, her fascination, quite plainly in her face. So it startled her to see that same lovely face cloud over abruptly, with angry wrinkles spoiling the purity of her brow. Vega glanced at Beth and realized her emotions were showing. Rather diffidently she nodded at a tableful of girls about ten feet from them.

"See those girls?" she said. There were five of them, all in tight pants, all rather dramatically made up, with the exception of one who wore no makeup at all. Her hair was trimmed very short and she had a cigarette tilting from the corner of her mouth. Beth's gaze rested on her with interest. She looked tough, a little disillusioned. Her blonde hair was unkempt but her eyes were piercing and restless and her face made you look twice. It wasn't ugly, just different. Quite boyish.

"They're disgusting," Vega said. "I can't bear to look at them."

Beth saw her hand trembling and she looked at her in astonishment. "For God's sake, why?" she said. "They're just kids. They look pretty much like the others in here. What's so awful about them?"

"That one with the cigarette—she ought to be in jail," Vega said vehemently.

"Do you know her?" Beth said, glancing back at the tough arresting face. Vega's heat amused and scared her a little. Vega was so frail. How mad could you get before you hurt yourself, with only one lung, a fraction of a stomach, and a bodyful of other infirmities?

"I don't know her personally," Vega said, stabbing out her cigarette, "but I know enough about her to put her in jail ten times over."

"Why don't you, then?" Beth asked.

Vega looked away, confused. Finally she turned back to Beth and pulled her close so she could whisper. "That lousy bitch is gay. I mean, a Lesbian. She hurt one of my girls. Really, I could kill her."

"Hurt one of your girls?" Beth could only gape at her. What did she mean? She sounded tense, a little frantic.

"One of my students. She made a pass at her," Vega fumed.

"Well, that couldn't have hurt very much," Beth said and smiled. "That's not so bad, is it?" She looked curiously at the girl.

But Vega was displeased. "I don't imagine you approve of that sort of thing?" she said primly, and Beth, once again, was lost, surprised at the changes in her.

"I wouldn't send her to jail for it," Beth said.

Vega stared at her for a minute and then she stood up. "Let's go," she said. "If I'd known she was in here I wouldn't have come." She was so upset, so obviously nervous, that Beth followed her out without a protest. They walked to the car, neither one speaking.

"Take me home, will you, Beth?" Vega said when they got in, and lapsed into gloomy silence. Beth began to see what Charlie meant by strange. Moody and restless. In fact, Vega's mood had changed so radically that the bones seemed to have shifted under her skin. Her face looked taut and tired and much older now. She slumped as if weakened by her angry outburst.

At last Beth asked softly, "Why do you go in there, Vega, if it bothers you so?"

"I didn't expect *her.*"

"What did you expect?"

"My girls, of course. They're in there all the time."

And Beth could hear, in the way Vega said *"my* girls," how much her students meant to her, how much she needed their youth around her, their pretty faces, their respect. "I like to let them see me in there once in a while," she added, trying for a casual sound in her voice. "Gives them the idea that I'm not a square. You understand. You see—I mean, well, they mean a lot to me," she went on, and there was a thread of tense emotion in her voice now. "Everything, really. They're all I have, really, I—" And unexpectedly she began to cry. Beth was both concerned and dismayed. She reached a hesitant hand toward Vega to comfort her, controlling the car with the other.

"It's all right, Vega, don't cry," she said. "Do I turn here?"

Vega looked up and nodded.

They turned down the new street and Beth ventured softly, "You have your mother and grandfather, Vega. And Cleve. Your family. You aren't alone. And you have friends."

"My family is worthless! Worse than worthless. They hang like stones around my neck," Vega said and the bitterness helped her overcome her tears.

"I'm sorry. I should keep my mouth shut," Beth said.

"And I haven't any friends," Vega cried angrily. "Just my girls. They're sweet to me, you know, they bring me things—" and abruptly, as if she was ashamed, she broke off. "I'd like you for a friend, Beth," she said. "I really would. I liked you right away. I've never been much good at making friends with women, and for some reason I get the feeling that you're the same way. It makes me feel closer to you. Am I right?" She paused, waiting for an answer.

Beth was alarmed by her behavior, afraid to aggravate her, and yet she felt it served her as warning not to get too close to Vega. The older woman was lovely, quick and charming. But Charlie was right—she was strange. Beth had a premonition of that wild fury with the world that displayed itself against the Lesbian and against Vega's family turning on herself someday. But she couldn't delay answering. You offer your friendship gladly, without deliberation, or you don't offer it at all.

"I'd like to be friends with you, Vega," she said, but it sounded hollow to her.

To Vega it sounded beautiful. "I'm glad," she said, and Beth felt that the mood had passed. Vega put a hand on her arm and left it there until they reached her house.

"Come in for a cocktail," she said. She was telling Beth, not asking her, and Beth was unable to refuse. "There's just one thing," Vega cautioned as they walked up the driveway to the small bungalow. "Mother can't drink anything. But *anything*. Really. It would kill her. She's an absolute wreck. You'll love her, of course, but she *is* a mess. I sometimes think she just keeps on living to remind me of the powers of alcohol."

Beth blanched slightly at this, but Vega laughed at her own remarks. "Anyway, Mother drank like a fish for twenty-three years and suddenly she went all to hell inside. Liver, bladder, God knows what-all. The doctor tried to explain it to me, but all I know is she aches all over and she has to make forty trips to the bathroom every day."

The little crudity brought Beth up short. It was so homely, so out of place on Vega's patrician lips. But Vega was full of contradictions; they were, perhaps, her only consistency.

As they paused, they were approached abruptly by a slight shadow of a man in worn corduroys and a jaunty deer-hunting cap. His arms were full of cats and his eyes full of mischief. What cats couldn't find room in his arms sat on his shoulders.

"Gramp!" Vega exclaimed. "You scared me to death." She

relieved him of two cats, the ones that were having the most trouble hanging on. "This is Beth Ayers," she told him. "Beth—my grandfather."

"How do you do, Mr.—?" Beth began clumsily, holding out a hand to him.

"Gramp. Just call me Gramp." He ignored her hand. Even with two of the cats transferred to Vega's arms he was still too loaded to let go and pursue the normal courtesies. "My best friends," he grinned, nodding at the soft animals.

"Your *only* friends," Vega amended. "The only ones he trusts, anyway," she told Beth. "We were just going in for a cocktail, Gramp. I was telling Beth about Mother."

"What about her?" His eyes snapped with good-humored suspicion.

"Just what a mess she is."

"Well, forewarned is forearmed," he said to Beth. "She's really quite harmless."

"Except for her tongue," Vega said softly.

The three of them headed for the front door again. "Fortunately she's much nicer than she looks," Gramp explained. "She likes to laze around in nothing but an old beat-up bathrobe. Saves pulling down her pants all the time. You see, she has to take a—"

"I know, I know, Vega told me," Beth said quickly. Why did they take such a delight in exposing all the ugly comical little family weaknesses to her? Did it make them easier to bear? Or were they punishing themselves for something? Beth stopped where she was.

"What's the matter?" Vega and Gramp asked with one voice, pausing and looking back at her.

"Vega, your mother doesn't want any visitors," Beth said. "She's *sick.*"

"Sure she's sick. We're all sick. It's part of the family charm," Gramp said. "Come on in and join the fun."

"You'll see what I'm going to look like in another ten or twelve years, according to Mother," Vega said.

"The last thing she'd want is visitors," Beth tried once more, but Vega shushed her with a laugh.

"Bull," Gramp commented. "Hester's sick and proud of it. She likes to show it off. She gave up appearances years ago. Actually takes pride in being a wreck. She's delightful. You'll love her. Even the cats enjoy her company."

And Beth, reluctant, bashful, but overwhelmed with curiosity to see what Vega would "look like in ten years," followed them in.

"Don't mention liquor," Vega hissed just before she pushed the front door open. *"Remember."*

Beth's first impression was that the house was stiflingly hot; and the second, that it was jam-packed with rickety furniture. Vega flitted around the room lighting lamps and dissipating the gloom, and Beth suddenly became aware of an old woman sitting in a corner who appeared to be broken into several pieces. She wore a gray, once-pink dressing gown; she had been listening to a speaking record until she heard Vega and Beth enter. Vega kissed her head briefly in salutation.

"Mother, this is Beth Ayers," Vega said "I told you about her. Mother's blind as a bat," she said cheerfully to Beth, who advanced to take the old lady's outstretched hand. "I forgot to tell you that."

"But not much else, hey?" her mother said, holding out a hand. "How do you do, my dear?"

Beth murmured something to her, grasping her hand gingerly. And then Vega said, with a wink at Beth, "Let's all have a Coke. Mother, you game?"

"Are you kidding?" Mrs. Purvis said. "It'll have to be Seven-Up, though. Gramp busted the plumber one with the last Coke. There's still fizz all over the john." And she cackled with pleasure. Gramp, unperturbed, was arranging himself in a harem of cats on the couch. Beth stared at Mrs. Purvis, repelled and fascinated and amused.

Vega in ten years? Utterly incredible! Never.

"What the hell did you do that for, Gramp?" Vega called from the kitchen. "The plumber hurt one of the cats?"

"No, they disagreed about the plunger," her mother answered, cutting Gramp off. "Gramp said the head was German rubber and the plumber said they don't make rubber in Germany. So Gramp pickled him in fizz."

"He deserved it. He was wrong," Gramp said mildly.

Beth smiled uneasily at them all, slipping out of her coat and feeling the sweat already trickling down her front. *God, it must be a hundred degrees in here,* she thought. *How does Vega stand it?*

Vega came out of the kitchen, apparently standing it very well, with some glasses on a tray and a bottle of Seven-Up. She poured it for her mother and handed Beth a glass with two inches of whiskey and an ice cube in the bottom. Gramp got the same and settled back into the cats with a conspiratorial sigh.

"Tell us what you did today, Mother," Vega said, while Beth made signs to her that she wanted some water in her drink. Vega took the glass back to the kitchen while Mrs. Purvis answered.

"Listened to a book," she said.

"A good one?"

"Good book, but a lousy reader. They cut out all the good stuff anyway. I guess they figure we poor blind bastards will die of frustration if we hear the good parts." She chuckled. "With me it's all a matter of nostalgia, anyway," she added. "How old are you, Beth, my dear?"

"Thirty," Beth said, taking her glass again from Vega.

"On the nose? Any kids?"

"Two," Beth said. "Boy and girl."

"Ideal," said Mrs. Purvis. "Just like the Purvis clan. You know," she said, leaning toward Beth, "what a harmonious family we are." There was a mischievous leer in her smile.

"I'm sure you are," Beth said politely.

Mrs. Purvis roared amiably. "Everything we ever did was immoral, illegal, and habit forming," she said. "Until Cleve turned straight and earned an honest living," she added darkly.

"God, Mother, you make us sound like a pack of criminals," Vega protested.

"We're all characters. But not a queer one in the bunch." Mrs. Purvis took a three ounce swallow of Seven-Up. "Too bad you never knew my husband," she said to Beth. "A charmer."

"Daddy was a doctor," Vega said, and Beth noticed, uncomfortably, that she was working on a second drink of straight whiskey.

"Yes," said Mrs. Purvis energetically. "Specialized in tonsils. Once a week he went down to his office—Monday mornings, usually—and sliced out eighteen or twenty pairs. That was all. Never did another thing and never lost a patient. Made a pile too, all on tonsils. Kept us quite comfortably for years. It's a shame he wasn't around to carve Vega up when the time came."

"My tonsils are the *only* things they didn't cut out, Mother," Vega reminded her.

"Well, it was a good life," Mrs. Purvis said. "Lots of leisure time, lots of money for booze and the rest of life's necessities. Of course, I drink tamer stuff these days. How's your Seven-Up, girls?"

"Oh, it's delicious," Beth said quickly, but something in the old lady's face told her that Vega's silent boozing didn't escape her mother. Whiskey didn't *sound* any different from Seven-Up, but it *smelled* different.

"I hope you split them up fairly, Vega," Mrs. Purvis said. "There were only two." She smiled inwardly at herself, slyly.

"There were three, Mother. One in the back of the shelf. You missed it," Vega lied promptly, with perfect ease.

"Oh." Her disappointment seemed to remind Mrs. Purvis that it was time for another of her incessant trips to the bathroom, and she heaved unsteadily to her feet.

"Can I help you?" Beth exclaimed, half rising, but Mrs. Purvis waved her down.

"Hell no, dear," she said. "This is one thing I can still do by myself, thank God. When I can't make it to the john anymore I'm going to lie down with the damn cats in the backyard and die."

"If they'll have you," Gramp murmured.

"Besides, she needs the exercise," Vega said. "It's the only walking she does, really."

"I get more exercise than you, my dear daughter," said her mother from the door. "You just sit around on your can all day and tell other people how to walk. You should try it some time. Every twenty minutes. Never gives the circulation time to get sluggish. There are many advantages to being old and diseased, as you will soon discover," she said, chortling with expectation at Vega. "Not the least of them are virtue and exercise."

"All right, Hester, get the hell in the bathroom before you lose it," Gramp snapped impatiently, and Beth saw Vega's temper rising too. Beth didn't know whether she was amused or repelled by the whole scene: the ugly crumbling old woman, the way Vega lived, the wise-cracking with the hint of violence under the humor. She didn't understand why she said yes when Vega fixed her another drink, then another. And Vega drank two for her every one.

Beth began to forget, or rather to get accustomed to, the hot-house atmosphere. She unbuttoned her blouse at the top and pushed the dark hair off her perspiring forehead, and talked and laughed with Vega and Mrs. Purvis. They were both a little daffy, she decided, but in a macabre sort of way they were fun. And Vega was so beautiful...so beautiful. Beth saw her now with slightly fuzzy outlines. Vega became animated in a careful sort of way, even laughing aloud, which was an effort for her. Every little while she would disappear with their empty glasses and come back with a couple of inches of liquor in them. Mrs. Purvis had long since finished her Seven-Up.

"No, thanks," Beth said finally, laughing in spite of herself when Vega offered her another. "I can't, really, I'm driving."

Vega raised an alarmed finger to her lips, and Mrs. Purvis said, "That crap will kill you, dear. It's the bubbles—they're poison, I swear. Whiskey is much better for you, believe me." And Beth

44

thought her sagging old face looked crafty and pleased with itself—or was it just the effort of trying to figure the two young women out?

Beth rose to go, throwing her coat over her shoulders.

"Oh, wait!" Vega pleaded. "Wait a little while. I'll make some dinner for us." She put a hand on Beth's arm and this time it didn't bother Beth at all. Or rather, the bothersome sensation was welcome; it was all pleasure. They smiled at each other and Beth felt herself on the verge of giving in. She felt at the same time a warmth in Vega that she hadn't suspected.

"Stay and have some dinner with us, Beth," Mrs. Purvis said genially. "Vega's a lousy cook unless she has company to fix for. The damn pussies eat better than we do."

"They're healthier, too," Gramp interposed.

Beth looked at her watch. It was past six o'clock, which struck her funny. "I can't, thanks," she said. "My kids, my husband—"

"Can't he cook?" exclaimed Mrs. Purvis. "Hell, I used to make the doctor sling his own hash three or four times a week. And we were sublimely happy."

But what happened? Beth wondered. *Your family split up and went all to hell. Everyone but Cleve, and even Cleve drinks too much. Charlie gripes about it.*

"Charlie can boil water," she said, "but that's all. It's past dinnertime now." She adjusted her coat and headed for the door.

Vega scooped up a couple of mewing cats from the couch and followed her, balancing her drink precariously at same time.

"Tell her to stay for dinner, Gramp," Mrs. Purvis said.

"Canned cat food. The finest," he offered with a grin.

But Beth suddenly felt the need to escape, and Vega, seeing it, took her hand and led her outdoors. "That's enough, you two," she called back to her family. "Don't scare her off!"

Beth turned and looked at Vega one last time before she left. She felt giddy and silly and she was aware that there was a smile on her face, a smile that wouldn't go away. "Thanks, Vega," she said.

"You know, you don't need modeling lessons, Beth," Vega said slowly, as if it were something they had a tacit understanding about. "I like the way you walk. It's not quite right for modeling—too free swinging—but I wouldn't change it for anything, even if I could. It would ruin you—the lovely effect you make."

Beth stammered at her, unable to answer coherently, only aware that she was deeply flattered.

"Tell Charlie you had a first-rate lesson," Vega went on. "Tell him you walked three miles back and forth in a straight line and you learned how to treat your hair with olive oil. Tell him anything, only come back on Friday."

Beth, smiling and mystified and pleased, said softly, "I will."

Chapter Six

SHE DROVE HOME LIKE A PUNCH-DRUNK NOVICE, LAUGHING AT the panic she caused and feeling light, giddy, peculiarly happy in a way that almost seemed familiar. She was unable even to feel guilty when she got home and found that Charlie had had to feed the kids and was waiting with stubborn hungry impatience for her to feed him.

She did her chores with a smile. Everything seemed easy. Even the children. The bedtime routine charmed her, the way it would have if she had to go through it only once or twice a year. She put her arms around her children and cuddled them, to their surprise. And Charlie, who was ready to bite her head off when she came in, traded his wrath for astonished love two hours later.

It did something to Beth to be in the company of a desirable woman, a woman whose interest was obviously reciprocal, and the first thing it did was make her happy. Her kids reflected the lighter mood gratefully and innocently, but Charlie...Charlie wondered where it came from, and, knowing his wife, he worried.

Beth was surprised two days later when Cleve Purvis called her. She had been in a state of wonderful tickling anticipation all day, picking out a dress, pondering what to say when she got to the studio. And now, at two o'clock in the afternoon, Cleve called.

"I know this is goofy," he admitted, "but could I talk to you?"

"Sure," she said. "Go ahead."

"Not on the phone."

"Why not?" she said, surprised.

"Don't ask me, I feel like enough of an ass already. I'll pick you up in half an hour."

"But Cleve—"

"Thanks," he said and hung up. So she got her clothes on and decided that whatever it was she'd make him drop her off at Vega's afterward.

Cleve took her to a small key club bar and sat her down at a table in the rear. They faced each other over the table. Strangers? Friends? Acquaintances? What were they exactly to each other? Cleve had left college before Beth met Charlie and they had only known each other fairly well since she had come to California. They had seen each other often, they had exchanged a few jokes, and now and then when Cleve was tight they danced together. But never alone. Never had they had a private talk. Charlie or Jean or the kids or somebody was always with them.

It made Beth feel odd, unsure, to be with him now in a private bar. Nobody knew about the meeting, apparently, and no one was there to see them but a few late lunchers and early imbibers. It gave the meeting something of the character of a secret tryst.

Cleve ordered a couple of martinis. "I know this must seem funny to you," he said, and covered his awkwardness with a gulp of gin.

"Does Charlie know you asked me here?" she said.

"Not unless you told him."

"No," she said, and somehow the fact that both of them *could* have told him and neither of them had made her feel part of an illegal conspiracy.

"Well, don't, Beth," he said. "Just keep it to yourself. I may not have any right to stick my nose in your affairs, but when your affairs get scrambled up with Vega's, somebody's got to tell you a few things."

Beth felt the hair on her scalp begin to tingle. "What things?" she said. Cleve finished his drink and ordered another. He drank like Vega—briskly and for a purpose. Beth looked hard at him, studying the face she thought she knew so well. It seemed different now, pensive under the thick dark blond hair. His mustache drooped and the deep cleft in his chin gave a droll twist to his frown. Cleve was not a handsome man, although Vega was a beautiful woman and they looked a good deal alike. It happens that way sometimes in a family. Two of the kids will resemble each other, yet the features that go so harmoniously in one face are awkward and out of proportion in the other. And still, Cleve's face was pleasant enough—not out-and-out ugly. Beth liked it. She liked the tired green eyes and the small wry grin he usually wore, and now and then, when she thought about it, she wondered why in hell such a man would marry a giggling good-natured idiot like Jean. Maybe her endless smile comforted him. Maybe it bucked him up through the dismal periods Charlie said he had, when he was more interested in booze than selling plastic toys.

Up until the present it had not interfered with his business. Charlie was willing to let him drink what he wanted, as long as he could do his job. So far, it appeared, he could. Beth, looking at him, wondered what strange, strong hold liquor held over the Purvises. Vega and Cleve both worshipped the stuff, and Mrs. Purvis was blind and crippled and leaking because of it.

Cleve had trouble telling Beth why he had brought her there this afternoon. It was easier after a couple of drinks, and by that time they were both looking at each other through new eyes.

"By God," Cleve mused. "I never realized you had violet eyes before. I always thought they were plain blue."

"Is that why you dragged me down here? To tell me that?" she asked.

He grinned sheepishly. "That's probably as good a reason as any. Better than the real one."

"You were going to tell me something about your wicked sister," Beth said. "And you better had before I get drunk. I have a date with her this afternoon at four."

"A date?" The phrase seemed to rock him a little. "Well, what the hell, drink all you want, you won't be any up on her. She's never sober."

"She's never drunk, either," Beth said.

"Yeah, how about that? I wish I were that kind of a drinker," he said enviously. "Never sober but never drunk."

"It doesn't seem to make *her* very happy," Beth observed. "Maybe it would be better not to be a drinker at all."

"No doubt about it," Cleve said, grinning, and ordered another.

"Cleve, I can't sit around all day," she said, giving him a smile. "Tell me about Vega, or I'll leave you here with only the booze for company."

"Okay, okay," he said. "Beth, I—I—Vega's queer." He threw it at her, curt and clumsy, as if it were hot and burned his mouth.

Beth stared at him, her face frozen with surprise, with a sudden fear and wariness. "That's a lousy word, Cleve. *Queer*."

"It's a lousy condition. I only tell you because she won't."

"Well, give her the credit of a little kindness, anyway," Beth snapped. "She's your sister."

"Nobody needs to remind me," he said. "Beth, this isn't a nice way to put it and I wish to hell I could laugh it off or forget it or put it some genteel way. But when Charlie told me she asked you to come in and model I thought somebody had better let you know."

"And that somebody was you? Is this what you tell all her girls? Must be great for business," She put all her scorn into it.

"No."

"Well, then why tell me? Why not let me find out for myself? If the other girls can be trusted with her, why can't I?" Her temper ignited quickly.

"You're special," he said. "You're different from the other girls—better, I mean. And she likes you more. That's obvious."

"Well, if Vega's so damn dangerous she probably would have made it clear to me herself." She was angry; her innocent idyll with Vega was jeopardized by his harsh words. How could she fool around now, just play a little, if Vega's own brother watched every move with morbid suspicion?

"That's the hell of it, Beth," he said, leaning toward her over the table. "Vega doesn't realize it. She doesn't know she's gay."

Beth's mouth dropped open slightly. "Good God, how can you be gay and not know it?" she exclaimed.

And it was Cleve's turn to stare. "I wouldn't know," he said finally, slowly, still staring. "I don't know anything about it, frankly. I've never felt that way."

Beth felt her whole neck flush and her cheeks turn scarlet. She was suddenly embarrassed and irritated. "Is that all you came here to tell me, Cleve? Vega's gay? Nobody in the whole world has figured this mystery out but you, of course, and you don't know anything about it. Not even *Vega* knows about it. Just you. Not your mother, not Gramp, not the people who live with her, not the models who study with her. Just good old Doctor Cleve, expert analyst. He doesn't know anything about the subject, by his own admission, but he's willing to damn his sister and smear her repu-tation on the strength of his own intuition. Oh, Cleve, come off it," she said, disgusted and disappointed.

He wouldn't argue with her. "I know she's gay," he said simply. "Shouting at me won't change that."

"Nuts!" said Beth—but she believed him. "Can you prove it?"

He smiled, a melancholy smile. "I'm glad you're defending her," he said. "I'm glad you're mad about it. I wouldn't have liked to see you take it for granted.... No, I can't prove it. I can only tell you things.... I say this, not because your eyes are violet, not because you have such a lovely mouth, not even because we're both a little high. I say it in honor of your innocence. I say it to spare you shock. I say it because I hope you and Vega can be friends, and nothing more. She needs a friend. She really does. All she has is Mother, and Mother has run her life since it began. Vega adores her as much as she hates her, and that's a lot. She can't get away from her, even though she wants to. In her heart, in her secret thoughts—I don't know—maybe she has some idea she's gay. But Mother hates the queers, she's always poured contempt on them.

How can Vega admit, even to herself, that she's the kind of creature Mother despises?"

"Your mother doesn't despise alcoholics, or quacks, or physical wrecks."

"Yes, but you see, none of those are *queer,*" he said earnestly.

"Oh, Cleve, that word! That ugly, mean, pitiless word!"

"I'm sorry," he said, studying her.

Beth finished her drink with a quiver of excitement and desire and disgust—all the feelings that Vega roused in her.

"Vega's going broke," Cleve said. "That's why the studio's so bare. Looks like a barn. She's had to hock a lot of stuff and return a lot. She used to support Mother and she told me they didn't want my goddamn charity. Now they're getting it—they can't live without it—but they let me know every time I hand them a check that they run right in and wash their hands as soon as it's deposited at the bank."

"Why?" Beth said, shocked.

"Mother thinks I'm a bastard because I didn't study medicine like my father. Gramp thinks whatever Mother thinks. And so does Vega."

Beth began to see what a tyrannical hold Mrs. Purvis, in spite of her debilities, had on her children.

"Vega and I understand each other," Cleve said. "We're both contemptible."

For a moment it seemed like he was begging for sympathy and Beth said, rather sharply, "Oh, you're not so bad. When you're tight."

Cleve gave a dispirited little laugh. "We know each other better than we know ourselves," he said. "Someday you'll understand us, too," he said, looking into his glass. "If you keep on running around with Vega." He sounded almost jealous. He sounded almost like a man warning another man away from his wife, not a friend warning another friend of his sister's emotional quirks.

Beth cautiously steered him back to finances. "Why is she going broke?" she asked. "She has a nice studio, lots of students."

"Not so many, not anymore. Their mothers are worried about them. There was a scandal a couple of years ago."

"I never heard about it," Beth declared, as if that proved it a deliberate fib.

"You don't hear about everything in the Purvis family," he retorted, and silenced her. "One of the girls had an affair with one of the others. Vega knew about it and she didn't exactly discourage it. And then some of the others found out and told their parents. Vega should have quit then and there and tried somewhere else, but she hates that kid who started it all and she wants to stay here and make a go of it in spite of what happened. Show everybody. Show the girl herself most of all. Damn!" he said, and finished another drink.

Beth thought suddenly of the strange tough little blonde with no makeup and a cigarette drooping froth her mouth in the caffè espresso place. "Who was the girl?" she asked.

"P.K. Schaefer is her name. Vega hates everybody but she hates P.K. worse than poison."

"Is she sort of a beatnik type? I mean, does she hang out in the coffee houses, does she dress like—"

"Like a goddamn boy," he finished for her, with the sound of his mother's disapproval plain in his voice. "Always has a cigarette hanging out of the corner of her mouth, as if that would make a male of her. As if that would take the place of—oh, hell." He ordered another drink, staring moodily at the floor.

And Beth knew it was P.K. she had seen. Did Vega love her or hate her? Or, as with the other important people in her life, did she feel both emotions for her? Beth felt a spark of jealousy.

"Vega doesn't hate everybody, Cleve," she said. "Maybe you two have had some bad arguments, maybe life with her wasn't all sugar candy when you were growing up, but, my God, she's a nice girl. She's fun, she's a lovely person. If you think you're going to make me drop her just by throwing a few old scandals and half-baked suspicions in my face, you're wrong. We get along fine and I enjoy her. After all, it wasn't Vega who had the affair, it was her students. She's not making any passes at me. And from what she's said about Lesbians I think she'd put the whole damn clan in jail if she had her way."

"Ah, she's had you over to The Griffin to see P.K.," he said, shocking her. "Exhibit A. She works fast, I have to say that for her."

"How did you know that?" She was mad again.

"She's given you her famous lecture on the beastly Lesbians."

Beth blushed. "Thanks for the drinks, Cleve," she said sharply, starting to rise, but he caught her wrist and pulled her down again. "Why do you think she talks about them if she doesn't have it on her mind all the time?" he said fiercely, his face close to hers. There was a high pink of excitement in his cheeks, as if he really, secretly, hated these women who were rivals for his sister's affection; as if he were admonishing Beth, for his own selfish reasons, not to become one of them.

"You said she didn't even know she was—*gay,* herself," Beth protested.

"Right," he said. "She'd quit spouting all that crap about putting them in jail if it meant she'd be going along with them." He sighed and gazed intently at her, and she smelled the whiskey on his breath. "Beth, you're a damn nice girl," he pleaded. "You're a lovely girl. You're bored as all hell with your life, it sticks out all over you. You stumble across my sister and she's charming, she's different, she shocks you a little and interests you a lot. You're looking for kicks; you're sick of that little house and that great big husband and those noisy kids, and Vega looks like heaven. She's got all the sophistication, all the glamor anybody could want. Hell, yes, I can understand it."

And Beth, thunderstruck, only gazed at him in silence, too surprised even to wonder when he had been observing her, when it began to matter to him what she did. *Not until Vega began to matter to me,* she thought, full of wonderment.

"Beth, she's nuts. Please believe me. She's goofy and she's pure trouble. I know; nobody knows like I know. I nurse her through her emotional storms; I have all our lives. She gets these desperate crushes she won't admit, or can't admit, or doesn't understand, and I go through hell with her. I don't want it to happen with you. Life has been too pleasant these past few months. No complications. Vega's been getting along so well."

"Why do you fight with her so much?" Beth said softly. "If all you're trying to do is help her. That *is* what you're trying to do, isn't it?"

"Yes," he said, and looked away. "God knows I love her. I just fight with her when I find out what she's done."

"Like what?" She felt as if he was almost on the verge of a confession of some kind to her.

"Like socking Mother right out of her chair. It's the only way she has of getting back at Mother for dominating her life. Or like getting stewed at seven in the morning when she's supposed to be at a Chamber of Commerce meeting that'll mean jobs for her girls. Like bugging me all the time about the money situation. And that goddamn blind spot of hers a mile square! If she'd only admit what she is and arrange her life accordingly. At least maybe she could live like other human beings then."

"How? What do you mean?"

"I mean face the fact there are two things she can't live with— whiskey and women. Put them out of her life. Get back to normal." He sounded bitter.

"But Cleve, *you're* normal, and *you* drink."

"Not like she does," he said quickly, untruthfully. "I go to sleep at night without a bottle by my bed." There was pride in his tone.

"Is it that bad?" Beth said. *Oh, Vega!* It made her want to nurse her, comfort her.

"She's sick," he said. "I don't mean the TB, I mean up here," and he tapped his head at the temple. "You can't provoke her, you can't cross her. She comes unglued. You haven't seen that side of her yet. You keep after her, you will."

"You've accused her of some pretty ugly things this afternoon, Cleve," she said quietly.

"I'm not accusing her of anything. I'm trying to show you what she's like. What she's capable of. I'm telling you not to let yourself get mixed up with a woman like that."

"You don't think I can handle myself, do you?" she said.

He shrugged. "I don't know. But Vega can't handle herself, that's certain. She leaves it up to me." He laughed, looking at his drink, but the laugh was mirthless. "Maybe it's from being so spoiled all her life, from being a favorite child and a worshipped wife who kept two husbands out of her bedroom for years."

Beth wondered, looking at him, his face dark and brooding, why he had really asked her there. Was he just trying to forewarn her of her potentially unhappy situation? Or was he threatening her? Beth eyed him suspiciously.

"You're warned now, Beth, and that's all I can do," he said. "Except, thank you for listening. And—ask you not to mention it to anyone."

"Are you afraid Charlie'd think you're as daffy as I think you are?" she said.

He laughed again, a short sad noise. "I'm afraid Charlie knew that years ago," he said. He leaned across the table and took her hands. "Beth, why in hell do you suppose I went to all this trouble for you? Exposed myself and my shameful family to you? Because I want to get laughed at, because I want to hear you say how buggy I am?"

"I don't know why you're doing it, Cleve. I really don't."

"You don't need to freeze up," he told her, his voice softening. "I just don't want to see you hurt, Beth. Jesus, I know *you're* normal. Don't get the idea I brought you down here to make you feel uncomfortable. You're as wholesome as cherry pie, you're no neurotic self-blinded Lessie. You're sweet and healthy. I guess I just like you that way. I guess I just don't want to see Vega *change* you." But Beth had the uncanny feeling that what he *really* wanted was to keep them apart, keep her away from Vega. Why?

"She won't change me, Cleve. I am what I am. It's too late for her to make me over, even if she tried."

"Thanks," he said, as if she had promised him she would never see his sister again. And then he let her go.

Vega's lips met hers a half hour later and this time Beth felt none of the resentment she had the first time, no desire to scold her and run. Instead, it was Vega who was irritable, rushed and nervous. She was preparing for a fashion show that night at the Hollywood Knickerbocker Hotel, and there were clothes and girls all over the studio.

Beth knew, without being told, that there was no time for her today, and it aroused a keen hunger in her for Vega's company. She watched the lovely woman glide smoothly about, her excitement showing only in her eyes, and Beth experienced an unwelcome qualm of jealousy for the second time that day. The girls, the young models, were so lithe and fresh. She found herself imagining their sweet young bodies full of tender untried places, and a sort of fever came over her.

It came as a shock when Vega asked her to leave. She pulled Beth aside and said in a warm whisper, "Darling, really, I'm up to my ears in this. I forgot all about it Tuesday. I just forgot everything Tuesday, all I could think of was you." And Beth wanted suddenly, urgently, in a sweat of fear and delight, to put her arms around Vega and kiss her indecently until her desire was satisfied.

"I hate to ask you," Vega said, "but—well, let's put it off till next week. I've got so much to do. Beth, don't look so disappointed!" She smiled like an angel of the devil and Beth said, almost humbly, "Don't kick me out, Vega. Can't I help? I'll do anything."

"No, you don't know a damn thing about it. I've got to do it myself. Now go, darling. Be a good girl and go." And she gave Beth a kiss on the cheek. Beth nearly suffocated for one lovely moment with the urge to pull Vega back into the shadows and tell her how beautiful she was, how unfairly beautiful.

But Vega left her and Beth was soon completely alone in the swirl of frenetic activity. Girls in tulle, girls in tights, girls in skin-fitted sheathes—all so young, all so feather-headed with excitement. Beth watched them a moment, enjoying the practiced movements, the bursts of nervous giggling, the fascinated preening at mirrors. Until she was jostled once too often and felt her solitude in the inconvenience she caused.

Shortly afterward she left. But she spent the whole evening in a misty fantasy of Vega that even Charlie could not penetrate with his grumblings about Cleve.

"I think he was out somewhere swilling booze this afternoon," he said. "He came in about five and he was loaded. If it happens again I'm going to raise the roof."

"Why does he do it?" Beth asked vaguely. "He's happy with Jean, isn't he?"

"I guess so. At least she never complains. He could shove a knife in her ribs and all she'd do is hand him that same old smile. But that isn't it. Something is bugging the guy. Always has been, since I first knew him, like he'd committed murder and gotten away with it, and then discovered he couldn't live with his conscience. It almost seems sometimes like he's trying to tell you about it. But he just ends up telling you to be careful."

Beth looked up at this, remembering her afternoon with Cleve. "Be careful of what?" she said.

Charlie shrugged. "Who knows? He never gets it said."

Chapter Seven

BETH AND CHARLIE BOTH JUMPED WHEN THE PHONE RANG AT one-thirty in the morning. Charlie grumbled, "I'll get it," but Beth had a sudden premonition and said, "Oh, never mind. I'll go."

Willingly he turned over, muttering, "Probably a wrong number. Some drunk, or something."

It was Vega and she sounded hysterical. "Beth! Oh, darling, thank God you're there."

"Where else would I be at this hour of the morning?" she said, keeping her voice low so Charlie wouldn't hear the conversation. She was both thrilled and alarmed to hear that cautious smooth voice, charged now with desperation.

"Beth, you've got to help me. I'm in a ghastly predicament. I'm just frantic."

"Where are you?" Beth asked.

"At the Knickerbocker."

"The hotel?" Beth was relieved; the trouble couldn't be too serious.

"Yes. It got so late. Some of the girls wanted to stay, so I said it was okay. Oh, I called their mothers and everything. You have to be so damn careful with them, with all these repulsive convention-eers around. It's like trying to smuggle a hoard of diamonds through a convention of international jewel thieves. And if any-thing happens to any one of my angels—holy God, it'd ruin me! I'd be run out of town on a rail." She stopped talking suddenly, as if to catch her breath, as if the tension in her had drained her resources.

"Vega, tell me what happened!" Beth demanded, worried.

"Well, I—we—" For a moment Beth feared Vega would burst into tears. Her honeyed voice broke and Beth grasped the phone in sweating hands, imagining the worst.

"Vega, did some bastard try to—" she began but Vega interrupted.

"No, nothing like that, I just—Beth, darling, would you mind driving over here?"

In the astonished silence Charlie called out, "Beth, for the love of God. Who is it?"

"It's Vega. And shut up, you'll wake up the kids," she hissed at him.

"Vega!" he spluttered. "What does *she* want?"

"I don't know. Please shut up."

"Well, tell her to go cram it, and come to bed."

"Beth, I need you. Will you come down?" Vega asked, her voice rough and soft and tantalizingly near to Beth. Beth stood in the dark, feeling her heart skip and a queer concentrated pleasure flash through her body. *Beg me, Vega, beg me,* she thought. *Work for me. I want you so.* "It'll take an hour," she hedged.

"Not at this time of night. Oh, darling, I'm so miserable. Please come to me. I haven't got a single cigarette and those s.o.b's at the desk won't send any up. I haven't even got enough whiskey for a lousy nightcap. You *will* come, won't you? And bring me some groceries?"

And Beth understood then why she was calling. Cleve had already warned her: Vega couldn't sleep without a bottle by the bed. There was a moment of acute disappointment when she wanted to throw the phone down and smash it. And then it came to her suddenly that Vega could have called somebody else, even Cleve. But she chose her instead.

"I'll come," Beth said weakly. "I'll come, Vega."

"Bless you, Beth, you're wonderful. I swear, nobody else is crazy like I am but you. I *knew* you'd do it. Darling, you make me feel so much less lonesome."

"I'll be there as fast as I can," Beth said, and hung up.

Beth tried to find her clothes in the dark without waking Charlie. But he was listening for her. Suddenly he switched on the reading light over the bed. For a second or two they were both blinded: Beth on one foot in the closet, pulling on a stocking, and Charlie leaning on his elbow against the pillow. When he opened his eyes and saw her he got out of bed and went to her without a word. Beth felt him come toward her and she was afraid of him; really afraid. He was a big man with a hard body and a strong streak of jealousy in him. His love for her was still alive but it was uncomfortable and a little the worse for wear and disappointments over the years. He was in no mood to deal gently with her.

She felt his angry hands close on her arms and jerk her forward so that her face snapped up to his. "Now what's all this about?" he said.

"I'm going downtown," she said.

"To Vega's?"

Beth looked away. "Let go of me, Charlie."

"*Answer* me, Beth." He had no intention of letting go until she confessed what she was up to. And maybe not then.

"Vega's downtown, at the Knickerbocker. She wants some cigarettes and things, and I told her—"

"Cigarettes!" he flared. "And *things!* What things?" When she refused, panting with indignation, to tell him, he said disgustedly, "And booze I suppose. And you're going all the way into Hollywood in the middle of the night to take them to her. Good God, Beth, I didn't know it had gone *this* far."

"What's *that* supposed to mean!" she cried. "I haven't done anything wrong! You have no right to hint that I have." She was furious with the strength of her fear; the fear that always rose in her like a red wall at the suggestion of abnormality and shut off her judgment and good sense. Her voice stirred the children, asleep in the next room.

"You haven't done anything wrong *yet*," he amended. "But you go down there tonight and you will." He was so cold, so bitter, so chagrined that she quailed at the sight of him. The moment his hands dropped from her arms, as if she were too wretched for him even to touch, she turned and fled from him, snatching up a coat from the hall closet. The liquor and cigarettes were ready in a paper bag on the hall table and she grabbed them on the way out.

In the bedroom Polly woke up and began to cry. Beth heard her when she started the car, and she wondered at every panicky second why Charlie didn't stop her, why he didn't run after her and shake her till her bones came loose, or strangle her. She could feel his fury like a tangible thing wafting to her through the mild night air. Backing out the driveway with dangerous haste she felt that if she had not been fighting mad herself, desperate and deter-mined, his anger would have swallowed her up and subdued her.

She drove down the Pasadena freeway and into Hollywood, her mind stewing. *If Charlie hadn't made such a fuss there wouldn't be any trouble. I'll be home in the morning, the kids don't ever need to know the difference. And if he could only realize—oh, God, make him realize—how happy I can be if I just have somebody to love. To have fun with. Somebody like Vega. Why doesn't he understand how good I can be to him? How patient with the kids? If he could only share me, just a little bit, just once in a while, with…with a woman.*

She was amazed to find herself reasoning like this: Beth, who hadn't given a conscious thought to other women for nine years; Beth, who thought she was solidly normal for so long, who even married a man on that conviction; Beth, who had turned Laura Landon out of her life one day many years ago with such reassur-ing feelings of superiority and normalcy. That Beth, that very same girl, was tearing through the night on a fool's errand at the whim of a beautiful spoiled woman who probably didn't give a damn what her personal feelings were.

Vega: Beth saw her in her mind suddenly, whole and clear, every detail of her, as she had seen Laura in her dream some weeks before. Strangely, life was worth living for a woman like that. Problems could be solved, boredom could be faced, chores could be accomplished, if Vega could only love her. With love, with passion, with romance in her life again, Beth's children would be more bearable. She could love them again because love was being reawakened in her and there would be plenty to go around. Why couldn't Charlie see it that way, see what joy and peace his family would know if Beth were only satisfied?

She felt a flare-up of stinging resentment at his apparent selfishness. He'd understand one of these days; he'd *have* to. Beth was so eager for Vega's company, so full of pleasure and trembling anticipation, that nothing could have stopped her then, not even the thought of Charlie's wrath.

She pulled off the freeway and into the stop-and-go traffic on Hollywood Boulevard. The great avenue was a strip of brilliants pasted on the black night. It might have been past two in the morning but it was Friday night, too, and the big brassy street was humming. Lights twinkled and flashed, announcing a hundred shows, a thousand succulent and sinful beauties, a million laughs. Posh shops displayed their slick wares in a weird radiance unknown to the daytime hours.

And the people swarmed down the walks and across the street looking urgently for fun, dressed in their courting clothes or their tourist sport shirts. They smiled at every light, every open door, every burst of commercial good humor. Beth watched them when she had to stop for lights, and they did not strike her as pathetic or lost or bored. They were having fun, they were all dressed up, and they were doing Hollywood right. She even found herself envying them.

The night clerk buzzed Vega's room for her, giving Beth a narrow-eyed examination all the while. "She says come up," he said, leaning toward her on the counter.

"Thanks." Beth turned away, but he called her back.

"Miss," he said and smiled at her sparkling eyes. "She's been giving us a rough time tonight. We're not supposed to take stuff up after midnight. And those girls with her are pretty noisy. I wonder if you'd tell her to tone it down a little. Would you mind?" He glanced at the paper bag full of whiskey under her arm.

"She'll tone it down," Beth said. "You won't hear a damn thing, I guarantee."

"Thanks," he said, and watched her fanny as she walked away toward the elevator.

She was full of a reckless elation, a taut and wonderful excitement that she didn't dare to analyze. She rode up in the elevator and all she thought about was Vega: the sight of her, the scent of her, the smile. Not what she would do once they were alone in that room together; not what she would say. Just a mental vision of that fine-featured face, that elegant body, too thin, almost too well kept, too pale. *But oh, deliver me! So beautiful!* Beth thought.

She knocked lightly on Vega's door. The hall was rather noisy, with half-suppressed laughter and an occasional squeal floating from the adjacent rooms. Beth had just time to hope that none of the girls was sharing Vega's room when the door opened and Vega herself nearly fell into Beth's arms.

"Oh, you're here!" she cried. "Thank God! Did you bring it?" Beth could feel the tremor running through Vega and watched her with fascination as she seized the package of whiskey.

Beth stood just inside the door, her coat and gloves still on, content to be in Vega's presence, content to smell her perfume and feel the air she stirred when she moved. Vega was swathed in a full peignoir of several varicolored layers that floated and swirled around her. It gave the illusion that she was rounder and softer than she was.

Vega busied herself with the bottle, opening it with a fingernail file and pouring herself a drink in the bathroom glass. Beth realized slowly that they were completely alone. The girls had banded together in the other rooms, and the fact that she and Vega were there by themselves, locked in a hotel room at nearly three in the morning, exulted her. She felt wonderfully strong and strange, gazing at Vega, who had softened and relaxed with the warmth of the whiskey and was settling herself on the bed.

Vega smiled up at Beth and said, "Come and sit with me and tell me how evil I am." Her smile was both sad and inviting, and suddenly the curious strength Beth had felt washed out of her and her knees began to tremble. She was afraid to move, afraid any move she made would be the wrong one.

Vega frowned slightly at her, perplexed. "Beth, darling, you can't just stand there in your coat for the rest of the night. Take it off and come here."

It was such a frank proposition that Beth wondered suddenly how Vega could be gay, as Cleve said, and not know it. It just couldn't be. She wanted to rush to her, grasp her hands and sink to her knees and say, "Vega, Cleve has been lying to me. He says you don't know yourself, he says—"

"What do you mean?" said Vega, and Beth realized, with a little gasp of horror and surprise, that the words had virtually spoken themselves, so intensely was she involved in her thoughts. Her face went a hot deep pink and she moved at last, slipping out of her coat, wordlessly embarrassed.

"What did Cleve say to you, Beth?" Vega was strung up tight again, leaning forward to catch each word.

"I shouldn't have said anything," Beth murmured. "I—I just had a drink with him this afternoon. He told me a lot of guff. I think he was just tight." She went anxiously toward the bed and suddenly Vega burst into a beautiful smile and laughed in her cautious, lovely way.

"He told you how charming you are and how wicked and depraved I am, no doubt. He thinks it's his mission in life to warn decent people away from his nefarious sister." Her laughter brought a breath of relief to Beth, who smiled gratefully at her. It gave her the courage to come and sit beside her, and when Vega offered her the glass and poured her a drink, she took it as a sign that there were no hard feelings. She didn't want the liquor, just Vega's esteem, Vega's warmth and favor. But liquor was one way Vega had of showing her approval and it had to be accepted.

"He's been telling people for years how rare I am," Vega went on. "How immoral. How faithless and frigid. I...was married, you know," she added abruptly, her eyes bright on Beth.

"I know."

"Oh, so he told you that too." And she laughed again, putting her head back a little. Her hair was loose, not wound into the graceful roll she usually wore, and it fell, two feet of it, in silky luxury down her back. Beth had an almost uncontrollable urge to touch it, and she was relieved when Vega straightened up and resumed her story. "I was married twice, Beth. They were nice enough guys. That wasn't the trouble!"

"What *was* the trouble?" Beth said and felt her throat constrict with excitement. It was such a perfect opening for a confession.

Vega turned her bottomless brown eyes on Beth and touched her knee gently, letting her hand rest there. "You blurted out a minute ago—to your own embarrassment, obviously—that Cleve thinks I don't know myself."

"Vega, I'm so sorry, it was thoughtless, I just—"

"No darling, I don't want you to explain." Her hand tightened on Beth's warm knee. "I just want you to tell me what Cleve thinks it is I don't know about myself. Tell me, Beth."

Beth opened her mouth to speak and found no voice. How could she possibly say such a thing? *He thinks you're a Lesbian, and you don't know it.* It could be torment for a sensitive person to have something that shocking, that personal, thrown at her from the blue.

"I can't say it, Vega," she admitted, and Vega read her pale face accurately.

"Well, then, I know what it is," she said. "And he's telling you what he honestly believes." Her face became pensive suddenly and she gazed downward at the whiskey in the glass tumbler. "I have never let him understand me very well. I have good reasons for it. He *thinks* he does, of course. It's rather painful sometimes, he thinks I'm so dense."

Beth felt herself in a state of tremulous anticipation. She didn't want to talk, only to touch, only to feel. And yet talking like this might bring her closer to Vega, help her understand her.

"If I tell you, Beth," Vega said slowly, "that I have never been attracted to men...I hope it won't give you wrong ideas." She glanced up to see how her remark was taken, but Beth said only, "Wrong ideas?" She sat holding her hands together tightly to keep from reaching out for Vega.

Vega smiled at her suddenly and said, "Relax." The squeeze she gave Beth's knee tickled her and they both laughed. "You didn't come here to get a lecture on me, anyway," Vega added. "You deserve some reward for your effort. Here, have another." She offered Beth the glass and Beth tried to turn it down. But she saw a quick shy retreat in Vega's eyes, as if Vega feared Beth were disapproving, and she took the glass anyway and drank.

"Was Charlie mad at you for coming?" Vega asked.

"Yes," Beth said simply. Her head was getting light.

"I'm sorry," Vega said. Her voice was tender and grateful.

"You know, I had an odd thought on the way over here tonight," Beth said, to change the subject.

"Tell me." Vega leaned back into the pillows and gazed up at her, the whiskey glass resting on her stomach. She held it lightly, almost casually, as if she could easily give it up, as if she could go to bed without a drink, without a bottle on the table beside her.

"I'd like to get lost with you in Hollywood. I mean—" Beth laughed, flustered. "See the sights, like the tourists."

"You don't go wandering in Hollywood at night without a man unless you want to get picked up, darling. Is that what you mean?"

"No, I just want to share it with you. You're fun to be with. I guess—to be frank—that's why I came tonight." She took the proffered glass again, avoiding Vega's penetrating smile bashfully, and when she returned it she felt quite dizzy. She leaned toward Vega slightly, steadying herself with both hands pressed into the bed in front of her. She found herself tilted close to Vega.

"Feel okay?" Vega asked. "You look way out. No need to keep up with me, you know. I'm more or less immune to the stuff. Ask Cleve."

"I feel fine. Wonderful," Beth said, raising her eyes to Vega's. She felt reckless, even. Their closeness was like a challenge, a dare that brought her pulse up high and visible in her throat and made her work for her breath. "Vega, you—you are the loveliest woman," she whispered.

Slowly Vega placed her glass on the floor and then her hands went up to Beth's shoulders, more to subdue her than encourage her.

"Beth?" she said, and the name itself was a question. "I never thought *you* of all people..."

In one quick painful second, Beth saw that she was caught; her fascination, her desire were clear and hot in her eyes and mouth. Vega could see them. There was nothing for it but to declare herself or retreat and run, spouting half-baked excuses that would fool neither of them. Back to Charlie she would go, back to the kids, back to Sierra Bella, humiliated and disappointed beyond her capacity to bear it. She could not give up so easily; she had come too far, risked too much.

"Vega, let me, you must let me," she said, trying to lean closer to her, but Vega's thin arms restrained her. Beth was afraid of hurting her and she paused.

"You know how I feel about this," Vega said, and there was something sharp, almost fearful, in her voice. Her eyes were quite wide. Beth felt her own strength and Vega's weakness and she forced Vega's arms down suddenly.

"You...of all people, you," Vega moaned. "No, Beth. *Please!*"

"Vega, forgive me," Beth said wildly. "I love you, I can't help it!" And she bent her head in one swift hungry movement and kissed Vega's exquisite mouth.

For the space of a heartbeat there was no response, only a chill, a palpable terror. And then suddenly Vega returned her kiss, and Beth, murmuring insanities, kissed her face and her mouth all over, holding her tightly and panting with the sheer forgotten glory of it: the marvelous sweetness and suppleness of a woman's body, the instinctive understanding that surpasses words, the indescribable tenderness two women in love with each other can create.

She became aware only slowly that Vega was desperate for breath. The weight of Beth's body was too much for her, and Beth rolled off suddenly, exclaiming, "Vega, darling, did I hurt you? Are you all right?"

Vega swept to her feet and nearly fell back again. Beth leaped up after her and caught her from behind, putting her arms around Vega and rocking her gently, her lips against Vega's throat.

"Come sit down," she said, and when she had Vega safely into a chair, she knelt and put her head down in Vega's lap, her arms around that tiny waist and her lips moving still against Vega's warm body, exploring, caressing, reverencing.

Until Vega pushed her head back and said, as if her breath had only then come back to her, "Stop it! Will you *stop* it?" with such anguish that Beth pulled away in alarm.

"Oh, I hurt you," she said, dismayed.

Vega got to her feet. "No, don't help me," she ordered. "Don't touch me."

"But Vega—"

"Shut up!" Vega turned a tormented face to her. She walked to a window and pulled it up, gasping up the air. "I told you not to get any wrong ideas," she said finally, when some measure of calm had returned to her. She gazed stonily at the street eight stories below, her face almost a mask now.

"I didn't know that was so awfully *wrong,*" Beth said, rising and coming toward her.

Vega looked up at her and her expression changed again, the fear showing quite plainly in the quiver of her muscles. "Beth, stop, hear me," she said. "It's not that I don't *know* what I am. It's just that I can't stand *being* what I am. If you do this, if you insist, you'll destroy me."

"All I want to do is love you, Vega," Beth said, and felt tears of frustration and passion struggling for supremacy in her. "Can love destroy a person?"

"The wrong kind can!" Vega said.

"But this *isn't* wrong."

"You only say that because you want it, because you're too weak to deny yourself," Vega cried.

"I've done without it for more than nine years."

"I've done without it for more than *twenty* years!" Vega said. But something in the parting of her lips, in the warmth of the kiss she had returned, gave Beth courage. Perhaps Vega feared her mother, perhaps she couldn't help knuckling under to her mother's ideas. But her body, her secret heart, seemed to beg for that proscribed love.

"I don't believe you," Beth said. "Your own beauty would trap you in a score of affairs."

"I'm not that beautiful," Vega said candidly. "I might have been once but I'm not anymore."

"I never saw anyone lovelier," Beth said. "I never saw anyone I wanted so much." The thought of Laura flashed before her eyes and reminded her that she was lying. But that had been so long ago, this was so here and now. "Vega," she said in a voice husky with pleading, with need. "Please come to me. Please, don't let me stand here alone in this strange room speaking love to a stranger. Let me know you, darling. Let me be close to you. Don't shut me out. Vega, do you know how long I've waited, turned this out of my mind and lived like a robot? No, *worse*—a robot can't suffer. I did it because there was no one I could love."

"You did it because Lesbian love is wrong and you know that," Vega said, and Beth could hear the echo of her mother's voice speaking, the way she had heard it in Cleve's speech. "And it's still

70

wrong, Beth. More for you than for me. *You* have a husband. And children."

"That's why I need it so!" Beth cried in a storm of misery. She was ready to explode with the feeling inside her, a whirlwind of contradictions and desires.

"Yes. You need *it,* not me," Vega said bitterly.

Beth couldn't stand it any longer. She rushed toward Vega, but Vega very swiftly and unexpectedly opened her diaphanous dressing gown, holding it wide away from herself so that Beth should see every detail of her white body.

Beth stopped abruptly, within a foot of her goal, and stared. She made a small inarticulate sound, and Vega searched her face with horrible anxiety. "If you can make love to that," she whispered, "then I'll believe you love me. I'll accept it."

She was a complex of scars that twisted every which way over her chest, like yards of pink ribbon in snarls. She had no breasts, and the operation to remove her lung had left a bad welt that Beth returned to once or twice with a prickle of revulsion. Even Vega's dainty little abdomen had its share. And the bones, the poor sharp bones without the ordinary smooth envelope of tender flesh that most girls take for granted and even rail against when there's too much. Vega's bones were all pitifully plain and frankly outlined.

Beth put her trembling hands over her mouth, to stifle her horror, and let the tears flood from her eyes. She shut them tight for a moment, but when she opened them Vega was halfway out of the open window.

With a little scream Beth lunged at her and caught her, pulling her to safety over the most violent protests of which Vega was capable. Beth held her, struggling and swearing hysterically, in her arms for some time, thinking all the while of Cleve and his unhappy eyes and his talk of Vega and their mother. She stroked Vega's hair and let her own unhappy tears fall.

After a while sheer exhaustion forced Vega into silence. Beth felt her drooping and she bent down and put an arm under Vega's legs and another around her shoulders and lifted her up. She was surprised at how slight the burden was. Beth was a big girl and she was strong, and she had always been proud of these unfeminine qualities in herself.

There was plenty of whiskey left, and Beth, after laying Vega down tenderly on the bed, poured her a drink. Neither of them had spoken a word.

Vega gulped the drink and then handed it back; she turned her face away and put one hand over it. Beth let her weep undisturbed for a while. At length Vega murmured in a broken voice, "You don't need to tell me how you feel now. I saw it in your face."

"Vega, you damn fool," Beth said gently. "Why didn't you tell me? Why did you spring it on me that way? I could have taken it, if you'd only let me know. If you'd only prepared me a little for it."

"No," Vega said, reaching for a tissue from her pocket and wiping her eyes. "No, what you mean is, you could have controlled the look on your face. You could have made up a kind little speech and said it right away, before your silence spoke for you."

"That's not what I meant," Beth protested.

"Don't you see, Beth," she said, turning to look at her and forcing herself to face those eyes that had seen her saddest and ugliest secret, "if I had told you beforehand you would never have confessed your love to me at all. You would never have tried to know me or touch me. That counts for something, believe me. That's one thing to be grateful for, even if it can't last. But aside from that it wouldn't have made much difference. You might have hidden your disgust a little better, that's all. No matter which way I did it, the ending would have been the same."

Beth lighted a cigarette. "This has happened before, hasn't it?" she said quietly.

"Yes," Vega sighed. "Now you know why I've been waiting twenty years. It wasn't pure virtue." She gave an acrid little laugh. "You thought my mother was ugly, didn't you?" she said. "I'll bet you didn't know how ugly a woman could be until now."

"Vega, please," Beth said, exasperated with her and with herself. She was in a state of tremulous nervousness, keyed up to a fever one moment with aching desire, and almost nauseated with shock the next. Somehow, in the space of a few short weeks, this lovely woman she had known well enough for a period of years had appeared to her as a lover. Suddenly Vega, who had been only Cleve Purvis's sister since Beth came to California, was all the promise of love, of womanhood to her. Vega became Beth's own passion resurrected in the flesh.

And now, with brutal suddenness, she had seen her mutilated body, repellent and pitiable, and she could not find her desire anymore. It had dissipated.

But surely I loved her, Beth told herself miserably. *When you love, you love more than a body. You love a mind and heart, too, or your emotion is a cheap fake.* She knew this was true. She knew that if her "love" had been real it would somehow have survived, even in platonic form. But all she wanted now was to get out, to leave, to breathe the open air, to be free of her cruelly misshapen dream.

The very sight of Vega, the small sounds she made, drove Beth's disappointment through her like a knife. She was ashamed of her selfishness but quite impotent with it. She had wanted a whole woman, warm and yielding. She had dreamed that her hands would touch the smooth perfumed flesh of a body that knew how to love. It had been a vital part of her desire and now she had little more than a face to hang her dreams on. Vega's face, covered with tears.

"You'd better go," Vega told her suddenly, and Beth wanted nothing mote than to obey. But shame and pity held her to the spot beside Vega on the bed.

After a moment Vega turned and gazed at her. "Surely you can't stay, after what you've seen?" she said in a leaden voice.

"Vega," Beth said painfully. "I said—I said I loved you. I've grown very fond of you over the last few weeks. I don't know how or why it happened. I only know that I can hardly bear to hurt you, to see you lying there in despair." It was meant as solace, to ease Beth's parting. Nothing more. But Vega in her desperation took it for more. She turned to gaze at Beth and there was a new look on her face. The eyes were less empty, the mouth less tragic.

"You mean you'll stay?" she whispered almost inaudibly. Once said, the words trapped Beth. For a moment she couldn't answer and her mind flew frantically from lie to lie, but there were no excuses, none that wouldn't hurt Vega mortally. She had seen Vega's ugliness and she had been sickened. Her passion had flickered and gone out, and now she was tired and ashamed and she wanted to be gone.

"Of course I'll stay," she said softly, hopelessly, to Vega. It was her conscience, her compassion, that spoke for her. If the incredulous pleasure, the stammering gratitude she produced in Vega could have reawakened the needs of Beth's body, Beth would have fallen on her with delight. Instead she lay wordlessly beside her, taking Vega into her arms and murmuring kindnesses to her.

"I knew you were better than the rest," Vega said, and her voice broke with emotion. "Beth, darling Beth, I knew it somehow. I had a feeling about you. Maybe because I wanted you so much. I did, you know. I do. Oh, Beth."

And Beth, as she kissed her, wondered with sad irony why Vega couldn't have said that to her before when she wanted so much to hear it, why she couldn't have played the game gently and broken the secret mercifully. Perhaps she hoped she could catch someone like Beth someday who had too much pride and pity to treat her like an outcast. Perhaps she hoped her pathetic condition would finally snare somebody the way it had Beth. She had waited a long lonely time for this, and she clung to Beth as if to let go for even an instant was to lose her forever.

Beth made love to her. It was restrained, partly because she saw with awful clarity in her mind's eye every part of Vega that her hands touched, and partly because Vega herself had not the breath or strength to throw herself into her feelings. Beth clung tight to her composure, swallowing her tears of frustration and giving Vega all she could muster of tenderness and patience. Vega could not be satisfied unless Beth appeared to be so, for otherwise it would be too clear that Beth was doing this for her out of charity. So there was the fatiguing necessity of pretending to enjoy it, pretending to feel the thrill that was nothing but a gruesome parody of the happiness she had anticipated.

Vega lay in her arms throughout the rest of the night and she slept like a guiltless child. Beth, beside her in the dark and afraid to move and disturb her, did not sleep at all. She stared into the night and cursed the unkind fate that had promised so much and delivered so little. All the dormant fires of her younger days had sprung to life and they burned in her still, tempting her, torturing her, until she knew she would have to find release somewhere or die of it. She even went so far as to imagine the young girls in the next few rooms and to wonder if it were possible to see them, to make friends.

At five-thirty in the morning? she said to herself, and smiled wryly at the dawn.

Beth drove home in the morning, dropping Vega off first and seeing her go with a sigh of relief. She was ashamed of her feeling of resentment and to cover it up in her conscience she berated Vega. *Jesus, I wanted to make love to a woman, not a carved-up scarecrow!* she cried to herself, and her own hard words dismayed her. Her attitude toward Vega was fast becoming one of bitter disappointment. She had been betrayed and she was near to loathing the object of her betrayal, so great had been her hopes and her needs.

At home in her empty house she put her head down and cried. They were tears of fury, tears of frustration, but not tears of despair. Not now. Her temper was too high and the blaze in her too hot.

For an hour or more she stamped around the house, picking up objects aimlessly and smacking them down again, kicking chairs and doors, and thinking. She walked out into the yard and pulled up a few flowers just because it felt good to ruin something. And then she went back into the house and threw herself down on her bed and slept.

She dreamed of Laura.

Just Laura, sitting on the studio couch in the sorority room they had shared, gazing at her. But though she didn't move, though she didn't speak, she was vibrantly alive this time. Beth could smell the remembered heady scent of her hair, and when she approached her and held out her hand she could feel Laura's breath upon it. She spoke to her, just her name. And Laura smiled, ever so faintly, over the gulf of years and the famous "well of loneliness."

Chapter Eight

BETH WENT THROUGH A PERIOD OF NEARLY TWO MONTHS, AS spring edged into summer, of emotional upheaval and torment that were all the harder to bear for being secret. There was no one to talk to, no one to explain to, no one to confide in. Charlie would never understand. His reaction would surely be one of anger and contempt for her. Her exclusive behavior, her moods, had already come close to damning her in his eyes. And *Vega*.

Oh, God! Beth thought with acute irritation. Vega was rapidly becoming a stone around her neck. She pestered her on the phone two or three times a day. She begged Beth to spend more time with her, and Beth, who was speedily growing sick and sorry about the whole affair, tried every machination to get out of it. But then came threats. Vega would sob over the phone, and her lovely voice, tangled in the gasps for air that plagued her when she was excited, would moan, "You love me. You *said* so. If you love me come to me, Beth. My God, I'm out of my mind I want you so much."

And Beth found herself yearning for the days when she and Vega were hardly more than acquaintances; even the days when she wanted Vega and couldn't have her were better than these when an unhappy and jealous Vega tried to force herself on her.

"I have to take Skipper to a birthday party," she would say. Or, "I can't, Vega, I'm bowling this morning."

"Oh, hell!" Vega spat. "You gave that up weeks ago. Jean told me. She said you just called up and quit and she thinks you don't like her anymore. She called me to cry on my shoulder." Her

77

voice was hard with jealous suspicions and Beth was obliged to concoct ridiculous fibs for her. Anything to keep her at arms' length.

But she couldn't keep her there always. There were meetings, awful exhausting affairs. Beth approached them with a dread that included an element of physical revulsion she found it hard to hide. Vega, who was sharp-eyed in spite of her infatuation, could see that Beth's response to her was only slight and that her thoughts were always with something or someone else. But she had fallen for Beth and there was no backing out. It was almost a fanatical attachment. Their relations became more and more trying, more strained, with Vega weeping pathetic angry tears and Beth snapping at her with wild impatience. They had really trapped each other and there seemed to be no way out.

Vega's most desperate fear was that one day Beth would simply refuse to see her at all. "I'd *kill* you if you did that to me," she told Beth once, thinking that by mentioning it before it had a chance to happen she might miraculously stave it off.

But Beth offered her no consolation, not even an answer. She knew quite well that soon it would come to a parting; that she had only delayed the break out of shame, cowardice, and a desire to lessen the pain for Vega.

Vega would often call her when Charlie was at home and Beth would be forced to talk quietly to her, to agree to her plans, just to avoid a revealing argument in front of Charlie. Beth upbraided her royally for it when they met

"Good God, Vega, I can't let Charlie know what's going on," Beth shouted at her. "That is, if he doesn't know already. Do you want me to stop seeing you altogether? He'd insist, you know."

"Beth, if you'd call me once in a while instead of forcing me to call *you*. Just *once* in a while. If you'd act like you cared—"

"Vega, don't throw a lot of sentimental pap at me."

"Is that what you call it?" Vega sprang to her feet, her face white. "Is that what you call my love for you? This affair was all your idea, Beth, in case you've forgotten. *You* insisted. *I* surrendered. And now you're obligated to me. I swear to God you are!" She would have gone on but lack of breath stopped her and she paused, panting, a hand to her throat.

"I'm not going to stand around and be hollered at," Beth said, picking up her coat with an angry sweep of her arm. "You're turning into a shrew, Vega."

"Beth, don't go! Please!" The last word was almost a sob and Beth didn't dare to turn around and see her face. She would have succumbed to her own sympathy and weakness again and hated herself for it afterward.

"Beth, I'm warning you here and now, if you leave me I'll tell Charlie all about this. I'll tell him everything."

Beth paused, her back to Vega, and her heart skipped a beat. She kept her voice under control when she answered. "He won't believe you."

"You know damn well he will. You said yourself he already suspects monkey business. Well, it won't take much to convince him."

"Try it," Beth said, still bluffing, still afraid to face her.

"You're goddamn right I'll try it," Vega said, with all the meager force she could muster.

Beth turned around slowly, reluctantly. "Vega," she said. "You're a viper. I can't think of anything else to call you. You're nothing but a lousy snake. You make me sorry I ever laid eyes on you."

"You've laid more than eyes on me, Beth, and don't forget it," Vega said, trembling with the fatigue of her feelings. "You owe me something."

"You owe *me* something, too, Vega," Beth said. Her voice was soft but furious. "You waited twenty years for somebody, remember? For some poor idiot like me to take pity on you—"

"Stop!" Vega cried, visibly hurt and beginning to reel slightly. Beth was forced to care for her, to help her to a chair and bring her a shot of whiskey. "Beth, don't say it," she begged. "Once those things are said there's no unsaying them. They hang there in the air and poison things. They destroy even the little white lies you tell yourself when things look blackest."

And Beth was touched by her misery in spite of herself. "You mean," she said quietly, "they make you face the truth."

"Hurt like that goes beyond the truth," Vega said. "When you're trying to hurt somebody else you kill them with truth like that. I couldn't bear it if you left me, Beth. I can't believe you will. I was so lonely before. It's not much better now, but it's better. When you're in a good humor I almost faint with love for you. I want to lie in your arms and die of joy. I wish we could live somewhere together, just the two of us."

And Beth, for whom the whole situation had taken such a sickening turn, was caught between pity and disgust. "I—I don't mean to leave you, Vega," she said at last, hoping that her phraseology would leave her an out. "But don't call Charlie. Things are bad enough as it is. Please, leave him out of it."

She hated to say it, for it gave Vega a powerful ace to play, but she spoke the truth when she admitted that things were already bad enough at home.

There had been a sort of armed truce declared between Charlie and herself. They had very little to say to each other, but for the children's sake they put on a show of life-as-usual. Beth reached a point where she hated to leave the house, as if her love affair—if the word "love" belongs there—had changed her physically and might give her away to her neighbors. She did the marketing and took the children out, but that was all.

Housework seemed an interminable chore to her. She had never liked it, any more than she liked cooking. But she had always done what was necessary. Now even that oppressed her to such an extent that she would often let things go until the last moment, sometimes failing to make up the beds until just before Charlie got home, and letting days, weeks, go by without dusting or vacuuming. The worse the house got the harder it was for her to do anything about it. She wanted to shut her eyes and forget it.

And all the time, every day, at every hour and in every imaginable posture, she dreamed of Laura. She dreamed of the romance, unfettered with family obligation or dishwashing, free of all the daily drudgery she so despised, free of a husband who was jealous and narrow-minded, free of children who were noisy and nerve-wracking.

Beth yearned for Laura. She was almost possessed with her. It was as if, out of the blue, she had fallen in love with her all over again; and, in a way, she had. She was in love with her own lost freedom, her own smooth young face, her college sophistication, her exotic love for a strange and fascinating girl. All the things that were once but were no more, all the things Beth had been and was no longer. These she loved. And Laura personified them.

To while away the hours, she read. On her shopping trips she picked up books—every book she could find on the subject of homosexuality and Lesbianism. She read them with passionate interest, and found a release in them she had not expected. Most of them were novels with tragic endings. Some were even dull, at least for those whose ruling interest in life had nothing to do with their own sex. Some of them depressed her, but all of them interested her and she gained a feeling of companionship with some of the writers which alleviated her solitude a little. She wrote letters to a few, the ones who impressed her most, who seemed to understand best what it was like to be gay and to be alone and starved for love; for less than love, even—for sympathetic companionship.

A handful of them wrote back to her and she established a correspondence with one or two that relieved her a little. She looked forward to their letters eagerly and poured out her desperate lonesomeness and bewilderment to them. After a few weeks they had all deserted her but one, who seemed really interested in her, named Nina Spicer.

Nina's letters came in oversized envelopes with the name of her publisher in the corner, and Beth read each one avidly. She knew dimly that although Nina Spicer was gay there was very little else they had in common. That became clear from her letters. But Nina had become intrigued with her and Beth was grateful for the interest. It was a bridge into another world where she longed hopelessly to be, and it comforted her.

The thought began to grow in Beth that the only way out of her depression was to go back to Chicago and search for Laura. Charlie would refuse, of course, and he'd fight it all the way, but she had to get out, shed her present life, try to find herself in a new environment with new people.

Chicago...it sounded beautiful, romantic as a foreign port to her, for the first time in her life. She had grown up there, she knew her way around. But it had never appeared as anything but huge and dirty and familiar, with sporadic excitements available.

Laura had grown up there, too. And suddenly Beth knew that she *had* to get to Chicago. She would go if it meant a divorce; even if it meant giving up her children. No sacrifice seemed out of line to her. Uncle John would take her in. She could always feed him stories and hide the truth from him. The idea of actually seeing Laura again awakened a trembling hope in her that came very near, at her best moments, to being happiness.

She spent three days trying to figure out a good way to broach the subject. Nothing had changed between herself and Charlie. He spoke to her when necessary and he spent the nights on his side of the bed, never touching her except by accident. His silent suffering both touched and exasperated her, like Vega's. Mostly it made her mad.

There was a secret woman in Beth, a woman capable of a wonderful and curious love for other women, and she wanted to dominate Beth. But, tragically for Charlie and her family, this tormented woman could not feel more for a man than a sort of friendly respect. If that was spurned she had nothing else to offer. And Charlie wanted passionate love and devotion, not a buddy who was more woman-oriented than he was. It all came out in a single bright and anguished explosion. Beth had cast about for a way to explain herself to him; a hopeless job before it was begun, for she could not begin to understand herself. And when she saw the futility of it, she gave up and recklessly threw the whole range of her misery before him, like a picture on a screen.

She waited until the children were in bed and Charlie was watching the TV in the living room. She came in and sat down in a chair facing him. He was stretched out on the couch with his head on a hill of pillows, looking intently at the glowing screen in hopes of forgetting his problems for a little while.

"Charlie?" she said, and because she had not approached him for any reason for several weeks he turned his head looked at her with surprise.

"What?" he said.

Beth swallowed once, to be sure her voice would come out clear and determined. "I'm going to go home. To Chicago."

He stared at her briefly and then turned unseeing eyes back to the set. "I doubt it," he said. "You wouldn't want to leave Vega that long."

"Vega can go to hell. She's driving me crazy," Beth confessed. He already believed the truth, although he had no proof of it. *So why in God's name am I pretending?* she thought defiantly. Suddenly it seemed easier and even cleaner to be frank.

"Don't tell me the great romance is fading?" he said, still not looking at her.

She gazed at his face she had once so loved and she wished, for the sake of that decaying love, that he would be kind, that he would say things that would not make her hate him.

"The great romance never existed," she said.

"If you're trying to tell me it was all platonic, don't bother," he said.

"I'm trying to tell you I'm not in love with Vega Purvis," she blurted. "I never was."

"That's funny!" said Charlie. "I got the other impression."

"Well, I thought I was in love with her," she said awkwardly, thinking, hoping the confession would unburden her at the same time that it destroyed Vega's worst weapon against her. But suddenly the words were ugly and hard to shape and she wished she had simply told him she was going away and left it at that.

"I—I thought I loved her the night I took her the whiskey, at the Knickerbocker. And I discovered that I didn't. That's all."

"After a little mutual exploration?" His voice was sarcastic. "Shall I send you a gold plaque in honor of your extramarital affairs?"

She stood up and stamped her foot and started to speak, but he added quickly, "And don't talk to me the way you talk to your children. I'll take you up and beat the hell out of you, I swear I will. For their sakes."

"Charlie, I'm going to Chicago!" she said flatly, finally.

"You're not going to run out on this, Beth. You have a responsibility to me and the kids. Nobody held a gun to your head when we got married. Why, you weren't even pregnant. You married me because you *wanted* to marry me, and by God, you're *still* married to me. And you're going to *stay* married to me until you grow up and learn to face your responsibilities."

"Charlie," she said, suddenly earnest and almost scared, "I can't *stand* this anymore."

"Can't stand what? No lovers? None of your lady friends suits you?"

For a second she thought she would explode with grief and fury, but she clamped her eyes shut and controlled herself. "I can't stand living with a man," she said, and suddenly the tears began to flow. She went on speaking, ignoring them. "It's not your fault you're a man—"

"Thanks," he snarled.

"And it's not my fault I need a woman. You have to understand that, Charlie. I'm not doing this because I want to hurt you. I'm not gay because I enjoy it. I don't even know if I'm gay at all. I wish to God, I wish with all my heart, that I could make a life with you and

84

the children. I wish all I needed to be happy was what other woman need—a home and a man and children. I thought I *was* like other women when we got married, or I never would have committed myself to a lifetime with you. I thought it was what I needed and wanted, or believe me I would have spared us both. I would have climbed aboard that train with Laura nine years ago. But I thought *she* was different and *I* was normal. And I was in love with you."

He sighed deeply, covering his face for a moment with his hands.

"I remember Laura," he said then, gazing into space. "I remember her so well, with that pale face, rather thin, and those big blue eyes. I remember how she adored you and how pathetic I thought she was. I remember how shocked I was when I found out that you had encouraged her. But I was always so sure, in spite of everything, that you were basically normal and that being married and having a couple of kids would straighten you out so easily. I was so sure of myself," and she saw his self-doubt and confusion now and it touched her. "I thought because I was a man and because I loved you so terribly that we'd be able to work out anything together. I thought that living with me would give you a lifelong preference for my love. Real love, a man's love. The kind of love that only a man can give a woman."

"That's not the only real love, Charlie," she said, sinking to the chair again, and leaning toward him, tense with the need to make him understand a little, now, at long last. "I thought I'd get over it too when Laura went away, and I thought I had. It was years after we were married that I began to feel like this, and at first I didn't even know what it was. It wasn't till Vega that I even realized what was wrong with me. Charlie, maybe if I could just have a sort of *vacation* from you."

"Vacation? How can you take a vacation from a marriage? It's a permanent condition," he said, and she could tell from his voice that it didn't make the first glimmer of sense to him.

"I know it isn't sensible, and I've tried to fight it, but it overwhelms me," she said. "I wonder, 'what in hell am I married for anyway? My kids are miserable, I'm miserable, Charlie's miserable.' If I were doing any good with all this suffering it might be worth while. If it made Skipper and Polly happy, if it made *you* happy, maybe it would be worth it all. But it doesn't. We're *all* unhappy. Charlie...please understand."

"You can help yourself, Beth," he said coldly.

"No, I can't," she said. "That's the awful part of it. That's what scares me so. I feel my irritation turning into hatred, almost. I want to get away so badly that I don't think I can stand it sometimes."

"Get away from what? Yourself? You have to take yourself with you wherever you go, you know."

"No, I want to get closer to myself, I want to *know myself,* Charlie. I don't even know who I am. Or *what* I am."

"You're *my wife!*" he said sharply, as if that were the argument to end them all, to end all of her doubts with one stroke.

"I'm myself!" she cried, rising to her feet again, her fists knotted at her sides. "And all I'm doing by staying here is creating agony for the four of us."

"The five of us. You forget Vega. Apparently she's not too happy with things, if you wish she were in hell."

"Oh, Charlie, spare me! God!" she shouted. Her voice sounded nearly hysterical.

"Keep it down," he said. "If you don't wake the kids up you'll scare the neighbors to death."

For a long trembling moment she stood there, unable to speak through her sobs and unable to look at his tired and disappointed face. Finally she said, whispering, "I don't know who I am, Charlie. Just saying I'm your wife doesn't tell me any more than I've known for years, and that isn't enough."

"You're either straight or you're gay, Beth. Take your pick." He couldn't yield to her, he couldn't be generous. He had been through too much and his restraint ran too high. He stood to lose a wife he loved, through that wife's lack of self-understanding. He might see her transformed into a type of woman he neither understood nor liked, before his very eyes.

"It's not that easy," she said, appalled at his attitude. "You aren't either black or white, you're all shades of gray in between. It might be the kind of thing I could get over and learn to live with, and it might be the kind of thing that will change my whole life irrevocably."

"What if you find out you're nothing but a goddamn Lesbian?" he said in that rough voice that carried his grief so clearly, and he wounded her heart forever with his words.

Her patience snapped like a stick bent too far. Without a word—words had never seemed so inadequate, so meaningless, so useless between two people born to the same native tongue—she turned and went into the bedroom and emptied all of her dresser drawers on the bed. Charlie watched her while she marched in white-faced fury into the basement and hauled two big bags up the stairs.

She dragged them through the living room and he leaned forward to say softly, "You fool, Beth. You fool!"

But she couldn't look at him. She thought she would either faint with her hatred or somehow kill him with the frenzy of it.

In the bedroom she stuffed things into the bags helter skelter. What didn't fit didn't go. The rest was left behind in a tangle.

Halfway through this frenetic task she went to the phone and called the Los Angeles International Airport. Charlie watched her, still on the couch, immobilized with disbelief. She made a reservation for that very morning at three o'clock.

And then she called her Uncle John and told him to pick her up at Chicago's Midway Airport the next day. Her reservation on the plane was for one person only.

"Just *you?*" Charlie said softly, staring at her. "You mean you'd really leave me here with the kids? You mean you really don't give a goddamn about your own children?"

"You said I couldn't take them with me!" she cried. "I'd take them if you'd let me."

"Never," he said. "But I thought—God, Beth, I though you'd try a little harder to get them than this. You've given up without a struggle." He was truly shocked; it blasted all his favorite concepts of motherhood to see her behave this way.

"I've struggled with you until I haven't any strength left," she said hoarsely.

"You never loved them," he said, hushed with shock and revelation. "You never loved them at all."

"I haven't a strong enough stomach to get down on my knees and beg for them," she cried. "I've begged you long enough and hard enough for other things."

"But they were *things*. These are *kids*. Your own kids!"

"I want them," she cried, "but I want my freedom more. I only make them unhappy, I'm not a good mother."

"Well, what sort of a *mother* do you think I'll make?" he shouted, and now it was Charlie whose voice was loud enough to wake the children.

She left him abruptly and finished her packing. In the children's room she could hear stirrings and she prayed with the tears still soaking her cheeks that neither of them would wake up and break her heart or change her mind. She forced her suitcases shut with the strength of haste and fear, and half shoved, half carried them out to the car.

Charlie stood in the center of the living room and watched her with his mouth open. When she passed him he said, "Beth, this isn't happening. It can't be. I couldn't have been that bad. I *couldn't* have been. Beth, please. Explain to me, tell me. I don't understand."

But she gave him a look of hopelessness, and once she snapped, "Is that all you can say? After nine years of marriage?"

Is he just going to stand there and let me go? she wondered. A sort of panic rose in her at the thought that he might suddenly regain his senses and force her to stop. But he let her get as far as packing both bags into the back of the car and actually starting the motor before he yanked the door open and shoved her over so that he could sit in the driver's seat.

"Beth," he said, and his eyes were still big with the awfulness of what she was doing to him and their children. "You aren't going anywhere."

Suddenly he kissed her urgently, holding her arms with hands so strong and fierce that they bruised her flesh. She felt his teeth pressed into her tender mouth and something in the despair of it, the near-terror she sensed in him at the thought of losing her, brought an uprush of unwanted tenderness in her heart.

He tried to kiss her again, but Beth struggled wildly, trying to hurt him. And all the while he was wooing her with violence, almost the way he had when they first met, as if he knew now too that words were long since worthless between them.

At last Beth grasped one of her own shoes and pulled it off. Desperately she struck him with all her strength on the side of the head. The sharp heel cut his scalp and he gave a soft little cry of astonishment. He pulled away from her at last and they stared at each other, both of them shocked at themselves, at each other, at what was happening, both of them crying.

Finally, without a word, he got out of the car and slammed the door.

Beth dragged herself over to the driver's seat and rolled down the window. "I'll write," she said, but their two white faces, still so near one another physically, were already separated by more than the miles Beth would fly across that night. He flinched at her promise, as if he knew that an envelope full of words would do no more good than those they had flung at each other in a huge effort to create understanding.

"Take good care of the kids," she said and immediately she began to back out because she could hear one of them starting to cry.

He walked along beside the car, one hand on the window sill as if that might keep her there longer. "What shall I tell them this time when they wake up and find you gone?" he asked.

"Tell them I've gone to hell," she wept. "Tell them I'm a no-good and the only thing they can hope for is that life will be happier without me than with me. It will, too."

She began to press the accelerator, gathering speed until he had to let go or run to keep up. He let go.

In the street she straightened the car around and gave one last trembling look to her house, her yard and garden, the lighted windows of the living room where the TV set played on to an audience of furniture. Skipper's little voice wailed through the night for a glass of water and Charlie stood at the end of the drive, a silhouette with silver trim, watching her.

Beth drove away. *God, let me never feel sorrow like this again,* she prayed. *Let this be my punishment for what I'm doing. I can't bear any more.*

Chapter Nine

IN PASADENA SHE STOPPED AND CALLED CLEVE. IT WAS PAST eleven o'clock and she hesitated, but she had to talk to somebody about Vega and had to make some arrangements about Charlie, and there plainly wasn't anybody she could turn to but Cleve.

"I'm in a little all-night joint on Fair Oaks, at Colorado," she said.

"God, Beth, you're on Skid Row!"

"Sh! Don't wake Jean up! Can you come down?"

"Sure, but you'd better find a cop to protect you till I get there."

"It's not a bar, it's a coffee place," she said. "Hurry, Cleve." And the catch in her throat warned him to heed her words.

He got there in less than fifteen minutes. She was waiting out in front and when he arrived they went in and took a booth and had a cup of coffee in the dirty brilliance of the fluorescent light.

"Cleve, it's not fair of me to dump my troubles in your lap," she said, "but you've got to help me. You're the only one who can."

He was alarmed by the look of her. Her eyes were heavy and scared, red with weeping, and her hair hung about her pretty face in neglected confusion. She breathed fast, as though she had been running, and she stammered—something Beth, with all her poise, had never done.

"If you're in trouble—"

"It's private trouble, Cleve. I'm leaving Charlie."

His jaw went slack and he stared at her amazed while the waitress placed the coffee in front of them. After a moment he lighted them each a cigarette, passing hers to her, and then he said to the coffee cup, "I'm really sorry. God! I thought you two were sublimely happy."

"Not everybody's as happy as you and Jean!" Beth said, and there was more wistfulness than envy in her voice.

"Thank God for that," he said wryly, but she was too wrapped up in her pain and perplexity to notice it. "Tell me about it?" he said.

"No," she said, shaking her head and making a tremendous effort to control herself. "You wouldn't understand any better than he did."

"What about the kids?" His voice was cautious. He had been handling Vega's flare-ups so long that frantic women were not new to him. He had some idea what to do.

"I—I left them. I'm no proper mother, Cleve. It was cowardly but I swear I think they'll be happier."

Like Charlie before him, Cleve was shocked. "But what in hell will Charlie *do* with them?"

"I don't know. I came to talk to you about Vega," she said quickly. If he persisted in that obvious shock she would go to pieces. His sister's name silenced him, threw him off the track.

"I went ahead and saw her, Cleve. I've been seeing quite a lot of her lately." She didn't know how to proceed. She couldn't blurt out the truth to him, and yet she had to say something. In her frayed emotional state Vega was likely to do anything, even scream the facts to strangers, unless she could be reassured that Beth at least thought of her before she left.

"I know," Cleve told her.

"You *know?*" Beth gasped. *"What* do you know?"

"That you've been seeing her," he said, and he was not pleased. "Who do you think gets the brunt of her bad temper?"

"I thought I got all of it."

He shook his head. "You don't even get half."

After an embarrassed pause she said, "I'm sorry, Cleve." She wondered how much of the truth he knew.

"So am I."

"She thinks she owns me. We've gotten pretty close. I can't disappear without giving her a message. Tell her I'm sorry, will you?"

"Okay." He looked at her. "Is that all?"

And she knew from his voice, his face, that he was disappointed in her, perhaps his feelings were even stronger.

"Vega took it all wrong, Cleve. She took it too hard."

"She did that with Beverly, too. The girl P.K. Schaefer took away from her."

It took Beth a moment to place P.K.

"I don't want her to do anything awful, Cleve," Beth said, pleading with him.

"Neither do I," he said and gave her a twisted little smile.

"I guess I loused things up for you, didn't I? I never meant to. It just happened. It got away from me. Will you talk to her?"

"I'll try." He was already bracing himself for another siege of fury and erratic temper and threats. When things like this happened to Vega he always had to nurse her through them. Her mother was too sick and Gramp was too frail and neither of them understood the problem. Mrs. Purvis, to judge from Cleve's description of her attitude, would have disowned her daughter at the very least had she known her true nature.

When Cleve made a move to get up she caught his hands, searching for the warmth, the desire to help her, that she so needed. But he was chilly, preoccupied with the problem she had thrust at him.

"Cleve, there's one more thing," she said and he paused.

"Beth, I told you not to get mixed up with my sister, but you went ahead and did it. Now you're sorry but it's too late. Don't you think that's enough?"

She was surprised and shamed by it. But not silenced. "I *must* ask you—you're the only one. Write to me," she implored. "Tell me about the kids and Charlie. He won't write, I know that. Besides I don't want him to know my address, if I should leave my uncle's house. Oh, Cleve, please! You *can't* turn me down!"

He looked at her a second longer, at her pale tremulous mouth and shaking hand, and then he took the address from her. It was one of Uncle John's cards from her wallet. He folded it solemnly and put it into his pocket.

"Thank you, Cleve," she said ardently. "You'll be my only link with them."

Cleve stood up. "I told Jean I had to go down to the corner drug store," he said. "I've told her that so often she thinks it means the corner beer parlor. I'd better get home and give her a nice surprise. Nothing but coffee on my breath." He was making an effort, at least, to be kind, to take the awful heaviness out of the atmosphere. She knew he would do as he said for her, and she was moved and grateful.

He took her arm and led her to her car. At the door he told her, "If this is half as hard on Charlie as it is on you, he's going to crack up fast. You look like hell, Beth."

"I know," she said. "I never did anything so awful—so hard—in my life. I feel like I'm going to die of it."

"Then you're a fool. Whatever your reasons were, they aren't worth it."

"That's what I have to find out," she said.

"Sure you won't tell me?"

"Yes, Cleve." She held out a hand to him and after a minute he grasped it and squeezed it. "I'm sorry," he said. "For you both."

"Thank you. Goodbye, Cleve. And write to me."

He nodded and then he turned and walked away and she watched him for a second, thinking how much he looked like Vega and what a hell of a mess she had handed him. Subconsciously she realized that her train of thoughts was enough to shatter her mind, her emotions. The load was already too great. She had to turn to something else, she had to move and do things and act ordinary and sensible or she would fly to pieces.

The plane took off three minutes behind time. She felt the ground fall away beneath her and the wide steel wings rise, heard the captain's voice moments later and saw her seat neighbor light a cigarette—all with a feeling of eerie unreality reinforced by the small morning hour.

"We are circling over Catalina Island," the pilot announced, "waiting for air traffic to clear over Los Angeles. In about five minutes we will be heading due east."

Beth looked out of the window and saw a wavy ribbon of orange lights—the shoreline of Catalina Island—and a cluster of white lights winking around the town of Avalon. She was on the side away from the mainland and couldn't see Los Angeles, but soon afterward the plane turned eastward and they headed inland again. She looked down, looking for landmarks in the night, and after a moment she recognized a few; the Colosseum, the brilliant green-white strips of the freeways, and then Pasadena with the winding pattern of Orange Grove Avenue discernible below. She followed it carefully with her eyes to where she supposed Sierra Bella began, and looked at the bouquet of lights there against the mountains, looked at it more with her heart than her eyes.

She closed her eyes then and for a short painful moment she could see the little town as it would look in tomorrow's daylight, bright with the colors of early summer, the lavender flowers of the jacaranda trees glowing over the streets, the pink and white oleander with its pointed leaves, the long palmy street up the mountainside to their small house, the sun frosting the purple mountains in the early morning, the sounds of her children tumbling out of bed and shouting for their breakfast, Charlie shaving and grumbling at the mirror.

Beth lighted a cigarette and said softly to herself, "Laura, I'm coming for you. Don't fail me. Be there, darling, or that's the end of me. I'll be destroyed, for I can never come back here."

Chapter Ten

UNCLE JOHN, GENIAL AND BUSTLING AND WORRIED, PICKED HER up in Chicago. He had to be content with the briefest and barest explanation from her. She was utterly exhausted and all she wanted was to collapse and sleep. She even took sleeping pills when it developed that her bitter self-recriminations would give her no rest. And for two whole days she refused to leave the room.

"I'll just say this," she told Uncle John when he pressed her. "I've left Charlie. He has the children; they're all fine. Everything is my fault. It would kill me to have to talk about it now. I'll try to explain it later. I'm so tired and miserable I just want to be alone."

So they gave her their hospitality and let her have her way. Uncle John was anxious and he even thought of calling Charlie and demanding the facts. But his wife restrained him. "Let's at least hear her side of it first," she said. "She *did* say it was her fault, after all."

Beth had no intention of explaining to them what couldn't be explained. She wrote to Charlie, just a note. She said she would be with Uncle John for a while and she'd let him know any new plans. Cleve wrote to her within a couple of days to say the kids were well but missed her badly, and Charlie had become very taciturn at the office. He had found a woman to care for the children during the day. Beth wondered impatiently what sort of woman she was—whether she was kindly and whether she liked children and whether she fixed them their favorite breakfasts, and what she looked like. There was no mention of Vega in Cleve's letter.

As soon as she had a little strength, a little sense, she determined to find Laura. The place to start was with Laura's father. Beth didn't suppose that Laura was still living with him; they had never gotten along, and Laura, when she left Beth nine years ago, had been an entirely different girl from the one her father thought he had raised. She had found herself and had begun to live for the first time, and Beth guessed that her first move had been to leave her father.

But Beth had to start somewhere, and so, when she had been in Chicago two days, she called Merrill Landon. It was midafternoon; it had taken her till then to get up her courage. She wasn't sure whether she was more afraid of finding Laura or of not finding her. What would Laura think of Beth, now that her former lover was no longer a radiant college girl? Of course Laura would be older too, but she was still four years younger than Beth, and Beth had lived with a mountain of dissatisfaction and discontent that had left its mark on her pretty face.

Merrill Landon was not in. Beth had to call again at seven. She approached the phone in a nervous sweat, afraid that her voice would break or her throat go dry and betray her nerves to him. She had to be very casual.

This time she got him from his dinner.

Damn! she thought while the servant summoned him. *He probably hates to be interrupted.*

"Hello?" he said, and his voice was deep and rough. He spoke in the same tone he would have used to bark an order to a subordinate at the newspaper where he worked. Beth gasped a little before she could say, "Mr. Landon? My name is Beth Cullison. I—I mean Beth *Ayers.*" Her maiden name! *God,* she thought in dismay. But there was no time to scold herself.

"Well, which is it?" he boomed.

"Ayers. Mrs. Ayers," she answered, trying to sound calm. She raced on, hoping to smooth over his first impression, "I'm an old college friend of Laura's. I'm visiting in Chicago and I thought it would be nice if we could get together."

Her voice went dry and she had to stop. There was an awkward pause. "A college friend?" he said, as if there were no such things.

"You *are* Laura's father, aren't you?" she asked timidly.

"Yes." He waited so long to answer that it made her wonder. "What do you want with Laura, Mrs. Ayers?"

"I just wanted to talk to her. If she's there."

"I haven't seen Laura for the last eight years," he said, and Beth's heart went cold. He added thoughtfully, "You said your name was Cullison. Were you one of Laura's roommates at the university?"

For some reason she was afraid to answer yes. Could it possibly be that Laura might have told him about the curious love that had sprung up between them? It was unlikely that he would remember her name unless it had special significance for him. What if he had forced the truth out of his daughter?

"Well?" he said, surprise and impatience in his voice at her delay. "Maybe you can't remember that far back?"

"Yes. Yes, I was her roommate. Excuse me, I—where is Laura now?"

"Mrs. Ayers, why don't you come over here tonight? I'd like to talk to you." And when she hesitated again in a welter of uncertainty he said, "Are you far from here?"

"I have a car," she said. "I'll come."

She took Aunt Elsa's Buick and drove out to the Landon house. It wasn't far; it was on one of the pretty shaded streets of Evanston. Merrill Landon lived there alone with his two servants. He had been there since he and Laura's mother first married and nothing could tempt him away.

There was nothing left of Laura's mother now but memories. But they bound Landon to her and kept him in the home she had furnished, where he could still see traces of her taste, her touch. No other woman had ever replaced her for him. Except, in a strange and uncomprehended way, Laura. And because she couldn't *be* her mother, because she was only a sweet shadow, a photo transparency, he blamed her and was very hard with her.

When Laura had at last understood where she had unwittingly failed him, she left him. She was his daughter, not his wife; that was her crime. And because he couldn't have her he couldn't forgive her for living. She was a constant threat to his virtue, a painful reminder of his dead wife. The knowledge of his tormented desire gave her the courage to turn her back on him and run.

He had found her once, after that, almost by accident, and they had it out in words, the awful incredible words that had never been spoken between them before. The rupture had been complete after that. He admitted that he wanted her. He took her in his bearish arms and kissed her mouth brutally. And Laura, in her shock, told him what she was, a Lesbian. And who had done it to her; her own father. So they knew the very worst of each other, had known now for years, and had lost each other. But the knowledge, though it hurt, washed away the bitterness.

Over the chasm of years and miles, Merrill Landon had come to love his daughter in a new way. He had never tried to pursue her, after that one shattering night in a New York hotel room when they had revealed themselves to each other, but he had spent the long years since then wondering about her, wondering how she might be living and with whom. His thoughts were mostly tender, sometimes resentful, always lonely. But he was proud and a little afraid of himself with her, and he would not seek her out again.

Beth rang his bell, ignorant of all that had passed between him and Laura in the years that preceded her visit. No servant opened to her, as she had expected, but Merrill Landon himself, as though he, too, was anxious for the meeting. She had never seen him before in her life but she knew him instantly. His flesh was Laura's and her whole body was suddenly covered with shiverings.

He was a huge man; not big like Charlie, not tall and long-muscled, but just big. Square-chested, slope-shouldered, powerfully built, with his dark hair and heavy beard. He stood high from the ground but you didn't realize it until you came close to him; the chunkiness of his construction gave him the look of a shorter man. In his heavy features she saw very little of Laura, who resembled most her mother. And yet there was something there, faint but visible, that kept the shivers coming in Beth.

He sized her up like a seasoned journalist. "Come in, Mrs. Ayers," he said, and showed her into a comfortable den stacked high with books and papers. It was apparently his study, the workroom where he wrote his daily editorials, read his books, did his dreaming, perhaps. Beth sat in a large ox-blood leather chair. She was afraid to lean back in it for fear of getting lost, of making herself look small and shy to this man she wanted so much to impress with her social ease. It would have helped immeasurably if she could have guessed by looking at him how much he knew of her love for Laura.

Landon mixed her a drink. "What are you doing in Chicago, Beth?" he asked with his back to her, and the sound of her proper name startled her.

Now he thinks he's got me, she thought. *I'm here in his house and he thinks he's going to find out about Laura and me once and for all. I'm not even Mrs. Ayers anymore, I'm just Beth. Just a schoolgirl.*

She told him she was visiting her uncle, she was living in California, she had two children. That was all. His questions were brief, as though she were a socialite he had to interview for the next day's paper, and she tailored her answers the same way. But Beth wanted to ask her own questions. She was the one who urgently needed to know, who had left her home and kids and husband and come all this way to find this man's daughter—and perhaps, at the same time, herself. She gazed around the room, taking in the working disorder, the handsome, slightly worn furniture. Laura knew all this, Beth thought; it was as familiar to her as her own room, and the thought made Beth ache for her.

She interrupted Landon to ask him, "Where is she, Mr. Landon? Maybe there's still time for me to see her tonight." He smiled at her over-bright eyes and somehow she expected his answer.

"I doubt it. She's not living in Chicago anymore."

Of course not. Goddamn! That would have been too easy. I should have known. "Where is she?" she demanded, and again he smiled at the pink flush in her cheeks, the line between her eyes.

"I'd like to know myself," he said. He was almost teasing her.

"You must have some idea," she cried, desperately afraid that Laura would slip out of her fingers before she ever touched her again. If she had been more observant she would have seen the understanding that began to show in his smile. He was needling her for a purpose.

"I do have some idea," he said calmly, sitting down behind his desk. "I'll gladly share it with you. If you'll do something for me, Beth."

"If I can."

"You can." She watched him while he listened to his memories. He could hear Laura's voice in his inner ear crying, "And that's not all! Remember Beth Cullison? Remember my roommate at school? Her too, Father! She was the first! I loved her! Do you understand what I'm telling you?" That voice, sharp with the saved-up sorrows and frustrations of a young lifetime, crying at him through tears and fury of what she had become, what her true nature was! And he had understood her, at last. His perverted love for her had twisted her whole personality. He had controlled his terrible desire for years, but it had cost Laura a normal childhood.

"When you find Laura," he said, "I want you to tell me where she is. That's all. Will you do that?"

Beth stared at him. "When I find her?" she said. "Where do I have to go?"

"Tell me her address, that's all," he bargained.

And she knew then that he could see plainly how badly she wanted Laura. She struggled to keep her face smooth, her passion under wraps. "Yes," she said. It was a whole confession of love, that word. It said, *Yes, I'll find her, I'll go to the ends of the earth, I'll do any favor for you if you'll tell me where to start, where to look.*

He smiled. He had her. "She's in New York," he said.

Beth's mouth fell open. "New *York!*" She was dismayed. She had only been there once, when she was a little girl of ten. She didn't know the city at all. And the size of it! "But, good God, Mr. Landon, there are millions of people in New York!" she exclaimed.

"There's only one Laura. She's been there a while, she knows people."

"What people?" Her discouragement showed now, too. She couldn't have hidden it from her extraordinary host.

"If I were you I'd start in the Village," he said. "She lived down there a while."

"I don't know the Village," she protested. "I don't know New York at all. I can't fly to New York just to scare up an old roommate of mine." It was supposed to throw him off the track, demonstrate her normalcy. But Merrill Landon was too far ahead of her. He knew too much that she didn't know. He saw the strength and determination in her chin, the trembling of her sensual mouth, and he smiled once again.

"You can't, but you will," he said. "Isn't that why you're here?" There was an embarrassed silence. She didn't know how to answer without exposing herself to him. "Beth," he said, and the gruff voice softened slightly, "I know you were in love with my daughter."

She gasped, and as he went on she gulped the rest of her drink.

"She told me so. You have a right to know that I know. She— well, she had to tell me; she didn't do it to hurt you. I've kept it to myself. I knew you from the pictures she used to have of you." She began to cry, and into the sniffly silence he added, "I love her too. Only I can't go find her now. Someone else will have to do that for me."

When they were able to look at each other again he said, "Did you come all the way from California to find her?"

She was undone. She had no secrets. He was too much for her, with his bright eyes that penetrated hers and saw so much and suspected so much more. "Yes," she confessed. "I had to get away from my husband. I was nearly cracking up. I just wanted to see Laura again. Everything was so wonderful then, so awful now. I thought it might help. I thought maybe that was what was wrong with me."

He lighted a cigarette for her and one for himself. "Laura doesn't want to see me again," he said. "With you it may be different. If you follow her to New York, Beth, you'll find her, somehow. I want you to tell me about her and where she's living. I won't give you cause to regret it. I've messed up her life enough as it is. Just tell me when you find her."

"All right." She seemed to have no will now. Only a need for Laura, a need for her love so great that it would propel her onward until she found her. "Mr. Landon," she said, looking at him with all her subterfuges stripped from her. "Why are you kind to me? Why don't you despise me for what I did to your daughter?"

"For what *you* did to her?" He gave a scornful little laugh that turned against himself. "If I were guiltless myself I could despise anyone I pleased. I could blame anyone I pleased. But I'm not guiltless." His words made her feel braver. "If it hadn't been you it would have been somebody else, Beth. You know that, of course. Laura is a Lesbian. Sooner or later she would have understood that, whether with your help or without it."

It was logical, it was sensible. But it had never struck Beth quite that way and it hurt. She stood up with a little gasp and walked away from him. "No," she blurted. "It was special, it was— almost sacred."

"To you perhaps."

"To both of us. She couldn't have done it with anyone else." She spoke positively because she was suddenly so unsure.

"I didn't mean to shock you," he said. "I thought you would have realized long ago that somebody had to be first with her and it just happened to be you. It was no divine choice, just blind accident."

Beth lighted a cigarette with trembling hands. "I guess it's because I've never known any other woman the way I know Laura," she said, talking fast to keep the tears back. "I guess it's because there never was anybody else I wanted like that."

"And you just took it for granted that Laura never wanted anybody else, either? You're fooling yourself, my dear. That's her nature. That's her life. For you, with a husband and a family, life has been very different. Now, when you want her again, you're resentful to find that Laura's life has gone on without you. That she's found other women, a whole new mode of living, other interests that you don't share."

It knocked her ego into a corner. "Oh, you spiteful bastard!" she cried in pure self-defense. And then clapped her hands over her mouth, sinking to a small straight-backed chair and weeping angry startled tears that nevertheless broke the tension and relieved her.

Merrill Landon laughed softly and she was unnerved to hear Laura's inflection in the sound. "You have a little spirit, after all," he said. "Good. You're mad because I'm right. Isn't that so? Of course."

And of course he was right, to her chagrin.

"I didn't even think about her after I'd been married," Beth said brokenly. It was the first time in all these weary months of wondering and experimenting with the wrong person, of deceiving Charlie and perhaps her own self, that she let go and spoke of it. And it felt good. Landon understood her language. That alone made it possible to speak.

"I was dissatisfied," she explained to him. "Oh, hell, I was just plain sick to death of the whole mess. The little things with a husband aggravated me even more than the big things. And the kids nearly did me in. When it got so I couldn't stand to have Charlie touch me, I knew we'd had it. *He* didn't, though. He still thinks I'm going through a phase.

"I guess when *I* changed so much it seemed to me Charlie should change, too. But that was unreasonable of me. Here I am, a completely different Beth, and he's just the same old Charlie."

"You fell in love with him that way," Landon reminded her.

"In love and out," she said.

"When did it occur to you that Laura might cure your ills?" He handed her a fresh drink and she took a swallow before she answered him.

"I began to dream about her," she said. "Just a little at first, but then all the time. I met another woman and I tried to find with her what I had known once with Laura, but it didn't work. Made me think that no other woman would be right for me." She glanced at him shyly, suddenly recalling that he ought to be shocked and disapproving, wondering where she found the guts to confess as she did. The whiskey? The house, Laura's house? The man, Laura's father? She saw no shock in his face, only interest and a certain remote sympathy, and it gave her a new respect for him.

"The other woman didn't love you?" he asked.

"Yes, she did," Beth said. He saw her chin quiver and knew she was understating things for him.

"When you find Laura, do you think she'll be just the way she was when you knew her in college?" he asked.

"No. That'd be pretty naive of me," Beth said.

"And yet that's what you're looking for in her. You don't know her the way she is now. You're setting out to find your old college roommate. Laura may disappoint you like this other woman did. Just by being different from your memories of her. Then where will you turn, Beth?"

It was a dismal thing to face. She had resolutely ignored the possibility until now.

"You'd better make plans," Landon continued. "A thing like that could crack you up if you're not prepared for it. It's been a while, Beth, quite a while. Nine years?"

She nodded. "She hasn't forgotten me, has she? Could that be?"

"She hadn't when I saw her. She remembers a college girl with no real experience of life, the way you do. She remembers an ingenuous romance. She remembers that you jilted her for a boy you knew, and probably married the boy. End of story. You'll have to take it from there yourself when you find her."

"If I find her," she said and emptied her glass again.

"You will, if you still want to as much as you did when you came in here tonight."

She put the glass down. "I do," she whispered.

He smiled. "You may get to New York and find her right there in the phone book. Who knows?"

Beth gave a wry little laugh. "Sure," she said. "I was thinking, on the plane, 'What if I get to Chicago and there she is, at home with her father.' It would have been too easy, though. But I *did* think she'd be living in the city, at least. Now...New York. God. When I get to New York they'll tell me she's living in Paris. And if I ever make it to Paris, damned if she isn't already on her way to Hong Kong."

"She's not much of a vagabond," Landon reassured her. "She'd have stayed here in Chicago if I'd made it tolerable for her. This was her home. She liked it here.... Have you any money?" he asked abruptly, looking directly at her.

"A little," she said with some pride.

"A little doesn't last long in New York."

"I have about three thousand in my bank account."

"Well, depending on how you live and whether you work or not, that might see you through a half year."

"I don't gamble," she snapped. "I don't eat at the Stork Club. And I don't throw the stuff away."

He laughed. "Okay, my dear. Go to New York with your three thousand dollars and live on it for the rest of your life if you can. I wish you only luck—the best kind. I was just thinking, if you should need a loan..." And seeing her face storm up he added, "I'm not laughing at you, Beth. I think you're a better girl—a braver girl—than I did at first. Maybe I hoped you'd be a disappointment. You see, I haven't liked you very well, over the years, since Laura told me she loved you. Simple jealousy. I haven't liked any of the others she told me about either. But I suppose it's only fair. I had her all to myself for eighteen years and only made her miserable." He turned away as he spoke. "When at last I had to share her, it was with her own sex. I was shocked when she told me, but after a while I found I preferred it to sharing her with men."

There was an awkward silence. Beth stared in surprise at his broad back in its brown tweed lounging jacket, feeling that his admission bound her to him, as hers bound him to her. They had a little something on each other now. They owed each other some small allegiance.

"I'll send you her address, if I find her," Beth said.

"Thank you. And your own. I don't think I'd better write Laura. I'll have to depend on you for news. Do you mind?"

Beth began to laugh and made him turn around to stare in his turn. "Is that funny?" he asked.

Beth shook her head and when she found her voice she said, "No, life is funny. I can't write to Charlie either. There's a friend in Pasadena who's doing for me what I'm doing for you. Writing to tell me all the news." They gazed at each other a little guiltily and still with amusement. "Are we a pair of cowards, Mr. Landon?" she said. "Or are we braver than everybody else?"

"Cowards, of course," he said. "We aren't really brave at all. But we do have a certain strength. You set out to find yourself, and that takes strength. I found myself long ago and had the strength to live with what I found—not a pleasant task. He grinned at her and suddenly she liked him. She liked him very much and in that instant she saw Laura in his face, his smile, again.

They were a pair of conspirators. If Beth found Laura and won her love again, she would be an ally for Merrill Landon. Through Beth he might come close once again to the daughter he adored; once again before time caught up with him and closed his life. For he was in his late fifties now and he had lived too hard. He was tired. He wanted a few years with her, and the idea had struck him when he interviewed Beth that this might be a last way to achieve the goal. He couldn't approach Laura himself. She would turn and run before he could speak, and she had a right to. But Beth might speak for him. She liked him. He could see it in her face.

They parted with an understanding—friends.

Chapter Eleven

BETH WITHDREW HER MONEY FROM THE BANK. THERE WAS nearly four thousand dollars. That was plenty. She felt extravagantly rich with the money her parents had left her lined up neatly in traveler's checks in her wallet. She took the precaution of getting the funds before she broke the news to Uncle John. Not that he could have stopped her; the money was hers, free and clear. But he could have slowed things down, and she wanted to be able to go now, at once.

"I've been thinking," she told him the next day, "that I'd like to take a trip."

"A trip?"

"Yes. To forget. To think about something else. I want to see some *new* places, Uncle John. I want to roam a little. I think it'd do me good."

He appeared unconvinced. He was a cautious man by nature and a provincial. If you could stay at home with your own comfortable bed and the food you liked, why go anywhere? His days of patient silence weighted his spirits down, too, and he suddenly asked his niece, with straightforward concern, "Beth, what about your children? How can you go traveling and just leave them?"

"They're all right," she said, looking away.

"How do you know? How long do you intend to be away from them? Is that good for children? Damn it, you haven't explained any of this to me yet. I don't like it."

"Uncle John, quit worrying!" she cried irritably. "The kids are with their father. They're better off with him, you must understand that."

"Why don't you take them away from him? You're their *mother,* for God's sake. If you're going to divorce Charlie you'd better start doing something about it instead of running around the country. Are you going to go through life married to a man who's unworthy of you, who won't let you keep your own children?"

"That has nothing to do with it. I told you it was all my fault!" she cried.

"What did you do, then? Just *what,* exactly, did you do? What's the *matter* with you, Beth? I have a right to know. I'm feeding you and sheltering you—I'm supporting you. Your husband should be doing this."

"You mean if I don't tell you everything you don't want me here?" she demanded, stunned.

"I mean you owe me an explanation!" he said, and she saw that his slow temper was finally roused. His balding head reddened. "Are you in love with some other man?"

"No!"

"Did you disgrace yourself? Or Charlie?"

"No!"

"Do you want your children, do you love your children?"

"Yes!" She was furious. Her voice broke.

"Then why in God's name don't you get them? It's unnatural! How is it that Charlie can keep them from you?"

"I gave them up!" she shouted. "I gave them up in exchange for my freedom. There! Make sense out of that if you can!"

She ran upstairs to her room and began to pack.

She made a one-way reservation to New York City and then she sat down and wrote a letter to Nina Spicer, the writer whose books about Lesbian life in New York had attracted her. She had almost forgotten Nina until her talk with Merrill Landon. Now, suddenly, the writer appeared to her as a possible starting place in her search. Nina knew New York; you could tell that from the books she wrote. She knew the Village, and she knew gay life both in and out of the Village. There was no reason to suppose she knew Laura, but perhaps she knew *of* her, knew where she could be found.

Beth had been candid, in a way, with Nina. She pretended she was gay, even when she wasn't sure of it herself. She painted a picture of herself as beautiful, lost, misunderstood, yearning for a passionate romance with any compatible female. When she wrote the words she believed them true and her belief carried conviction, for Nina answered her with a certain condescending kindness and sympathy.

So Nina Spicer had a passel of half-facts from which to form an opinion of Beth. And Beth knew even less of Nina—only what she could guess from the books: a half-dozen violent, lively, coarse stories, loaded with deaths and beatings and perversities. They had some of the interest of good newspaper reporting, with a sort of gusto in the gory details and a lot of tormented screwballs for characters. Occasionally the love scenes were moving; more often, blunt case histories, skillfully dissected.

Beth pictured her as a casual hardheaded girl, fast to take up an affair, fast to drop it; hard to know and only partly worth the effort. But she was grateful, terribly grateful, to Nina for her letters. She wished there were some way to know her without having to meet her, for she sensed a bridgeless difference between herself and Nina that might make enemies of them. But she needed help now and Nina was the only person she knew who could give it to her.

Beth escaped at midafternoon the next day, taking a bus from the Conrad Hilton on Michigan Boulevard to the airport. It was that simple. No one even saw her leave the house.

There was no crushing despair, no gnawing panic and indecision this time. This time she was on the last leg of the journey, the all-consuming quest to find Beth Cullison Ayers and make a human being out of her. Laura was at the other end.

But Laura was not in the Manhattan directory when Beth checked it at the airport.

What if she died? What if she got sick and died, or left the country, or went to jail? What if she can't stand the sight of me? But she banished such painful musings as fast as they came up. She couldn't really believe in them or there would be more point in jumping out of the plane than riding it to New York.

She went directly to the Beaton Hotel on First Avenue near the U.N. Building. She remembered the name from the time she and Uncle John and Aunt Elsa had stayed there when she was a youngster of ten. It had seemed like the marvelous castle in the fairy tales to her then, and the name remained in her memory.

They gave her a room on the fourth floor. She took the least expensive one they had, the kind where you share the bathroom with two or three other rooms. Perhaps it was an unnecessary economy, but she had Merrill Landon's sardonic warnings about money ringing in her ears and she wasn't going to be caught spending hers foolishly.

She unpacked a few things and hung them in the closet, and all the while her heart was high and going a little faster than it should have. She was in New York. Laura was in New York. Things would work out, they had to.

And what if they did? What if Laura could be found, and fast? And what if she fell into Beth's arms as though the nine years between them didn't exist, their lives apart didn't exist? Then what?

Then, Beth thought, almost timidly, *divorce. I'll have to divorce Charlie. I'll never get the children back. My children. My babies. My own flesh. But I'll have Laura again.* Was it worth it? It had to be.

Quickly she went to the phone book, the Manhattan directory, and looked for Laura Landon. Maybe the one in Chicago was wrong. After following her shaking finger down several columns she got the answer she secretly expected; the answer the phone book at the Chicago airport had already given her: no listing. She sighed and lighted a cigarette. It was not going to be a cinch, this strange mission of hers. She checked the book again for Nina Spicer's name.

Nina was there. With relief and some trepidation she dialed the number. It was ten-thirty in the morning, but the voice that answered was obviously newly roused from sleep. It was a low pleasant feminine voice, almost sultry. Beth liked it. It made her curious to meet the owner, curious to see what she looked like.

"Nina Spicer, please," she said.

"This is Nina."

"This is Beth Ayers, Nina. Do you remember me?"

"How could I forget? The girl with all the problems."

"I'm sorry I woke you up."

"Sure." Her breezy lack of courtesy threw Beth for a moment.

"Did you get my note?" she asked.

"I did."

"Could we meet for lunch?" *Damn, I sound like a question box,* Beth thought. But Nina was playing things her way. Beth had to go along.

"Let's make it dinner. I'm tied up at noon," Nina said.

"Okay. You'll have to name the place. New York is all new to me."

"Where are you?"

"The Beaton."

"Good enough. They have a decent bar on the top floor. I'll pick you up in the lobby about four-thirty. We can go on from there."

"Fine." Beth was both repelled and attracted by the girl on the phone. The voice was lovely, but the attitude was hardly warm and welcoming. Curious, amused, a little supercilious, somewhat intimidating.

Beth hung up. She wasn't afraid of Nina, just on her guard. And she was so eager to meet her, to ask her about Laura, that the day dragged unbearably. She was too excited to rest. She ended up writing letters, one to Merrill Landon, one to Cleve.

"Did you have much trouble with Vega?" she asked Cleve reluctantly. "Tell me everything's okay. It would mean so much. I'll send you a box number in a day or two. Don't know how long I'll be in New York."

When there was nothing left to write and no one to write to, she walked. She saw the United Nations buildings and she poked around the shops. A tailor across the street from the Beaton sewed a button on for her and told her about his international clientele.

She was in her room by four, in case Nina should come early, but Nina was late. It was a quarter to five when she called Beth's room, and Beth, almost beside herself with impatience, went down to the lobby to meet her. She looked for a light blue linen suit, which was Nina's description of herself, and found her standing by a square pillar near the desk.

Beth walked straight to her and took her hand, pleased to see that her directness threw Nina offstride slightly. Nina expected to have that effect herself, mainly by fixing people with a go-to-hell stare. But Beth was not interested in Nina for Nina's sake and it made her less susceptible to Nina's notions of who was running the show.

They went directly up to the bar, speaking softly, feeling their ways with one another. They ordered martinis.

"How long will you be in New York?" Nina asked.

"That depends."

"On what?"

"A lot of things. You, maybe."

Nina smiled at her martini glass. She was not a pretty girl, though her eyes were green and well shaped, and she wore her brown hair long in a soft bob. Her nose was too sharp and prominent and her mouth too small and irregular to be pretty, but she had a nice figure. Unusually nice, Beth had noticed on the way up in the elevator.

"What have I got to do with how long you stay in New York?" Nina asked, sizing her up silently. "You don't even know me." She spoke suggestively, with the hint of a smile on her face, as if she had only to keep leading a little and Beth would soon take a pratfall.

"I'm looking for someone," Beth said. "I thought you might be able to help me find her."

"Oh. Romance?"

"No," Beth lied, speaking briefly and annoyed at Nina's tone of voice.

"You're not at all horsey, are you?" Nina said, changing the subject suddenly and grinning.

"Horsey?" Beth stared at her. "Should I be?"

"Frankly, yes. I got the impression from your letters."

"It's not the impression I meant to give." Beth didn't like Nina's expression. It was too cocksure, too well acquainted with all the ins-and-outs of gay life in New York City that Beth yearned to know herself. She felt suddenly reluctant to bring Laura's name up. Maybe later in the evening, if Nina got more congenial.

"So you're leaving your husband, hm?" Nina said. It was part of her technique with people to startle them, embarrass them, leave them stammering.

"I didn't say that," Beth protested.

"You don't need to. Your letters said enough. He isn't here in New York, is he?"

"No. But that doesn't mean I'm leaving him."

"From the things you wrote me, I'd say you could hardly wait to ditch him."

"I haven't written you for a while," Beth said in a chilly voice. "Things change." Beth was being played with, to see if she would snap or take it in stoic silence. She was aware of this, aware that no matter how she reacted Nina wouldn't care—just as long as there was some reaction. Nina didn't give a damn for anything else. It was seeing people squirm, seeing them enmeshed in their own poor little problems that amused her. Beth was a good case history. And she was new and different to Nina. She would help to pass the time. She might even show up, slightly distorted, in Nina's next novel.

Beth made up her mind to ignore it. Nothing mattered but finding Laura, and if Nina could help, Nina would have to be catered to.

They had another martini and then Nina took her out to dinner. It was a little place down in the Village, but expensive; the tourist trade had discovered it. But the food was excellent. Beth ate gladly. The lack of rest and the martinis made a bad combination, and she felt a little slap happy.

"I want to learn my way around down here," Beth said. "I want to get to know the Village." Just being in it gave her a tingle of hope, of excitement. The Village. The end of the rainbow. How she had wondered about this place! And Laura had lived here; Laura knew it, too. Perhaps better than Nina.

"Sure," Nina said. "Sure you would. Just like the rest of the tourists."

"I have a special reason."

"What's her name?"

Beth finished the drink beside her, distinctly nettled. "She may not even be here," she said tightly. "I lost track of her years ago. The last I heard she was in New York."

Nina put her head back and laughed and Beth knew, with tongue-tied resentment, that she was being laughed at again.

"So you gave up your husband and kids to come on a wild goose chase after your long lost love," Nina said. "How romantic! That's why you wanted to meet me, I suppose. So I could lead you to her."

She laughed again and Beth thought with disappointment that she could never like this peculiar girl. It was apparently not possible for Nina to be friendly. You made her acquaintance and then you either knuckled under to her or else you had to drop her. One way or the other she got a good show, and that was all she wanted out of life, besides a few affairs. She didn't need friends and she didn't especially want them. Lovers, yes. Friends, no. Lovers kept boredom out. Friends let it in. At least, that was the way Beth sized her up.

Somehow the mere idea of exposing Laura's name to the malicious laughter of this worldly girl who faced her over the dinner table disheartened Beth. She couldn't do it; not just then. She looked at the writer, feeling sure that Nina would tolerate her good humoredly as long as Beth was still "new," still good for laughs. And Nina looked back at her, always with her mocking little smile, so different from Jean Purvis's endless good-hearted grin.

Physically Nina and Beth pleased each other. Nina took in her visitor's long, strong limbs, well shaped and smooth, and her intense violet eyes. She was ever so slightly, even fashionably, boyish. And Nina laughed softly to herself at the idea of filling Beth full of moonshine and bull and letting her find her way out of the mess.

After dinner Nina took Beth around to some Lesbian bars. It was the first time in her life that Beth had ever been in such places. They recalled scenes from Nina's novels to her and she asked ingenuous questions, unaware of the fact that her voice carried too far, far enough to make one or two other customers smile.

"Not much noise tonight," Nina said, after shushing her. "Monday night," she explained. "Always dead."

Beth was thinking, *What if Laura's here somewhere? At least she's been here before. Did she meet people here? Fall in love?*

They took in three places. The first was another tourist trap. There was a long dark bar in front and a dining room with sketchy floor shows in the back. No show on Monday nights. But the waitresses were interesting. Beth found herself staring at them in fascination, as they lounged against the walls waiting for the sparse crowd to fill out. She even wondered if they drank orange juice in the morning like everybody else. It shocked her to realize how far out of her depth she was, how far removed from her collegiate sophistication. She wondered how obvious it was to Nina, but a glance at her revealed only the supercilious little smile.

Nina watched her closely and her scrutiny made Beth nervous. *She wants me to put my foot in my mouth,* Beth thought, and it made her stammer a little. But it didn't stop her from asking questions.

Beth was surprised to see so many men sitting at the bar. "Who are they?" she asked. "Johns?" She remembered the word from one of Nina's novels and she asked her question in a firm clear voice that made Nina duck and laugh.

"Quiet, for God's sake, they'll think we're cops," she said. "Or a couple of gaping hayseeds."

"Well, are they?" Beth said. "Do they hang around gay girls all the time?" But she lowered her voice.

"Um-hm," Nina said, her eyes wrinkled at the corners.

In the next place there were only women, except for the man behind the bar, and he apparently enjoyed the confidence of the girls he served. There was only a handful of young women there when Beth and Nina arrived, and Beth looked them over quickly, always with Laura's lovely face in her mind. But Laura wasn't there.

Nina seemed to know everybody. She was getting more gregarious as she had more drinks. Not loud at all, just bold; bold in the way she looked at people, in the things she said.

"So you want to go back to your husband," she needled Beth.

"I didn't say that, either."

"You don't say much, do you?" Nina laughed. "What'd you get married for in the first place if you're gay?" she said. "Think it would cure you?"

"I didn't know I was gay," Beth said.

"You seemed to in your letters."

"They were easier to write that way."

Nina laughed at her and called one of the waitresses over. "This is Billie," she said to Beth, and the girl sat down and talked with them. She was extremely pretty; very small and dainty-looking, but with cropped hair and a decidedly aggressive swing in her walk. She spoke softly, however, almost timidly, and left the bulk of the conversation to Beth and Nina.

"Beth is looking for her long lost love," Nina said, pleased to see the consternation her announcement created in Beth. "What's her name again?" She glanced at Beth.

"Maybe she comes in here," Billie said helpfully. "I know them all."

"I doubt it," Beth said.

"Come on, her name," Nina demanded.

"She's not here," Beth said, feeling cornered and stubborn. She hated the phrase "long lost love," so lightly, even sarcastically, spoken.

"So maybe she comes in other times," said Billie, innocently unaware that Beth and Nina were sparring with each other.

"Bring us another drink, will you, Billie?" Nina said, still staring Beth down. As soon as the girl had left their table she leaned over and said confidentially to Beth, as if making it up to her a little, "Do you like her?"

"I don't know her," Beth said warily.

"She likes you," Nina said. "She's been cruising you like mad since we came in."

"Cruising me?"

"Looking you over, sizing you up."

Beth didn't believe her. Nina only wanted a rise out of her.

"She wants to be a boy," Nina said. "She boards with a family on Bleecker Street. She thinks *they* think she's a boy. She always wears pants."

"She had on a skirt tonight."

"That's because she has to wear one in here. City ordinance. No women in bars in pants. But she won't wear the skirt to work. She carries it in a paper bag and changes in the john."

"She's crazy if she thinks she can pass for a boy," Beth said seriously. "She can't be over five-feet-three. And she's so pretty. Her features are very feminine."

And again Nina laughed at her. And again Beth realized she was being made a fool of. Was any of it true? Was Billie so blind as to think she could transform herself into a boy with a pair of pants? Or was Nina showing her at least part of the truth, a sad, even pitiful, intensely interesting little corner of life, cut from the Village pattern?

At the last bar there were other men, but they never seemed to join the girls at the tables. They rather intrigued Beth, who wondered why they spent all their free time sitting quietly on bar stools watching the flirtations, the loves, the dancing and social-izing of these women they could never touch. Some of them seemed to know the girls and were greeted affectionately with a nickname or a slap on the back. But they never presumed to follow a girl or to talk before they were spoken to. It was their solitary pleasure simply to watch, and now and then to be permitted a few words, a little sharing of this odd way of life

Beth observed one who seemed particularly pathetic. He was overweight by quite a bit, balding and with blue pockets under his eyes, and he looked not only sad but outright bored—something none of the others did. She wondered why he bothered to come by at all if it depressed him so. His face stuck in her mind later and she pitied him. This third and last place they were in had a larger clientele than the others, probably because it was eleven o'clock by the time they got there.

Beth was absorbed by it. She wanted to wander all night around the Village, look into all the windows and share all the secrets. Behind some curtain, in some doorway or shop window, she might find Laura.

But when she stood up suddenly to go to the ladies' room she realized with a start that she was drunk. Quite drunk. Nina had been telling her to quit for some time.

"You don't want to be hungover tomorrow," she said. But it was so condescending, so solicitous for the "country cousin," that Beth had defiantly ordered another. And another. She knew now, gripping the table with both hands, that Nina was right, aggravating though her attitude was. Beth should have stopped early in the evening.

Nina appraised her skillfully. "You're going to feel like hell in the morning," she said. "Too bad. I was going to take you out for lunch, too. One of my favorite places."

"I'll make it," Beth said. She *would* feel rotten, all right—that was a cinch. But she'd go. She had to learn her way around here somehow, and doing it with Nina, however embarrassing or even upsetting, seemed safer than going it alone.

They drove home in a taxi, and Beth was disconcerted to find that the warmth and closeness of Nina's body in the rear seat pleased her. Nina said nothing and that made it easier to enjoy her. When she opened her mouth it threw Beth on her guard automatically and destroyed the sensual pleasure.

Beth left her with a queer feeling of dislike and desire that disturbed her sleep, tired as she was. She couldn't fathom Nina and the only thing she thought it was safe to count on was that Nina was playing the game only for herself. She had no special favors to grant Beth Ayers, and when Beth ceased to interest her, that would be the end. Kaput. End of guided tour through the Village, and end of information, such as it was. Beth thought fuzzily that she had better ask Nina about Laura, whether Nina laughed at the idea or not, before Nina got it into her head to drop her. For, strangely, on this first night of their acquaintance, she felt the break coming. It was inevitable with a girl like Nina. Things never last, things aren't meant to last. That would be her way of seeing it. So why not break it off as soon as it bores you? And Nina's philosophy, Beth was soon to learn on her own, was typical of many a weary Greenwich Villager. It was not the attitude that comes with sophistication, but the attitude of boredom and disappointment.

Chapter Twelve

THEY HAD LUNCH THE NEXT DAY, THOUGH BETH FELT GRAY
with the hangover. And somehow, over the salad and crackers, she
found she couldn't speak of Laura. It was like trying to swallow a
pill that was too big for her throat. She made the usual try at it, but
it reached the back of her mouth and suddenly scared her, and she
choked a little and finally gave up.

But several nights later, things changed. Nina unexpectedly
asked her to come to her apartment for dinner. Beth had been
hoping to see where she lived, how she lived, even what she ate.
Nina was her link to the gay world, and though she couldn't quite
like her she still was deeply interested in her, in the things Nina
could teach her. She accepted the invitation gratefully, and was
astonished, when she got there, to see that Nina had cooked the
dinner—or was in process of cooking it—herself.

Nina fixed her a drink and Beth stood in the tiny living room
looking at the books that banked one whole wall from floor to ceiling. It made her feel more comfortable with Nina to see that she
read or, at least, had books around. Beth liked to read and when
she found others who did she ordinarily cottoned to them. It
helped her get over her suspicions with Nina, the shadowy feeling of being *had,* of being taken for a ride, that she couldn't quite
pin down.

They ate in a corner of the bedroom, a room that was even
smaller than the living room and literally gorged, like an overfed
animal, with a bed, a desk, and three typewriters, to say nothing of
the card table from which they ate.

"Apartments up here are damn cracker boxes," Nina said. "If you want a good address, you pay for it." She was in the East Seventies, just off Fifth Avenue, in a staid old building that was eminently respectable. It was like her to look down on the Village, part of her philosophy to get out of it, or, at least, to *live* out of it. She could never stay away fulltime.

The dinner was good, to Beth's surprise. Nina had put candles on the table and turned out the lights, and Beth began to feel, in spite of the shivers of warning that flashed through her when Nina smiled her knowledgeable little smile, a curious intimacy. After all, they had written many letters to each other. Nina had been kind, in her off-the-cuff way. Nina was being good to her now, taking time off from the book she was working on, showing her around.

Maybe I'm taking the teasing too hard, Beth thought, as she ate.

"Lord, I'm stuffed," she said, when Nina offered her more. They smiled at each other and there was a small pause. Nina's was a different kind of smile. There was almost warmth in it; at least, there was an absence of the mocking twist that bothered Beth so.

Perhaps out of uncertainty, or stubbornness born of accustomed shyness, Beth refused to drop her eyes first. And Nina, her bluff called, had to keep her own eyes on Beth. And somehow—as though the two pairs of eyes, one sparkling green, the other misty violet, were magnetized—they leaned toward each other. Beth reached out without consciously directing her hand and cupped it gently behind Nina's neck, pressing the warm brown hair beneath it and pulling Nina closer still.

In utter silence, in the calm light of candles, over the steak plates, in the night of the city, they kissed each other. And leaned away again slightly to gaze at each other. Beth was inanely surprised to see that Nina's lipstick was smeared. And Nina smiled, the good smile, and they kissed, again. And then she suddenly rose, as if it occurred to her she was risking a true affection for Beth by playing with her, and began to clear the plates as if nothing had happened.

Beth picked up a stack of plates and followed her into the cramped kitchen. She put the slippery crockery on the little table and her arms around Nina, and a voice inside her urged, *Tell her. Tell her it's Laura you're looking for. Tell her now, before she gets bored and you lose her.*

But I can't, Beth thought. *She'd burst out laughing at me if I asked her now. It would ruin the mood, it would make her sarcastic again. And I'd hate myself for asking.*

Nina slipped away from her and brought in the rest of the plates, and they did the dishes together, speaking softly of small irrelevancies, enjoying each other's physical presence.

And still Beth hesitated, with that name on the tip of her tongue and some ineffable misgiving freezing it there.

Nina showed her an album full of snapshots she had collected, and startled her by pointing to a nice-looking crew-cut boy and saying off-handedly, "That was my husband."

"Your husband? You never said you were married."

"I'm not. I was. Besides, why should I tell you?" And for an instant Beth felt the wall of sarcasm rising.

"No reason," she said. "What happened?"

Nina shrugged. "What happened with you and Charlie? It didn't work. We divorced years ago."

"Did you love him?"

"Hell, no. He was just a nice kid. We had fun."

"And no children."

"And no children. You were a fool to have children, Beth."

"I love them," she said humbly.

"Ha!" Nina cried. "Then what are you doing here? Why aren't you with them?" After a suggestive pause she prompted, "Was the old long lost love *that* tempting?"

In the midst of such sharp and painful needling Beth couldn't speak Laura's name. She couldn't bear to have it laughed at and she clammed up for a while. When she could control her voice a little she tried to explain.

"I left my kids because I treated them badly. I was unjust, I was unreasonable, I hurt them over and over. Even if there had never been any 'long lost love,' I think I would have left them. The more I hurt them the worse I hurt myself until I thought we would all go crazy."

Nina saw what a whirlpool of guilt and resentment she had stirred up, and, interested, she stirred it a little more. "So your solution was to dump the kids in the river and run to New York in search of a girl you haven't seen in nine years? Not very sensible, was it?"

"Not very!" Beth conceded. "Not much fun, either," she added sharply.

Nina dropped her smile at once. "I'm not laughing," she said with a solemn face. But of course she was, inside, in the dark and silence of her private self. "My first husband and I had it worked out a little better than that, that's all. You should have used your head."

"Your *first* husband?" Beth snapped. "Where in hell is your second?"

"Oh I mean my ex-husband. My *former* husband," Nina corrected herself.

"Well, say so, then." Beth had caught her lying. She had never married. It simply pleased her ego to say she had, to make Beth feel that no experience Beth had ever had was unique or different from any Nina had had. Nina had to be one up on you, or at least on a level with you, or she couldn't enjoy herself. Ordinarily she lied to this end with great skill, gracefully and casually. It gave Beth her first peace of mind with Nina to catch her in a blatant fib, to see that startled look flicker over her face.

Nina had the good sense to take it lightly. She passed over it, coming to the couch where Beth sat and settling beside her. She cocked one foot against the coffee table and said slowly, "Would you like to spend the night?" The conflict of desires on Beth's face tickled her, restored her self-assurance.

"I don't think so," Beth said.

"Why not? Afraid of me?"

"Not of you." *Damn her! She would make a test of it, a challenge, How can I turn her down now?* But Beth wasn't absolutely sure she *wanted* to turn her down.

"Afraid of what, then?"

"You don't really want me to stay."

"Why do you think I asked you?" Nina had made her mind up. Beth was moody, she was pretty, she was new. Nina smiled at the swell of her breasts beneath the simple suit she wore and wondered how they looked undraped.

"Stay," she said. And when Beth didn't answer she added, "I have a nightie you can borrow. Go take a shower and I'll get you a towel. Go on!" She shooed her as she might have a wayward child or a chicken, and Beth got up and obeyed her. It exhausted her to try to make a decision. It was easier to let Nina make it for her.

She showered and dried herself, gazing at herself critically in the mirror of the medicine chest, wondering just how big a fool she was to stay, to walk into whatever trap Nina might be laying for her. The small consolation was that you could only walk into Nina's kind of trap once. Nina had a way of stripping your innocence off with both hands. It hurt, but Beth was learning. She sensed that the lessons Nina taught her would bolster her when she faced the gay world alone.

"Finished?" Nina called outside the bathroom door. "Here's some pajamas."

Beth opened the door a few inches and grabbed them and saw Nina grin at her modesty. She slipped the blue cotton pants on and found they were too short. The jacket was too tight through the bust and she laughed silently at the picture she made in the mirror.

Nina was waiting for her, curled up on the foot end of the sofa-bed she had pulled out from the love seat in the living room.

"You can sleep in here," she said. "There's plenty of room." There was in fact room for two, but Nina had her own bed in the other room and Beth was relieved to know they would sleep apart.

She sat down on a pillow as far from Nina as the length of the bed would permit, and Nina fixed them both a nightcap. They drank in silence for a moment, and then Beth spoke. Maybe it was the liquor that prompted her, or the informality of the pajamas that were too small and looked silly, or just the need to know. At any rate, she spoke of the things closest to her then.

"How do you know if you're gay, Nina?" she asked.

"Simple. You go to a fortune teller," Nina said.

"Is that how you found out about yourself?"

"No." And Nina's face became more serious. "No, I did it the hard way."

"What's the hard way?"

"I got hurt."

"Well, I've been hurt before," Beth said. "A thousand times, a thousand different ways. It didn't teach me a thing."

"You weren't a good student, then."

"I don't mean with women, Nina."

"I thought you were in New York trying to find some woman."

"I am. But she never *hurt* me. I hurt her, but she never did a thing to me."

"Well, there must have been others."

There had been Vega, of course. But Beth couldn't talk about her, and there seemed no reason to confess that sordid little chapter to Nina, who would only have laughed at it anyway.

"No," Beth said. "No others." She finished her drink quickly and Nina reached to refill it, but Beth held back.

"You mean that once nine years ago you had a fling with some girl," Nina said, letting her hand drop, "and now you wonder if you're *gay?*" She spoke with exaggerated incredulity and the curl in her small mouth was not kind. But it was amused.

"I loved her very much," Beth said. "I just happened to meet my husband at the same time. I've been wondering all these years if I made the right choice. Lately, with things so bad at home, I thought seeing her again would help me make up my mind. Help me understand myself."

"What makes you think she'll be so eager to see *you?* Or help you out? What makes you think she cares a damn about you after nine years? Especially if you hurt her the last time around?"

"I have no idea how she'll react," Beth said. She resented the probing mockery Nina subjected her to, but if it was the price of knowledge she was ready to pay it. "I only know she was a very gentle, affectionate girl and when we parted there were no hard feelings."

"Oh, swell," Nina said. "She's had nine years to sit and stew over it, remember. She's known other women by now, if she has any sense. She can evaluate what you did to her. She couldn't before when it first happened. Or weren't you her first?"

"Yes. I was." Beth glanced up at her. It was true. Laura had experience to measure Beth with now, but Beth had nothing but memories with which to judge Laura. Memories and one abortive sad little romance with a sick woman that only made Laura look the lovelier in her imaginings.

"She may look good to *you*," Nina pointed out, "but you may look like hell to her. What if you barge in on a new romance? What if you finally find her and the poor girl is madly in love with somebody new? How glad do you think she'll be to see you? You could louse up her whole life, throw a monkey wrench into her romance. What's she supposed to do, laugh it off for old time's sake? Welcome you with open arms and let the other girl go jump?"

In a burst of irritation and arrogance Beth leaned across the bed, her hands planted deep in the mattress just inches from Nina and the rest of her weight on her knees. "You know something?" Beth said. "I don't give a damn. I don't care what I do to her life, as long as she lets me back in it. I want her so badly I can see her in every female I meet. I can smell her the way she used to be after her shower at night when she was covered with scented powder and her hair was still damp. God, God, I can even taste her!"

And Nina twisted her mouth into a laugh. When Beth started to protest she put a hand up and exclaimed, "No, I believe you. You're in love."

Beth came down to a more reasonable sitting position. "Does that make me gay?" she asked seriously.

"For the time being." Nina sized her up. "Why do you worry about it, Beth? Why are you so anxious for a label? What do you care what category you fall into? Just be yourself."

"I don't know myself."

"Then just be however you feel like being and pretty soon the pattern will emerge."

"I've been doing that for thirty years," Beth said. "There is no pattern, there's only chaos."

"Well, maybe that comes from living with a man. Maybe you were never meant to settle down. I know some perfectly nice girls, all straight, who can't live with men. They can't live without them, either, of course. It's a matter of balancing their lives between the men who are important to them, and the other things. It doesn't necessarily mean you're gay. It doesn't necessarily mean you should go live with a woman and make love to her, just because you've made a flop of your first marriage. So maybe you got the wrong guy. Try somebody else."

"It isn't that easy. If you'd ever been married you'd know that."

"I have been married. I told you," Nina said quickly

And Beth, seeing that she meant to stick by her fib, said, "Oh, sorry. I forgot." She hoped Nina liked the sarcasm in her voice. Nina was used enough to dishing it out. But Beth was glad for her words. They put a new light on things, made her see them from an angle that had been closed to her when there had been just her own ramblings in the dark to guide her.

"If Charlie was a mistake, I'll be paying for it all my life," Beth said.

"Don't be silly. What did you pay him for this trip?"

"A lot of misery, Nina. A lot of soul searching and misery."

"You'll get that out of life anyway, Beth. You have no corner on misery. That's everybody's business. That's the growing-up process, you might say." It sounded familiar to Beth. She wondered if she might have read it somewhere in one of Nina's books. "Your long lost love can probably teach you a few things about misery. Anybody who's gay knows that subject backwards and forwards."

Beth reached over to a small end table to squash out her cigarette. When she sat up Nina unfastened the central, cornerstone, button on the tight pajama tops. It was accomplished with one quick movement that caught Beth off guard and the straining button yielded gratefully before she had time to catch Nina's hand and stop her. At once, the whole thing came unbuttoned, the jacket top failing open over her bare chest.

Rather than protest or lose her temper or button the thing up again, or even use the gesture as an excuse for making a pass, Beth just sat there as if nothing had happened. Her expression, her attitude, were a dare to Nina. She gazed into space, apparently preoccupied, and Nina, who was fishing for a hard reaction, was nonplussed. Beth could sense it without looking at her. She continued to sit, inwardly amused and relieved to see Nina's consternation. Beth's full high breasts were disturbingly visible and Nina could neither move away, nor mention them until Beth did something without making herself look idiotic. So Nina sat still beside Beth, both exasperated and interested. The gambit forced an unaccustomed respect for Beth on her. Perhaps Beth was something more than a passionate hayseed trying to scare up an old crush. Perhaps she was good for something besides laughs.

At last Beth leaned back into the pillows, settling down with a sigh, her arms and legs flung out and the unbuttoned jacket flung carelessly out on either side of her. She shut her eyes and said, "Forgive me, Nina. I'm beat."

"Sure," Nina said. Released by the words, she got up and took the glasses and full ashtrays into the kitchen. Beth listened to her moving about, smiling to herself. She felt better about Nina now, less at her mercy.

"I'll be in the next room," Nina said. "If you have any bad dreams, that is."

"Thanks. I'll remember," Beth said. She heard Nina take a few steps and stop, and make a few odd noises with her tongue and then with an ashtray, as if to attract Beth's attention, make her open her eyes. But Beth kept them shut, ignoring her. "Did you like the dinner?" Nina said.

Beth had. She had said so several times. So it was plain that Nina was looking for an invitation, a more intimate talk, a caress, maybe even a night in bed with Beth. And Beth was both surprised and flattered. But she had no idea of yielding her small lead then. Let Nina squirm. It was her turn.

"Yes, thanks," she said noncommittally. "It was delicious."

And seeing that she would get no further without stating her intentions in plain English, Nina gave up with a smile, put out the last light, and climbed into her own bed.

It was black early morning when Beth was slightly roused by a movement of the bedclothes. She continued to breathe slowly and softly as if she were still asleep, letting Nina slip under the blankets and lie beside her. Nina didn't touch her and didn't move for fully ten minutes, for fear of waking Beth.

They played cat and mouse for a while. Beth was at first dismayed to feel Nina's presence. Not so much because she didn't desire her as because she didn't *want* to desire her. She didn't want to feel an attraction for this odd girl who was teaching her some valuable facts in such a humiliating manner. And yet she did. She couldn't imagine living with Nina or sharing the things that mattered with her. But she could imagine, vividly, making love to her. She could see in her mind's eye the well-shaped legs and trim torso, the long brown bob and green eyes, the small passionless mouth that nevertheless felt so strangely soft and sweet when they kissed over the steak plates.

It was a lovely body that lay next to her, not like the poor tortured thing that was Vega, with her heart all twisted inside by the mutilations on the outside. After a while Beth knew she wanted to touch Nina; she knew she would have to pretty soon if Nina didn't make the move first. She wanted extremely to control herself, to withstand the temptation, to prove the stronger, and this desire gave her a few moments more of resistance. She wondered if Nina meant to sleep beside her all night, without making a single gesture toward her. Maybe she wanted merely to wake up in the morning with Beth beside her and enjoy Beth's surprise. She wondered if it was just another trap to make Beth look silly.

Beth held her breath for a second and then her breathing came faster with the speed of excitement and even fear. Nina heard it, lying so near her in the bed, and she tensed, knowing there was nothing more she needed to do. But Beth startled her by reaching over her and snapping on the small pink lamp on the end table, flooding the room with a soft rosy radiance that made them both visible to each other. Beth couldn't have explained the action; it seemed better somehow than simply grabbing Nina like an animal after bait. Maybe it was just another effort to resist, to do anything but touch Nina.

Nina rolled over on her back and stared at Beth, her eyes opening wider slowly as they became accustomed to the light. "What the hell did you do that for?" she asked. But she wasn't angry.

"What the hell are *you* doing in my bed?" Beth said.

Nina smiled. "I had a bad dream," she said. And Beth had to smile too. Nina looked boldly at her. "You're still unbuttoned," she said. In the sudden intimacy it was possible to speak of it.

"I like it that way. Your pajamas are too small for me."

Nina reached up slowly and put her hands on Beth's warm breasts. "You can never know for sure if you're gay, Beth," she said softly, "unless you can respond to more than one woman. You'll never know if you save yourself all for the long lost love. How do you even know you'll find her? Maybe she's gone for good and you'll go home to Charlie and never know what you left him to find out."

There was a pause. In a way it was true, and in another way it was a satin-covered, thorn-lined invitation to infidelity. Beth wondered if she would be unfaithful to Charlie by making love to a woman. It had never seemed so to her with Vega, probably because making love to Vega was a depressing chore. But Nina made her feel suddenly that she was a faithless woman. Nina made her feel that the things she was doing were both silly and wicked, and wonderful. At the same time, she made her believe they were natural and inevitable.

Beth looked down at her, with her soft brown hair scattered on the pillow. Her eyes were very green in the rosy light and her skin was very fair. Beth caught her hands, pulling them gently away from her breasts and kissing the palms. And then Nina took them back to slip out of her own pajamas. Beth watched her in silence, letting things happen as if she had no will to stop them; she didn't even try.

Nina wriggled out of the bottoms and threw them on the floor, at the same time pushing the covers off her body with a couple of long quick thrusts of her legs. Suddenly, almost unexpectedly, for Beth was not well prepared for anything that happened that night, Nina was lying beautifully naked beneath her, her fine legs crossed at the ankles, her sharp restless eyes searching Beth's.

Beth looked away and said in a low voice, "Do you want a yokel like me to make love to you? I don't know what I'm doing, Nina. I'll disappoint you."

"You couldn't, honey. Try it."

"You mean, in the mood you're in, *nobody* could disappoint you." Beth gave a sad little laugh. "It just happens I'm the one who's with you."

"In the mood I'm in, nobody could touch me but you." Beth felt the smooth tingling drift of a hand over her back underneath the loosened pajamas. She bore it for a moment in silence and then, with a little groan, she struggled out of the tops, nearly tearing them in her hurry. She turned on Nina, leaning over her and bending nearer until her weight rested partly on her, and then she kissed her and a flash of pleasure, as sharp and dreadful as a sword, impaled her. She had wanted to tell Nina, "Don't laugh at me. Don't make me feel clumsier than I am. I think I could kill you for that." But there had been no time and now there was no need.

Nina, for once, was not laughing. She was spread beneath Beth like a carpet of warm silk. She moved with her, she murmured to her, she was as absorbed as Beth was in the fantastic luxury of sexual pleasure. When she tried to pull away a little Beth caught her from behind and kissed her bare neck and shoulders, her fingers pressed around Nina's lovely breasts and their legs entangled. Nina was surprised at the strength she felt in Beth's arms, and let herself be pushed back down on the bed with a sigh of ecstasy.

Nina showed Beth things that night that Beth never dreamed existed. "I'm going to do things to you you never even heard of," she whispered, and she did. With her mouth, her fingers, the warm tickle of her breath, she called up feelings in Beth that had never been there before. She made Beth aware of parts of her body, her own familiar comfortable body that she thought she knew so well, that Beth had never discovered for herself. A thousand sensual subtleties were revealed to Beth in Nina's arms: all the tricks and caprices of a lovely body, all the scented shapes, the astonishing joy of uncontrollable physical reactions, the enormous force of a woman's ecstasy flowing unfocused through her whole body, claiming her absolutely and reverberating in her for hours after the act of love.

Beth kissed Nina with a hungry mouth, amazed at her own appetite, at how much it took to satisfy her. She would settle against Nina, holding her in her arms and thinking *now* sleep would come. And she would half doze off for a while and then shift her weight a little and the mere feel of Nina's hair brushing her face, or a length of perfumed leg, would jolt her desire to the surface.

"Nina," she murmured wildly once in the night, "am I exhausting you?"

"No," Nina whispered. "You surprise me but you don't exhaust me."

And once Beth tried to recall if it had been this way with Laura, if it had been this good, or if it could be. There wasn't any reason for anything to be so beautiful. After what she had done, after what she had been through, Beth could hardly believe this was happening to her at all. It seemed as if all her days were fated to be gray and worried, all her nights empty and tragic. And now suddenly she was incredibly happy. There was no time to wonder whether the happiness was purely physical. She didn't stop to think about her ambivalent feelings for Nina, about how Nina might look in the daylight, with irony in her air again and sarcasm on her lips. There was no daylight, no night, no time, nothing but that moment on the bed with Nina in her arms. Beth was unable to think ahead or to care what happened.

Nina's voice came softly out of the dawn to her. "You're gay, Beth," she said positively.

"I know." It came as a wild wonderful relief, just to know for sure after years of tormented wondering.

Nina stroked her cheek with one finger. "What was her name?" she asked.

After a long pause Beth answered her. "Laura."

Nina smiled. "Good," she said. "I don't know any Lauras."

Beth felt a small stab of dismay. And then she wondered if Nina could conceivably be jealous now, unwilling to share Beth, unwilling to reveal anything she might happen to know. Beth considered Nina's curious incapacity for friendship. Nina might be able to come close to her as a lover but never as a friend. She might even learn to love Beth for a little while, but she could never like her and it would never last.

"You know what you'd be if you let yourself go?" Nina said playfully into her ear. "You'd be a butch. You'd cut your hair off real short and live in the Village. Oh, yes, you would. Don't smile.

135

And I'll bet that's exactly what you will do, too. You won't be interested in me very long. Not after you find out how many beautiful women will be interested in *you*."

Beth squirmed uncomfortably at the idea. "I don't want a lot of beautiful women, Nina," she mumbled.

"What do you want?" Nina asked, and when Beth hesitated, silent for over a minute, she teased, "Me?" And then, with spite in her voice, "No. Laura. *Laura* she wants, after all I did for her last night."

"I don't know," Beth said. "I really don't know...now."

"Now? You mean now that I've corrupted you?" Nina laughed quietly. "I'm glad I mixed you up a little. I hope you don't find your Laura. Not for a while anyway."

Chapter Thirteen

WHEN BETH LEFT NINA'S APARTMENT TWO DAYS LATER, SHE found a letter waiting for her in the post office box she had rented. She half expected Nina to ask her to move in before she left. But it would have inconvenienced Nina too much, with the lack of space and the long hours she had to spend at her typewriter. She didn't want to be bothered and Beth understood, even though she was sorry not to have been asked. Nina should have known Beth would refuse, out of consideration for her. But Beth never got the chance.

The letter was from Cleve, and Beth tore it open in the elevator on the way up to her room at the Beaton. She got as far as, "Dear Beth, How do you like New York? Charlie and the kids are as ever. Not very happy but getting along. The kids like Mrs. Donahue pretty well now that they're used to her. Charlie works like a dog— too damn hard if you ask me. Puts all of us to shame and gives me a guilt complex."

Beth asked herself if he might not be drinking still more and neglecting his job down at the office. Of course, he was still half boss; Charlie was the other half. But she knew Charlie would be hard on him if the alcohol became more important than Ayers-Purvis Toys.

She stepped out of the elevator and went to her room, fumbling with the key in her purse and pushing the door open with her shoulder. The morning sun was coming in her windows and she sat down on the bed to finish reading the letter.

"Charlie has some big idea for a new toy," Cleve went on. "He wants to call it 'The Scootch.' It's a sort of spring, a great big thing you can crawl inside or sit on top of and bounce. It travels when you bounce on it, or you can roll down hills in it. Sounds kind of goofy probably, but the neighborhood kids go for it in a big way. So do your kids. Skipper says it's better than a kite any day. Charlie is hoping it'll take up where the Hula Hoop left off. If it does we'd make a fortune. He's been working on it night and day, try to get the right materials and colors, and working up a marketing scheme for it. I haven't seen all the plans yet. Jean and I have been away on a vacation, and I haven't been feeling so red hot lately. But don't worry about me. You have enough on your mind."

It was kind and restrained, with hardly a trace of reproach. Beth lowered the letter to her lap for a minute, not quite finished with it, and stared out the window at the shaded side of the building across the street. "Not feeling so red hot." *Drunk, maybe?* She hoped not. She liked Cleve too well, she owed him too much, to wish him any ill. But the thought of his mother, ravaged by liquor, and his sister, who devoted her life to it, frightened her.

"You ask about my family," he went on in reference to one of her notes. "Mother is about as ever. Gramp still feeds his cats and vents his temper on the delivery boys or the plumber or whoever gets in the way. Vega is at Camarillo. We all thought it would be for the best—"

Camarillo! *Camarillo!* All the sense was suddenly shocked out of Beth. Camarillo—the state mental institution. "Oh, God!" she cried aloud, too stunned to read any further for a minute, unaware that she spoke aloud. "Oh, good God! *Vega!*"

"We all thought it would be for the best since the studio folded two weeks after you left. Do you remember P.K.? The girl she said she hated so much? Well, P. K. managed to spread some pretty ugly rumors about her, and that, on top of the shaky state of her finances, did the trick. The students she had left, and there was really a surprising number—they all liked her a lot—had to leave. Their parents heard about it and disapproved, and that was it.

"The doctors say she has an excellent mind and she is very reasonable most of the time, and they hope she can come home in another few months. The oddest part of it is, she copies Mother all the time. I mean, all Mother's sicknesses. She acts as if she's crippled, has to run to the bathroom every five minutes, even says she's blind and can't see a thing. The doctor says it's almost as if she wanted old age to catch up with her and incapacitate her to punish herself for her feelings. Or maybe to stop her from *having* any feelings. Another angle occurred to me. If she is Mother, how can she be anything Mother *disapproves* of? Like gay? I don't know—make any sense?

"Don't worry too much about this, Beth. It's been in the wind for many years now. I'm surprised myself it didn't come sooner. She'll be okay. The important thing for you is to get yourself straightened out and come home. Charlie needs you. He used to be a nice guy but now there's no living with him.

"Best to you, Cleve."

Vega at Camarillo! Of all the things in the letter none affected her any more than that. Vega had had to bear the loss of her lover and the loss of the girls she adored and her business, her only means of support, within two weeks of each other. Beth bowed her head and cried, without bothering to cover her face or wipe away the tears. Vega had had to face the scorn of a teenage torturer in the person of P.K. all alone. It must have been godawful, terrible even for Cleve, who had to hear it all from her hysterical lips, who had to try to comfort her and care for her.

P.K....

"Oh, Vega," Beth said. "Vega, I'm so sorry. Forgive me. I wish you could hear me, I wish I could undo what I did to you. Please Vega, get well."

Just telling it to the walls was better than keeping it all inside and getting sick on it. Even at that there was a sick feeling in her stomach and it didn't go away for a long while.

For three days she stayed in her hotel room. Not the lure of seeing Nina or even the search for Laura Landon that had propelled her this far could stir her. She simply lay on her bed and tried to disentangle her thoughts. Now and then she had some food sent up.

She told herself that nothing that had happened was her *fault,* exactly. It was fate, it was an accident, it was foul luck. But one single person couldn't have caused it all. The Purvises were wrong to drink so much, Charlie was wrong to be so bad-tempered, Uncle John was wrong to be so inquisitive. Laura was wrong to have walked out of her life nine years ago. Everybody was wrong but Beth, who was only an innocent girl trying to find herself. She had to see it that way or get sick on herself.

She had been in New York for over a week but she hadn't found Laura. There was Nina—an unexpected discovery—but Nina wasn't what she came for. It was time, and overtime, to find Laura.

Beth thought about these things as she rode up Fifth Avenue in a bus. She was on her way to Nina's apartment, just off Fifth, near the Metropolitan Museum of Art, sitting wedged between two ample women with their arms full of bundles, and silently cursing the humid warmth of the late July day.

It was early afternoon. Nina would still be sleeping but Beth wouldn't disturb her. Being away from her for several days had generated a number of feelings in Beth, all of them at odds. She had to get back and try herself against Nina again. She had to know for sure what she already suspected: that her desire for Nina was mostly a desire for physical love, a desire that required only a pretty body and a certain skill in using it.

Still, and most important, she wanted to find Laura. She had only been down to the Village once, but she would make Nina take her again. Tonight. If Nina didn't know any Lauras there must be plenty of people down there who did. It was a Saturday night this time and things would surely be busy. Maybe Laura herself... But it both frightened and excited her too much to think about it, to visualize that actual meeting that would come, had to come, some day, when she and Laura would be face to face again, when they would search for the right words, the right gestures, to show their love. It would all be so clumsy at first and then so beautiful, and Beth ached to have it happen. Soon.

Across from her on the bus sat a small heavy man suffering so visibly from the heat that Beth almost smiled to herself. He looked enough worse than the rest to make Beth almost feel cooler. He was balding, with shadows of weariness under his eyes and a hopelessly rumpled seersucker suit, and he reminded her sharply of one of the "Johns" she had seen with Nina the night they had met and gone bar hopping in the Village.

Forlorn and hot and friendless, she thought. *He's probably on his way home to a wife he can't stand. He's probably mired in a life that bores the hell out of him. But he hasn't the guts to get out of it.*

She pitied him, for it seemed to her then that escaping from a life you didn't like was a matter of courage. She had that courage and she was trying to be proud of it. She didn't dare to wonder if she had the *right* to leave her life and everyone in it or if the dumpy little man across the aisle had that right. She only saw his dissatisfaction and she scorned him for enduring it. Everything that touched her now she saw in terms of her own problem.

The rest of her thoughts were of Nina as she approached her apartment. They had had three days together, three strange long days and nights when Nina didn't write anything on her new book or call anyone or even go anywhere. They had simply lain around, not bothering to make up the beds or dress themselves. They had made love and talked and when they got hungry Nina ordered sandwiches from a nearby delicatessen and that was what they lived on.

Nina had made her keep her voice down for fear her neighbors would hear them. "I don't know what they'd think," she said. "I can't afford to have them thinking *anything.* I had enough trouble finding this apartment and I don't want any nosey cops coming around answering complaints. It's not the same as the Village. You can do things there you wouldn't try uptown."

Beth had stared at her. "I'm not making any noise," she said. "Well, don't."

Beth thought back on this, bemused. Nina had dodged any commitments to her. She was lavish with compliments, telling Beth how pretty she was, how delectable her body was, how Charlie probably didn't appreciate her. But she never had a word to say about how much she really liked Beth, how often she wanted to see her, what her presence meant to her. Beth was in the dark. All she knew was that Nina thought she was pretty and had handled her life like a fool.

Beth wasn't prepared for what she found when she walked into Nina's apartment ten minutes after her bus ride and found Nina in bed with a girl of eighteen. The girl was still asleep but she woke up hard when Nina sat up in bed and said, "Who the hell told *you* to come over? At *this* hour?" Her eyes were narrow with anger and Beth recoiled, shocked.

"I'm sorry," she said. "I'll leave."

But before she could turn around and get the door closed behind her Nina said, "No. You're here now. So stay."

Beth looked at her doubtfully and at the sleepy-eyed and rather scared girl beside her. "I don't think that's the best idea," she said, but Nina's anger had passed as quickly as it had come. Suddenly she saw the possibilities of the situation: Beth's embarrassment, the charming consternation of Franny, the girl in bed with her, and herself, Nina, mistress of their feelings. What a scene! It was worth playing out.

"Make yourself some coffee," she told Beth. "We were just getting up."

And Beth could tell by the sudden change in Nina's voice, by the look on her face, that she was playing with her two guests.

"I didn't expect this, Nina," she said frostily. "I have no claim on you, I realize, but I didn't expect *this.*"

"Oh, come off it, Madame Queen. What *did* you expect?" Nina asked, smiling at Beth's white-faced annoyance. "I don't wear a chastity belt, you know."

Franny, the teenager, got up abruptly, sitting down again in humiliation as she remembered her nakedness, and then covering herself with a blanket and going into the bathroom. Beth collapsed in an armchair and preserved a chilly silence while Nina dressed herself, smiling all the while, wondering whose temper would blow first.

Franny came out of the bathroom a few minutes later with her clothes on. She walked over to Beth and spoke, facing her. "I didn't know I was muscling in on anything," she said. "This just happened, almost by accident. We weren't even going to sleep together. I feel as bad about it as you do, believe me. And she gave Nina a dirty glance but it only made Nina laugh.

"Thanks," Beth told her softly, surprised at the dignity the girl had mustered. "But never mind. I didn't come for that anyway."

"For what, then?" Nina said cheerfully, going into the kitchen.

"I want to go back to the Village tonight, Nina. I want to see the places we missed last time."

"There are quite a few," Nina said ironically. "Couple of dozen, at least."

"That doesn't matter. I want to see them all."

"Laura, hm? Got Laura on the brain," Nina said. She was fixing some frozen orange juice.

"Yes," Beth said simply.

"Well," Nina grinned. "I didn't make such a big impression on you after all. Did I?"

"Let's forget it," Beth said. The whole episode made her feel mildly nauseated. The sight of Nina no longer aroused desire in her—just regret and a powerful longing for Laura. She wasn't sure exactly what caused it—the other girl in Nina's bed, the fact that Nina held Beth's regard so cheaply, or Nina's selfish and peculiar pleasure in running people.

"I have to find Laura," Beth said in a flat, positive voice. "Will you help me?"

"Sure," Nina said airily. "We'll do the town tonight. Franny, want to come along?"

Beth expected a pointed "No" from the girl, but she said, "Yes, I'll come," instead. Beth looked up to find that Franny was gazing at her, not Nina. Nina saw it too, and was not so amused. For what reason Beth never clearly fathomed, Nina dressed as nearly like Beth as her wardrobe would permit—same color dress, same style of shoes, similar white bag. Was it to show Beth that Nina could wear the same things and look better in them? Was it because she thought Franny was admiring Beth's clothes? Beth stared at her curiously but Nina gave no hints away.

Chapter Fourteen

IN NINA'S PHRASE, THEY DID THE TOWN THAT NIGHT. BETH drank very little at first, but as the evening wore on the little mounted up and she realized, sometime shortly after midnight, how tight she was. She was quite fascinated, as she had been before, with the people she saw. Many of them knew Nina and came over to talk to her. There was one pretty, rather boyish girl at the bar whom Nina had never seen before who caught her eye, and Nina kept calling her "Farley," after a movie star she resembled, until Beth in embarrassment asked her to quit.

The rest of the time Nina needled Franny. Beth was glad it wasn't herself that night. She thought she couldn't have taken it. She would have lost her temper in one big spectacular blast and that would have been the end. She would have had to walk out on Nina and maybe on her chances of finding Laura.

For Nina asked everyone, all her friends, if they knew any Lauras. And some of them did, but none of them knew Laura Landon.

"It's going to be all over the Village that there's a great search on," Nina said. "Maybe that'll help you."

"Thanks, Nina."

Toward two a.m. Nina succeeded in getting Franny on a crying jag and Beth told her indignantly to stop torturing the girl. But Nina laughed and said, into Franny's face, "She's enjoying it." Whereupon Franny got up and ran into the ladies' room and didn't return for a half hour.

Beth had nothing to say to Nina. She was afraid any words between them would be angry and she kept quiet, answering Nina in monosyllables. Nina saw it and was both amused and annoyed. When she got drunk she liked a fight. She felt mean. At the very least she wanted to embarrass somebody.

"You don't really think I give a damn if you find that girl, do you?" she asked Beth.

"I don't care what you think."

"You know something? I don't believe there is any such person as Laura Landon."

Beth shrugged, determined not to get nasty.

"I think you're just leading me on. You just want a free tour of the Village," Nina said. And when Beth still maintained silence she went on, "You think you're something, don't you, Beth? Just because Franny has been eying you all evening."

"Has she?" Beth was surprised. She hadn't noticed it.

"Don't play innocent with me," Nina said, and Beth wondered if she was jealous. Perhaps Nina had dressed herself like Beth in at least a partial effort to snag Franny's eye.

But when Franny got back she slipped a little penciled note into Beth's hand under the table. Later Beth got a chance to read it. There was a telephone number and a plea for a call scrawled in pencil on lined paper. Beth smiled slowly across the table at Franny, largely for Nina's benefit.

And just then she noticed, out of the corner of her eye, the entrance of a woman whose face and manner captured her interest entirely. She was big, nearly six feet tall, wearing slacks and a man-cut jacket. She was a little over her best weight but strikingly handsome with the black-and-white hair—still mostly black—curling closely around her head, and light eyes. She walked with a slight swagger, her hands thrust into the pockets of her pants, and Beth wasn't the only one who turned to look at her as she made her way up to the bar.

The bartender apparently knew her and fixed her something to drink in response to a nod she gave him. She stood alone at one end of the bar, seemingly preoccupied, although now and then she smiled at someone near her who spoke to her.

Beth watched her, captivated by her manner and the world-weariness in her face, for five or ten minutes. Finally she leaned over to ask Nina who she was.

Nina gave a quick glance at the bar, reluctant to turn her attention from Franny, and said, "Oh, God! Beebo Brinker. You don't want to talk to her."

"Why not?" Beth demanded.

"You won't get anything straight from her. I mean that both ways."

"Do you know her, Nina?"

"Hell, yes. Lousy bitch."

"Why lousy?" Beth asked.

"Oh, it's a long story. Leave her alone, Beth, she's no good."

"She might know Laura," Beth said.

"If she does, Laura'll never be the same. They never are when Beebo gets through with them."

"What does she do to them?" Beth said.

"I don't know, Beth. Don't bother me about it."

"I want to meet her," Beth said stubbornly.

"Okay, damn it!" Nina flared suddenly. "Go meet her, I don't care a damn what you do. She knows everybody in the Village. If Laura Landon is living here she'll know."

"Nina," Beth protested, "you brought me down here to help me find Laura." She stared at her bewildered. "Now you don't want me to find her. Is that it?"

"Go on, Beth. Go talk to her. It's about as bright as most of the things you do. But for God's sake don't bring her over here. I can't stand her."

Beth looked at her a moment longer, and then at Franny, who was afraid to talk to her. She turned on her heel and walked away from them.

Beebo had found a bar stool and was sitting down by the time Beth reached her. Beth stood a little behind her, nervous and hesitant for a moment, and then she touched her sleeve. Beebo glanced up and to one side, seeing a girl there but not looking at her.

"Hello," Beebo said. Her face was nearly expressionless.

"Beebo Brinker?" Beth said.

"The same." She didn't seem to care who Beth was.

"Beebo, I'm looking for a friend of mine. It's urgent that I find her. Someone told me you knew everybody down here." Beth knew she sounded breathy and frightened but her voice, her manner, were out of her control. "I was wondering if you could tell me where she is."

"Try me." Beebo lighted a cigarette and Beth watched, mesmerized. Her gestures were perfectly masculine right down to the snap of the match, almost more masculine than a man's, carefully learned, carefully studied, tellingly imitated.

"Well..." Beth leaned against the bar on one elbow, facing Beebo's profile. Beebo still had not really seen her face. She smoked, or drank from her whiskey and water, and gazed into the mirror behind the bar.

"Well, her name is Laura," Beth said, once again with the frightening feeling of exposing her love to laughter.

Beebo's eyes narrowed and in the mirror she looked at Beth for the first time.

"Do you know a Laura, by any chance?" Beth said.

After a long tense pause Beebo said, "Laura? What's her last name?"

"Landon."

Slowly, very slowly, like someone moving in a dream, Beebo turned around and looked her full in the face. Her lips parted slightly and she studied Beth so closely that Beth involuntarily drew away a little, clinging to the edge of the bar for support. She felt suddenly weak, although Beebo's gaze was not unkind and Beth liked her face. It even seemed to resemble Beth's own in some ways, though Beth's was softer and smaller and feminine. Beebo, still in her early forties, looked like a college boy—gray-haired to some extent, but still collegiate.

"Beth," Beebo said, very softly, and it sounded like thunder in Beth's ears. "You're Beth. *Beth!* Goddamn! I never thought we'd come face to face, you and I."

For a long bewildered moment Beth simply stared at her. "You know me?" she murmured at last. There was no other sound for her in all that noisy bar but Beebo's voice.

"Know you?" Beebo grinned. "Honey, I know you better than you know yourself. I've spent the best years of my life hating you. You were the only real rival I ever had with Laura."

Beth's eyes grew huge with astonishment for a moment and suddenly full of tears. She turned her head away, one hand over her eyes, and Beebo explained gently to her.

"I met Laura when she first came to New York," she said. "I thought I brought her out. I mean, I thought I was the first woman she had ever loved. Until she called me Beth in bed one night. That was how I met you. Beth Cullison." Beth looked at her again, unable now to look away.

"That is your name, isn't it?" Beebo said.

"It was. It's Ayers now."

"Married?" Beebo said.

Beth nodded and Beebo gave her a little grin. "It figures," she said. "Laura used to tell me about how wonderful you were, how kind you were to her when she was so young and scared and didn't know what she was. She never talked about you except with love. God, how I used to hate the sound of your name. Have you ever had a rival that didn't exist, Beth? Have you ever been jealous of a shadow, a snapshot? I could tear up the snapshots but there were always more. She had dozens of copies lying around. She showed them to everybody. When I gave her hell for it she said I should be glad we looked alike. And you know something? We do. I didn't used to think so from the pictures she had of you, but seeing you now...Of course, you're pretty. And you're a woman." She turned away and drank the rest of her drink.

"Have something with me?" she said.

"Thanks. Scotch and water," Beth said, still too shocked to think sensibly. Beebo ordered it for her.

"So now you've come back to find Laura," Beebo mused. "Why?"

"Do you know where she is?" Beth said eagerly, her heart floating over the things Beebo had told her. "Is she still living with you?"

Beebo laughed a small private laugh. "No," she said. "Not for the past seven years. We broke up long ago." And something she left unsaid made Beth feel that, though they had broken up, Beebo still felt love for Laura. "She was an extraordinary girl," Beebo said. "I loved her very much." And then she stopped abruptly and Beth knew she would speak of that part of it no more.

"What happened to her?" Beth said. "Is she all right? Where is she?"

"She's in New York," Beebo said.

Beth gave a sigh of relief. "Where?" she said urgently. It was almost a groan of impatience.

Beebo swiveled in her seat again to look at her. "Why do you want to find her so badly, Beth? Who's Ayers? Doesn't he have anything to say about this?"

"I—I left him," Beth said. "It's all over."

"Do you think it's such a good idea to take up with a woman just because you left off with a man?" Beebo said.

"I'm gay," Beth said quickly. "It was never right with Charlie."

"Any kids?" Beebo said. Her skeptical eyes went deep and made Beth feel suddenly guilty.

But she answered with a brazen show of assurance, "No."

Beebo took a drag on her cigarette, watching Beth through narrowed eyes. "That's good," she said at last. "You'd be in bad trouble otherwise."

Beth had a momentary spell of sinking, of sickness, that made her shut her eyes and wipe her forehead with one sharp nervous gesture. The faces of Skipper and Polly were very clear before her during that moment.

"Something wrong?" Beebo said quietly.

"I—I guess I've had too much to drink," Beth said.

"Where are you staying?" Beebo said.

"The Beaton."

"Are you here alone?"

"No, I came in with Nina Spicer. Do you know her?" She looked up at Beebo then to see if her reaction to Nina was as harsh as Nina's to her. But Beebo only grinned and said, "Sure I know her. Everybody knows her."

Beth liked Beebo's face even better, now that it was becoming more familiar to her. She felt secure with Beebo, as if Beebo were a friend. It wasn't logical. Beebo had frankly admitted an unreasonable hatred of her of some years' standing—something Nina had never felt. And yet there was nothing fishy, nothing odd and egotistical about Beebo.

"How did you meet Nina?" Beebo said.

"I wrote to her, after I read some of her books. When I left Charlie I came here to find Laura and I thought Nina might help me. She knows the Village."

"Well, she can teach you a few things. But they won't have much to do with true love and happy endings," Beebo said. "Still, I guess that's something to know. There isn't much true love in the world. Did she give you a few scars?"

"A few, I guess." Beth smiled a little, "Nothing I won't recover from."

"Good. You're lucky. Now tell me one more thing. Since you won't tell me why you want to find her, are you sure you do want to find Laura?"

"Yes. Absolutely." She spoke ardently and made Beebo smile again, but such a different smile from Nina's. Warm and friendly and concerned, somehow.

"What do you think it will accomplish?" Beebo said.

"I still love her. I want her back."

Beebo finished the drink she had before her and then she said gently, "Beth...Laura is married."

There was a moment of deafening silence between them and then suddenly it seemed to Beth as if the whole bistro was coming apart at the seams. She staggered a little and Beebo got up quickly from her stool and steered Beth expertly onto it.

"You're okay, baby," she said when Beth had recovered a little. "Don't tell me it never occurred to you. Don't tell me you never thought of it. Damn, you got married. It happens, you know. Here, drink this." And she forced half a glass of scotch and water down Beth's throat.

After a moment, when she could talk, Beth whispered, "I thought of everything. Everything but that. I thought she might have gone to Europe or somewhere. I thought she might be in love with somebody else. I thought she might have disappeared. I even thought she might be dead. But, God help me, God help me, I never thought she would be married. Married! I hate him!" She whispered the words with near-despair, too stunned even to cry.

Beebo half lifted and half pulled her off her stool. "Come on, sweetheart," she said in her hoarse low voice. "You're coming home with me. I'll tell you about it. Believe me, I felt just the way you feel now when I found out. But that was seven years ago, after she left me. I didn't think I could stand it but I did." She spoke with a sweetness that amazed Beth in one so gruff and strange, and Beth clutched at her words for courage. She never thought to argue with Beebo about going home with her. She never even tried to stop and tell Nina where she was going.

But Nina saw her go out with Beebo's arm around her and Nina said softly to herself, "Damn!" She knew that was the end of her influence on Beth, and Beth had held promise for more pleasure. It was for that reason that she had tried to discourage Beth from meeting Beebo. Nina liked to control her visitor, and she loved to make love to her. It piqued her vanity to see Beth so easily slip out from under her only go to someone she disliked and feared. With alcoholic malice she watched the two of them leave.

Someone else watched them go: a small rotund man, balding, with bags beneath his eyes and an air of fatigue and boredom that seemed never to leave him. When the door of the bar swung shut behind Beth and Beebo, the small heavy man got up and walked slowly toward it and followed them into the night.

Chapter Fifteen

BETH STAYED WITH BEEBO THAT NIGHT AND THEY SAT UP AND talked through most of it. Beebo told her about the two years she and Laura had lived together, what a paradise it had been at first, what a red hell it had become when Laura had fallen out of love.

"She was looking for a substitute for you when I met her," Beebo admitted. "When I turned out to be myself, not you, she was disillusioned. She held it against me, in a way. And in another way, after a while, I think she learned to love me for myself. But it was never good enough. I was so much older; I'd done my running around and I wanted to settle down. Laura was It as far as I was concerned. The end of the trail. I was through looking over the field, through chasing after new affairs.

"But for Laura it came too soon. She was too young. She hadn't seen more than a little corner of life and I wasn't enough for her. She needed variety, she needed to know other women, and that was more than I could bear. And at the same time, she needed security. Somebody had to take care of her, watch over her, provide for her. All of that. I wanted to desperately, but I didn't qualify. I was a woman and I was a disappointing lover to boot. She needed a man, one who understood that she was gay and would always be gay, and not interfere with that part of her life."

"Where did she meet him—her husband?" Beth asked. She was sitting cross-legged on the floor in Beebo's living room, drinking the coffee Beebo had fixed for her, while Beebo sat on the couch above her with her legs split casually over the long coffee table. She was still drinking whiskey and water.

"She met him on a blind date," Beebo said. "And a few weeks later he introduced me to Laura. He lived down here at the time."

"What's his name?"

"Jack. Jack Mann."

Beth memorized it. "But you and Laura lived together for couple of years before she married Jack?"

"Yeah. They loved each other all along, though. They got very close. The worse things were between me and Laura, the closer they were between Laura and Jack. She always ran to him when anything went wrong."

"Was she *in* love with him?"

"No. And he isn't in love with her. Maybe that's why they're so happy. No romance, no jealousy. No matter what passionate affairs they may be having on the outside, their marriage is sacred to them. And it works. It works a hell of a lot better than a lot of straight marriages I know."

"Do you mean Jack's gay too?"

"Yes, honey. He's gay." Beebo looked down at her, and smiled. "He had 'Beth' problems when he married her, too. She was still thinking about you even then. Used to drive him nuts. I remember he finally gave her a lecture about it. Said you'd never see her again, you were gone out of her life and probably married, and Laura had better grow up and realize it."

"Did she?" Beth asked shyly.

"I'm inclined to think she did," Beebo said. "As a matter of fact, I can't help wondering what good it'll do to open a closed chapter, Beth. If it's no good for Laura it can't be much good for you."

Beth hung her head, watching her cigarette burn and feeling the smoke sting her eyes, without moving the thing or blowing at it.

"Maybe no good at all," she admitted. "But I have to know. I've come so far and I've had to face so much. I can't run out now when I'm so close to finding her. I wonder how she thinks of me now."

"Probably pretty much the same way, *when* she thinks of you. Romanticized. You symbolized everything good, everything wise and beautiful for her. You were an ideal love that just by accident, wasn't so ideal after all. If you ever hurt her or crossed her up, you were forgiven. As far as Jack and I could see you never did any wrong."

Beth smiled ironically at her.

"I think she realizes now that you weren't perfect, if only because you were human. She's not in love with you anymore, but she still idealizes you to some extent. That's the way I see it, at least."

"Is she still so beautiful?" Beth asked softly.

"Yes." Beebo was watching her carefully, deeply interested in this pretty young woman who had caused her such exasperation and heartache years before. "Some people don't think she *is* beautiful, you know."

"Some people are blind. She's lovely—I mean, unless she's changed?"

"No, not so much. Not to look at. But in other ways she's changed a lot. Remember, when you knew her before, you were the sophisticated one. You were the one with experience and you taught Laura. Now it's the other way around. Laura's the woman of the world and you're the provincial housewife. Do you want to start all over with her on that basis? Can you?"

It was an acute observation. Beth had never thought of her relationship with Laura. "Well, I—I'm not *that* provincial," she said in stammering defense of herself. "I've been married, I have a couple of children. That counts for some experience, doesn't it?"

"Laura's married too. Laura has a daughter six years old. And why the hell did you lie to me about having children?"

Beth flushed crimson, overcome by the revelation of Laura's maternity as much as her own lie. After a moment's confusion she said, "Beebo, I—forgive me. I didn't know you, I didn't know whether to trust you. I—" and she had to cry. It was the first time since she had met Beebo that evening that her feelings unwound enough for her to let the tears come. The storm was brief and hard but it cleared the air. "I love them terribly, but I can't live with them," she confessed brokenly when she could talk. "I left them with Charlie, my husband."

"You ran away?" Beebo frowned at her.

"Sort of. He knew I was going; I didn't try to hide it. But he doesn't know where I am now. He thinks I'm with my aunt and uncle in Chicago."

"And where do they think you are?"

"God knows. I blew up at my uncle and when I left, I sneaked off like a thief in the night." Beebo tossed her a white linen handkerchief and Beth blew her nose gratefully.

"That's too bad, honey," Beebo said gently. "You're in a hell of a situation. Me, I told off all my relatives twenty-five years ago, and left before I had any obligations. They all predicted I'd go straight to hell. But when I look back on it, I'm not sorry, strange to say. Some of it's been hell, all right. But some of it's been…wonderful. Just wonderful. Makes the rest of it worth the pain. Like the first year with Laura."

Beth gazed up at her and caught a faraway smile on her face. "You must be lonely, Beebo," she said. "Living alone like this. Or aren't you alone?"

"I live alone," Beebo said. "But I have a lot of company. A lot of drinking buddies."

"That still makes you pretty lonely, doesn't it?" Beth knew that loneliness, and she sympathized eagerly.

"Yes, honey, it does. I had a couple of dogs, once. Dachshunds. They helped for a while. But they died."

"Oh, I'm sorry."

"Actually, they were—killed."

"How awful." And Beth sensed a whole story, a whole miniature tragedy behind the words. But she dared not press Beebo for it.

"What's Laura's little girl's name?" Beth asked.

Beebo came back from her reverie and smiled at her, pouring herself another inch of whiskey from the bottle by her feet. "Elizabeth," she said. "What else?"

"For me?" Beth said.

Beebo nodded. "They call her Betsy, though. Jack put his foot down on Beth."

And oddly it struck them both funny and they laughed together, and Beth found herself reaching for Beebo's hand. Just to grasp, just to hold for an instant in gratitude. "God, I'm so glad I found you," she said. "I was so depressed. It all seemed so hopeless."

"I can imagine," Beebo said with a humorous edge in her voice, "if Nina Spicer was showing you around town."

"Is she like that with everybody?"

"She tries to be. Too bad. She's a shrewd girl and she's made quite a success of this writing bit. But she has to analyze everybody. She learns enough about human nature to use people but not enough to help them. It's not in her nature to give a damn what happens to them after they cease to amuse her. She just likes to pull the strings and see them hop. That's not saying she can't teach you a few things, Beth. But she can crack your ego at the same time and it's not worth the aches and pains involved."

"Are most gay people like that?" Beth asked.

"No. But a lot of them are. Too many. That's the most valuable lesson Nina can teach you, honey. It doesn't last long in the gay world and when it's over it keeps on hurting for a long time. You're on your own. You watch out for yourself. You haven't any of the safeguards or the consolations or the help that straight people have. There's nobody you can run crying to when you're the loser."

"Nina taught me something else. I'm gay," Beth said.

"Oh, hell," Beebo said and laughed good-naturedly. "You learn that yourself, nobody teaches you."

"She said if I cut off my hair and went to live in the Village, I'd be a butch."

"Good God, you're no butch!" Beebo exclaimed. "She's filling you full of bull just to amuse herself."

"I thought so," Beth sighed. "But I'm so damned ignorant. I'm not sure of anything. I thought maybe Laura could help me understand myself. Show me what I am."

"Nobody's going to draw you any diagrams, sweetheart," Beebo said.

"I've been wondering about it for all these years. Wondering if I did the right thing in marrying Charlie and leaving Laura."

"Why did you marry him?"

"I loved him."

"Do you still?"

"I don't know. Yes, in a way. I hate him too, though. There were times when I think I could have killed him."

"How do you know it won't be like that with Laura?" Beebo asked. "How do you know you weren't cut out to be a loner? Bisexual, maybe. Or the kind who can only love from a distance, no matter which sex, no matter how much passion?"

And Beth had to turn away from Beebo's brilliant, absorbing eyes, too troubled by her ideas to face her squarely. To change Beebo's train of thought she asked, "Why doesn't Nina like you?"

"I jilted her once. A few years ago. And I don't read her books. And, I suppose, she didn't want me to waltz off with you tonight. Sort of lets the air out of her balloon."

Beth smiled silently into her near-empty coffee cup. "Beebo," she said. "Will you tell me where Jack and Laura live?"

"Made up your mind?" Beebo said.

"Yes."

"You're going to see her?"

"Yes."

"In spite of all the pitfalls?"

"I'd walk through hell to see her," Beth whispered.

Unexpectedly Beebo reached over, putting a hand on each of Beth's shoulders and pulling her back so that she leaned against the couch between Beebo's knees. The hands were strong and firm as a boy's, disconcerting in the warm grip. Beth could feel Beebo looking down on the top of her head and she wished she could see her face.

"Okay, honey," she heard Beebo say. "I'll call them tell them you're coming."

"Oh, God, no!" Beth cried. "No, Beebo. Please. I don't want her to know in advance. I want to surprise her. If she knows she'll change things, she'll clean the house, she'll fix a big dinner, she'll have something fixed to say to me that won't be genuine. It just won't be the same. Please, let me surprise her."

"She won't thank me for that," Beebo quipped. "But if that's the way you want it."

"That's the way."

"Okay, okay," Beebo sighed. "They're up at 528 North Lexington. Eighth floor. His name is J. F. Mann. And Beth—just for the record—she's interested in somebody right now. I don't know how seriously."

"Okay. It's okay. That's something I expected," Beth said. She turned her head to Beebo's leg and kissed it fervently, impulsively. "Thank you," she said, and experienced a strange, unexpected flash of pleasure at her own boldness, at Beebo's nearness and warmth.

She stayed the rest of the night, sleeping in spite of her excitement. Beebo gave her the bed and slept on the couch in the living room. She had gone out by the time Beth got up the next morning, but there was a note for her to help herself to some breakfast and to keep in touch with Beebo. Beth scribbled down her room number and phone at the Beaton on Beebo's telephone pad and drank some orange juice. Her mouth was dry with excitement and she found it hard to eat, but she made herself take something. At the same time she riffled through the pages of Beebo's telephone directory. And there it was. There it had been all along, but without Beebo's help she wouldn't have found it. "J. F. Mann," and the address. Beth tore another sheet of paper off the phone pad and made a note of the number, slipping it into her purse.

Before she left she cleaned up her dishes and the ones Beebo had left, including the coffee cup and the whiskey glass from the night before. She made the bed, thinking as she did it that Laura must have slept in this bed too, once. After that she straightened up the living room. It wasn't the same as keeping house for Charlie. She actually enjoyed the tasks, enjoyed the feeling that Beebo would come home to a clean house and a tidy kitchen, and it would be due to Beth's care.

She took a long look at the rooms before she closed the front door after herself, and she had the feeling that sooner or later, someday, she would be back. She hoped so. She liked Beebo, she had learned from her, and it hadn't been the sharp, painful sort of lesson Nina Spicer taught. But just as effective. Perhaps more so.

Chapter Sixteen

BETH WALKED OVER TO SEVENTH AVENUE TO GET A TAXI. SHE walked with a light, swinging step, feeling a small new joy in her heart that almost amounted to hope for a happy ending to it all—the mess and bewilderment and misery of the past few months.

As she walked she noticed a short balding man ahead of her with a noticeable aura of ennui about him, standing buggy-eyed and uninterested before a window full of leather-work. He looked familiar, though she was sure she didn't know anybody in the city outside of Nina and Beebo.

Still...Maybe I saw him at one of the bars, she thought, vaguely disturbed by his face yet unable to recall it. She walked briskly past him as if she had not noticed him at all. *He probably lives down here. He probably goes bar hopping at night. I've seen him in a bar, that's all.* But it piqued her not to remember where.

She had the taxi driver let her off at Fifth Avenue and 38th Street, near the public library. She wanted to buy something, some little house gift for Jack and Laura that would make her appearance less awkward, give them all something to say. For half an hour she wandered from store to store, north and south, trying to find the appropriate thing, ignoring Merrill Landon's strictures about budgeting her money. It had to be something really nice or it just wouldn't do.

She stopped to look into the toy window at F. A. O. Schwartz, thinking suddenly of Polly and Skipper and wondering if she could send them something without upsetting them. In the middle of the window, prominently displayed, was a big, gaudy, orange giant spring, with an elaborate bow attached to the top like a gift wrapping. A big sign leaned against the bottom: "THE SCOOTCH— bounce on it, roll in it, dive through it. The new sensation!"

After a moment she went in and asked one of the clerks about it.

"Yes, it's quite unusual, isn't it?" he beamed. "We can't keep them in stock. The kids adore them. Just like those hoops a couple of years ago. I'd be willing to bet the Scootch will outsell them."

"Who makes it?" she asked faintly.

"Who? Uh—let's see." He up-ended a carton behind the counter. "California firm," he said. "Ayers-Purvis Toys." He read the name slowly. "That must be a new one, I don't recall it," he said. "All the new ideas come from California," he explained, smiling. "Don't know why. They breed out there like cats."

"Thank you," she said, turning to leave.

He called after her, "Excuse me, wouldn't you like to buy one? I mean—you'll have to get one sooner or later for your own kids."

"My own kids probably have twenty of them," she said, and left, knowing he would go to the back of the store and tell the others about the wacky customer he had.

She felt a tormented tenderness for Charlie, standing there gazing at his supreme achievement in the window. It was so silly. It was so ingenious. It would make him and Cleve a fortune. She wished him well; she wished for the first time in along time that she had been able to adapt to him better than she had. She wished fervently that they might have made each other happy, that the children could have brought a sense of fulfillment to her life. She wished that she had been there when he came home with his face lighted up and that happy, abstract look in his eyes to tell her about his wonderful new idea, wished she could have seen Polly and Skipper with their daddy's great invention.

She leaned momentarily against the wall of the toy shop and a woman stopped to inquire if she needed help.

"No," she said, and straightened up and walked into the crowd. She finally bought a pair of crystal candlestick holders at Black,

Starr, and Gorham's. While they were being gift-wrapped her spirits revived a little. She thought of Laura, thought of her very hard. Tried to picture the man she married. Was he good to her, was he rich, was he intelligent? He was gay—did that make him swishy, too? A nancy? Or could a man be gay and reasonably masculine at the same time? She burned to meet him. She was prepared to hate him.

At the hotel she collapsed on her bed and slept the rest of the day. When she awoke, late in the afternoon, she wrote Merrill Landon a note to say that Laura, his lost Laura was found. She gave him Laura's address and told him she was married. "And you have a granddaughter," she added. "Betsy." She asked him to forward a note she enclosed to Charlie, so it would have a Chicago postmark on it.

To Charlie she wrote: "I saw the Scootch in the shop windows today. For what it's worth, I'm proud of you. I hope you make a million dollars. The kids must love it I'm fine, don't worry about me. I haven't made my mind up yet on anything. Take care of yourself and give the children my fondest love. Beth."

She cried while she wrote it, knowing she had no right to the tears. They were tears of self-pity more than anything else. She had given up a lot when she gave up her children, her home, her conjugal rights. She had given them up on a gamble, in the hope that she might someday find something else, something that would mean more to her. But she hadn't found that something yet and it scared her to feel herself suspended between two worlds, belonging to neither. And she had done it all, deliberately, to herself.

Beth took a taxi to Laura's apartment building. It was a short ride in the pleasant twilight, with the sun almost down and the air cooling.

She asked at the desk for Mr. and Mrs. Mann.

The clerk telephoned up and then asked Beth who was calling, one hand judiciously placed over the receiver.

"Mrs. Ayers," Beth said doubtfully.

"Mrs. Ayers," the clerk repeated, gazing down at the floor and speaking into the receiver. He glanced up again at Beth and then handed the phone to her.

"Hello?" she said, her heart pounding, rising in her throat, her ears geared for Laura's light voice.

"Mrs. Ayers?" It was Jack. He sounded rather growly, but pleasant.

"Yes."

"I'm afraid I don't know you."

"I—I'm an old school friend of Laura's," she said, wishing the trembling in her would go away just long enough for her to make a serene first impression on him.

"Oh," he said. And then, with just a hint of enlightenment, *"Oh.* Well, then, won't you come up?"

"Thanks, I'd love to."

She got into the elevator, feeling the light nervous sweat break out all over her body, trying not to clutch her present too tightly in her clammy hands and ruin the wrappings. She watched the numbers of the floors flash above her until they got to four. It seemed an eternity.

She found the door promptly, but it was another matter to ring the bell. She felt suddenly faint and hated herself, trying to take up her courage and smooth her dress and compose her face with a multitude of ineffectual fluttering gestures. At last she stopped and stood rigidly still for as long as she could bear it, her eyes tight shut and the sweat loosed uncontrollably all over her. And then she reached for the bell.

Before she could push it the door opened and she gave a small but audible gasp. A short dark man, crew-cut and horn-rimmed, smiled at her.

"Took so long I thought you must have gotten lost," he grinned. "Mrs. Ayers? Come on in. I'm Jack Mann."

"Thanks," she said from a husky throat, and followed him into the living room, grasping the box with the candlesticks in it so closely that the white tissue paper pulled apart under one of her

164

thumbs. She looked about the room with quick scared eyes, her whole being prickling with the possibility of Laura's presence.

"Sit down," Jack said. He watched her with a mixture of amusement and curiosity that was friendly enough. Beth obeyed him, lowering herself halfway into her chair and suddenly remembering her gift.

"Oh, here," she blurted, rising abruptly and thrusting it toward him "I—I brought you a little something. I remember Laura used to like crystal and cut glass, things like that."

"Thanks," he said, accepting it "Yes, she still does. Shall I keep it till she gets home? She ought to be the one to open it."

"Isn't she here?" Beth stared at him, still half out of her seat.

"If you froze that way," he said with a grin, "you'd be a pretty unhappy girl."

And she sat down suddenly, embarrassed.

"Yes, she's out," he went on. "I mean, no, she's not at home." He put the gift on the table in front of him and sat down opposite her in a leather chair, asking if she'd like a drink, how long she would be in New York, a dozen urbane civilities that they batted back and forth with a show of casualness. And all the while they studied each other surreptitiously, Jack with the bemused air of a man trying to place a face, and Beth with the intense interest of a rival.

"So you and Laura went to school together," he said.

"Yes. Just for a year." She thought she liked him, which was something she hadn't planned on. He was ugly, in the nice sort of way that women like. There was a friendly intelligence in his face. And he was short. Beth guessed that he and Laura might be near the same height. Beth was taller than he, quite a bit taller in her high-heeled shoes. But he was quick and graceful and very much at ease, and it made her easier within herself, for which she was grateful. He went to a small built-in bar in a corner of the living room and fixed her a drink. It gave Beth a chance to look around. It was a spacious room, an unusually roomy apartment for midtown Manhattan.

He must be doing well to keep Laura like this, she thought.

"When do you think she'll be in?" she asked in a voice loaded with careful disinterest.

"I don't know. She's out with a friend. They were going to a concert, so it could be rather late. If you'd told us you were coming..." He smiled and shrugged, handing her the scotch and water.

"Thanks. I guess it was silly not to. I wanted to surprise her."

"Well, it sure as hell will surprise her if she hasn't seen you in nine years. If you'd gotten here ten minutes earlier you would have caught her."

"Probably just as well I didn't. I might have ruined her evening." She was thinking of the "friend" Laura went to the concert with, and Jack, though his eyes opened wider at this, pretended not to have heard.

"Where's your daughter?" Beth asked suddenly. "I thought you had a daughter."

"Really? What gave you that idea?" he asked with a little frown of curiosity visible between his eyes.

Beth cursed her own clumsiness silently. "I should have told you right away," she stumbled. "I ran into a friend of Laura's—oh, just by accident—or I never would have found you. She told me about—Betsy."

"Oh. That explains it. I was about to ask how you found us." He said it slowly and she knew he was amused but somehow she didn't mind. She had the feeling he was being amiable because he liked her, not because it was his obligation to a guest. "Who was the friend?" he asked.

She didn't want to throw it at him as if she had been down in the Village sleuthing and run into Beebo as a likely well of information—as if she and Beebo were in cahoots. But his smile broadened at her delay and she finally said, with a little sigh that meant she was surrendering all her subterfuges, "Beebo. Beebo Brinker. You know her pretty well, I guess."

"Pretty well," he said with the emphasis of understatement, and laughed outright. "Good old Beebo. How the hell did you find *her?* Well, I guess it's not so hard at that," he answered himself. "Anywhere south of Fourteenth Street you can't miss her. Was she wearing her boots?"

"Her boots?"

"Yes. She wears them when she's mad at the world. Makes her feel manly." He said it without ill-will but full of old familiar affection.

"No boots," Beth smiled. "But lots of advice. Lots of stories."

"She must have been bowled over when she found out you knew Laura," Jack said. "She's still in love with her."

A queer little flash of disappointment, almost alarm, went through Beth. "She recognized me," she said. "I guess Laura told her quite a bit about me. Showed her some old snapshots, or something."

"Then you must be Beth," he said. "I thought so but I didn't want to embarrass you.... Beth the Incorruptible."

"What?" she exclaimed.

"That's what I used to call you," he said. "In the days when I couldn't stand you. Purely sarcastic, you can be sure. But that was before I met you. Laura used to make you seem that way when she talked about you."

Beth began to grin. Suddenly, strangely, she felt at ease. "You know, it's the damnedest thing," she told him. "I met her father in Chicago a couple of weeks ago, and he knew me right away. I met Beebo in a bar last night and she said, 'My God, you're Beth!' And now you've got it figured out too. I feel like a celebrity."

"Around here you were a celebrity, for quite a while," he said. "We all had to learn to live with you—all of us who lived with Laura. Papa Landon got you thrown in his face one night at the McAlton Hotel—all about that year you and Laura roomed together. After Laura told him she cracked him over the head with a glass ashtray and beat it. Gave him a concussion, but he recovered. They've never seen each other since."

"My God!" Beth breathed softly. "He spoke of her so lovingly. As if it had all been forgiven, if not forgotten."

"I suppose it has," Jack said. "I suppose he'd like to find her again and patch things up." His eyes were bright on her. "But it wouldn't be a very good idea."

"No? Why not?" Her mind flashed to the note she had mailed that very afternoon with Laura's address and married name in it.

Jack shrugged. "Well, Laura's happy now. We're happy, I should say. And Landon never did anything but upset her. At least when they were together."

"It's been a long time. Maybe he deserves another chance," Beth suggested.

"I think that's up to Laura, don't you?"

"Why not to him?"

"He wasn't the aggrieved party," Jack said. "Whatever was unhappy between them was his doing. It's up to Laura to forgive, not Landon."

"Oh." She lowered her head, a small alarm inside herself. But Merrill Landon had given Beth his promise not to visit Laura, not to interfere with her life. He said it was because he had no right to bother her. All he wanted was a link, an address, a reassurance. And remembering him with confidence, even a sort of affection, her trust returned and she calmed herself.

Before she could ask Jack more a little girl about six years old burst out of a door behind him and said, "Daddy, will you fix the TV? The picture's all crooked."

"Sure. Come here, honey, we have company," he said. "This is Mrs. Ayers."

"Hello, Mrs. Ayers," she murmured and came forward shyly, her hair long and blonde and floating like Laura's, her features dainty and her face fair, though she wore glasses like her father. She was shy and unspeakably sweet and small, and Beth thought of Polly, her Polly...and of Laura and all Laura's reflected beauty and reticence. And she held out her arms to Betsy with a full heart and full eyes and clasped the astonished child to her.

"Oh, you're lovely!" she exclaimed. "You look just like your mommy."

The little girl backed away, frightened at her strange behavior, but Beth caught her hands and said, "Don't be afraid. You know, I have a little girl—" She stopped, suddenly wary. She meant to keep that part of her life separate and apart from this. "I was a good friend of your mommy's years ago," she said, brushing impatiently at a tear. "We went to school together. And I'm so happy to see she has a beautiful little daughter that looks so much like her."

Betsy smiled. "You're beautiful, too."

Beth had to resist the impulse to hug her and probably scare her again. Jack had adjusted the television for Betsy in the meantime and he came to take her by the hand. "You go in and watch," he said. "You can have another half hour," he told her. "Then bedtime. School tomorrow."

Beth watched her retreat across the living room and turn in her bedroom door to say again, with the same little dip of her head that Laura gave before people she didn't know and was a bit shy with, "Good night, Mrs. Ayers."

"Good night, Betsy," Beth said solemnly.

Jack gave her a kiss and closed the door behind her. He looked up to see the tears in Beth's eyes and, surprised, he said, "She's just a kid like any other. Except to Laura and me. We've got her pegged for President of the United States, naturally."

"I didn't mean to be silly about it," Beth said. "She—looks so much like Laura."

"That's nothing to cry about," he smiled. "That's something to be grateful for. Before she was born I had nightmares that she'd look just like me."

"It wouldn't have been *that* bad," she said, forced to return his smile.

"Not for a boy, maybe," he said. "A man can be ugly and nobody cares. But a woman can't. Her whole life is twisted up if she is."

Beth gazed at him with a new respect. His words recalled Vega's shocking hidden ugliness to her and for a minute she was nearly overcome with the thought of her former lover. She concentrated on Jack for the sake of composure. He was a father, he had proved himself a man. He had a lovely child and a lovely home. He had Laura.

All Beth's stereotyped ideas about homosexual men were getting a bad jumbling. He seemed as normal, as comfortable to be with as any man she knew. Only, he wasn't normal, and it gave her an odd feeling inside. She asked herself how much he knew of her, and what he supposed she was doing there, trailing Laura after all these years.

They talked and the time passed quickly. He told her how he and Laura had met and how their love had grown and Beth thought, watching him, that Laura must love him very much to have let him marry her, to have taken his name and shared his home and borne his child. It amazed Beth that Laura could have done that, gone that far. Laura was not a selfish girl. She wouldn't have objected to children on that ground. It was the mechanics of it, the necessary intimacy between a man and a woman that preceded children that Beth could hardly picture Laura accepting. But she had and with *this* man, Jack, who faced Beth now over a friendly nightcap and described his life with Laura.

"The one thing I never thought she could do," she confessed to him, "was marry anybody."

"I didn't think she could, either," he said. "Gave me some bad nights till she said yes."

"I remember when we were in college together, how she used to talk about—about men."

"She didn't think much of us as a group," he said and his eyes twinkled. "Chalk that up to Papa Landon. He set a sterling example as a slob. I had quite a prejudice to overcome before I could talk her into tying the knot."

"You don't mean you had to talk her out of women?" Beth exclaimed.

"Hell, no," he said and laughed. Now that it was out in the open they both felt better. "Nobody could do that. I'd have been nuts to try. She can't be talked out of women and I can't be talked out of men—emotionally, that is. It would take more words than there are. But that doesn't matter to our marriage. Nothing goes on in this house that might hurt our life together. We keep the other stuff apart; it always comes second."

"Does Betsy know?"

"No," he said simply. "It's not that we hide things, it's just that she's too young to understand, even if we made a point of it to her. She knows we have our own friends, she knows we go out occasionally. Like Laura tonight. Now and then she meets some of our friends. That's all. She's a happy kid, thank God. And we're happy."

"I'm glad," Beth said, and she truly was. "I've been expecting to hate you ever since I knew you existed. But I don't. I don't even want to anymore. I'm glad things have worked out for you. Only..."

"Only, you'd like to see Laura again. See if she's changed and all that?"

"Something like that." She looked away from him timidly.

"Why did you come to New York, Beth?" he said quietly. "It wasn't just to find Laura, was it?"

"Oh, it was a lot of things," she said.

"Laura said you were married. Or nearly married when she last saw you. You said your name was Mrs. Ayers. Is Mr. Ayers here with you?"

"No, he's in California," she said. "As a matter of fact, we're divorced. I haven't seen him for quite some time."

"Too bad," he said, but he said it too quickly, too lightly, without comment, and she sensed his doubt, sensed that he only accepted her statement to put her at ease, not because he believed it. She had no idea why she felt compelled to lie about her marriage. Maybe because she thought Jack would not let her get close to Laura if he knew. Maybe because she was at heart so desperately ashamed of the mess she had left in California. At any rate the lie was spoken and she had to stick by it now.

"Any kids?" he said and she shook her head, unable to speak the monstrous fib aloud. How could Laura take her back, how could she learn to love Beth again, hold her and come close to her, if she knew what Beth had done to her own children? She must never know and Beth realized suddenly that she had to keep the whole past in the shadows, to pretend it was no more real than she said it was. Or it would poison the happiness she felt so near.

"You must be a little older than Laura," she said brightly to Jack, switching the subject abruptly and making him blink at her.

"A little," he conceded. "Twenty-two years."

"My God!" she cried. "That much? I don't believe you."

He shrugged and smiled. "You don't have to," he said.

"But that makes you damn near fifty years old," she said, incredulous.

"Damn near. Forty-seven."

"But you look as if you were in your thirties."

"Thanks," he said with a grin. "You make me feel extremely generous. Have another drink."

She handed him her glass. "You look so—Joe College," she said and he gave a laugh that was more of a snort of self-mockery and said, "That's going too far." But he did look remarkably young and moved his spare body with a suppleness that belied his age.

She took her glass back filled and looked at it intently, as though in search of poise. "Is—is Laura in love with anybody, Jack?" she asked.

"Not seriously," he said, studying her, wondering just how much she wanted from his wife.

"Either she is or she isn't," she said.

"Well, on that basis," he said, "I'd have to say she is. But remember you forced me into it."

"Then it is serious." Her face was very pale and her eyes were on him now.

"Hell, she's not going to marry the girl."

"Has she known her a long time? Does she dream about her all the time?" The questions tumbled out of Beth and she was suddenly humiliated by her eagerness, her concern, and her gaze dropped from his again.

"She's known her for a while now," he said. "I think it's beginning to fade. But they still see each other just about every day. They're pretty compatible."

"Who is the girl?"

He chuckled a little. "Betsy's piano teacher," he said. "Betsy's getting free lessons all over the place. Very economical."

After a long pause Beth said, "Are you in love with anybody?"

"You have designs on me, too?" he grinned and she blushed a quick red. "I'm always in love with somebody. How about you?"

She had left herself wide open for that and she knew he wanted to know why she was there and what she was seeking from Laura.

"I'm never in love with the right person," she said softly.

"I'll bet," he said, but though he teased her it was not malicious. "You must have been once," and when she glanced up at him, he added, "to hear Laura tell it."

"You mean—my husband?" she faltered.

"I mean Laura," he said bluntly. "She was terribly in love with you, for a very long time, Beth. Long after she left you."

"Is she still?" she asked. She had to say it; her heart and tongue would not be still even though the asking of it shamed her.

He looked at her a moment and then he shook his head. "Her life has changed," he explained. "There are other things, now. I don't know exactly how she feels about you anymore, Beth. I can only say she's safely out of love with you and has been for a long time. We don't talk about it much. On the other hand, I think she'll always feel a special tenderness for you. It's just that you don't seem very real to her anymore. You're more like a beautiful dream that's over and done with. Something to remember with gratitude and affection, but something more like a mirage than a fact."

Beth finished her drink. "Do you suppose I'll ruin it all by seeing her again?"

"You could. Depends on why you want to see her," he said, urging a confession from her with his voice, his attitude, everything but his words.

She looked at him out of tormented eyes. "I wonder if I could explain it, even to you," she murmured.

"Try," he said.

"Jack," she said helplessly, "there's no way. I don't know myself. I won't know why I'm here until I see her face before me. Until I touch her and hear her voice. Maybe I'll know then, if I'm lucky." She felt herself getting shaky and she stopped talking. He took her glass again and refilled it.

"She'll be along," he said. "These things are never very late."

But it did get late. Later and later until it was after midnight and she could no longer bear to sit there and face him and keep her dreadful secrets from coming up in her throat and gagging her. She got up at last and thanked him and told him, "I can't wait any longer. I'll come by tomorrow. Please don't tell her I was here. I have to surprise her. Don't ask me why, I can't explain."

"There's a lot you can't explain," he said mildly. "Why don't you spend the night?" he went on. "We have plenty of room."

Her heart jumped at the chance.

"Get up, you're on the sofa-bed," he told her. "Won't take a minute to make it up."

When he brought her one of Laura's nightgowns to wear she took it with a sudden gesture and look of pleasure she made no attempt to hide. He smiled at her.

"Still want to keep it a secret?" he said. "From Laura, I mean."

"Won't she see me when she comes in?" Beth said. "Right here in the living room?"

"She won't know who it is in the dark."

"Don't tell her, then."

"It'll probably knock her for a loop in the morning," he said. "But if you want it that way."

"I do. Thanks, Jack."

"Sure." He smiled at her, showed her where the bathroom was, and left her to herself.

She lay down after a while, turning out the light and lying in the dark. She didn't expect to sleep with her mind whirling and full of Laura, but she did. Very suddenly she dropped off as if a switch had been flipped inside her and stifled her thoughts.

Chapter Seventeen

IT WAS ALMOST DAWN WHEN SHE HEARD THE FRONT DOOR opened carefully, and shut with a small click. She was lying on her stomach with her face obscured by crumpled bedclothes and the pillow. She heard Laura come in, heard her pause as she caught sight of the sofa-bed open and occupied, heard her rustle softly across the room and felt her presence, her scent, only scant inches from her. The room was full of a deep gray light and Beth was sure it wasn't enough for Laura to distinguish her face by. She lay almost breathless on the bed until Laura turned and moved quietly away, going into her own bedroom.

Beth rolled over and gazed at the faintly visible ceiling with a tremendous happiness inside her that called for singing, shouting from the rooftops, hilarity. It made her smile at the ceiling and hug herself, and after a while it got her out of bed and sent her to the door of the bedroom where Jack and Laura were sleeping. She just stood there, one hand pressed against the door and a smile on her face, for half an hour. There was too much excitement and anticipation in her for the unhappy parts of her life to bother her. She never once thought of Charlie or of Vega.

She got up and dressed. There was no point in trying to sleep any more; she was too keyed up. She put her clothes on and washed her face and then she made up the sofa-bed, folding the sheets and blanket carefully and stacking them in a chair while she closed the hinged mattress and put the cushions back in place. All slowly...all quietly.

She picked up a magazine and looked at the pictures. And finally, after what seemed like an eternity, she heard stirrings in

Jack and Laura's room. She heard a sleepy male voice speaking softly and then someone answering him, and her whole soul thrilled to that light feminine voice. It had been so long, so abysmally long and lonesome a time since she had last heard it. She even wondered, half laughing at herself, if she would have recognized it as Laura's voice without the sure knowledge that it was actually Laura who spoke. She heard her so indistinctly; the words were unintelligible, just a faint murmur of sound.

Fifteen minutes went by, during which Beth could hear sounds of running water in the bathroom, small sounds of drawers opening and shoes dropping and things being moved and things being gotten into. Suddenly the bedroom door opened and she looked up—almost leaped up—only to see Jack emerge.

Jack gave her a pleasant grin. "She's still sleeping," he said. He gave three sharp raps on Betsy's door and said, "Get up, honey." And then, turning to Beth, he said, "Come on, I'll fix you some breakfast."

She got up and followed him into the kitchen and helped him make scrambled eggs and bacon and coffee and orange juice and muffins.

"I believe in big breakfasts," he told her.

"You're some cook," she said. "You really know your way around the kitchen. I'm a flop in that department."

He smiled, unabashed. "Worked out very well," he said. "Laura's not a great cook, and she doesn't like it much. I do most of it."

"Under protest?"

"Hell, no. I enjoy it. I wouldn't do it otherwise."

Betsy came in as Beth was pouring the orange juice and she exclaimed brightly, "Hi, Mrs. Ayers! Did you stay all night?"

"Sh!" her father told her. "Come here and let me button you. Mrs. Ayers is going to surprise Mommy. We don't want her to know she's here."

"Oh," she said, turning big eyes, made bigger still by the lenses in front of them, on Beth, while Jack did up a row of pearl buttons on the back of her dress.

"There," he said. "Eat."

Beth had the uncanny feeling that everything she saw and heard, every bit of this little morning ritual she was sharing with them, would tie Laura closer to her and help her understand herself. Nothing was unimportant. She remembered it all.

"When does Laura get up?" she asked while they ate.

"Not till ten or so. It depends," he said.

"She isn't working, then?"

"No." It was emphatic. She sensed that he didn't want his wife to work.

"Who did you tell her I was?"

"She asked me this morning," he said, grinning. "I told her you were my mother. Stood her on her ear."

"Did it? Is your mother dead or something?"

He laughed. "No. Laura's never laid eyes on my mother, and neither have I for thirty years. But I call Laura 'Mother.' It started out as a joke and ended up a family institution. I was calling her Mother long before I had any notion of marrying her. A Freudian slip, I suppose."

Betsy giggled, more at the tone of his voice than at his words, for they didn't make much sense to her.

"I'll be home after five," he told Beth when he finished. "We'll go out for dinner or something." He got up and Betsy followed him. At the kitchen door he turned to add, "Say, tell Laura to call George McCracken and cancel that order, will you? I've changed my mind. And tell her to mail a check to Dr. Byrd. It'll save me writing it down."

"Sure," Beth said.

When they had gone she felt suddenly scared, suddenly on her own without anyone to help her through it, and she almost wished that Laura knew she was there. It was going to be such a hard shock for her. Or was it? Would she take it in stride the way she seemed to have taken the rest of her life?

Beth cleaned up the breakfast dishes, leaving the coffee and wrapping the muffins in waxed paper for Laura. She smoked incessantly out of sheer nervousness and she began to wonder if it would ever be ten o'clock.

But Laura was quicker than that. It was only a little past nine when Beth heard her getting up, heard the familiar morning sounds that Jack had been making an hour ago. And all at once Beth was overwhelmed with the significance of it. It seemed as if all she had suffered and begun to learn so painfully and searched for so clumsily was about to be revealed to her, as if her very soul would come walking out of that bedroom with Laura and show itself to her for the first time and answer all her questions.

She was almost more afraid of seeing her true self than of seeing Laura now and she sat on the edge of the chair with her whole spine shivering and her hands hot and sweaty.

The bedroom door opened and from her seat Beth heard Laura cross the living room, the dining area. For a shattering second she felt the gray faintness that possessed her in tense emotional storms and she clamped her eyes shut. But the feeling passed and she opened them again. They opened on Laura.

She was standing in the doorway of the kitchen, and at the moment Beth saw her she was still too stunned to speak. There was not even a trace of amazement yet on her face, just morning sleepiness and the heart-piercing beauty that Beth had loved so passionately long ago.

For some moments they simply stared at each other, both too full of feeling to speak or move. And then Laura raised trembling hands to her face and Beth heard her voice, clear and familiar now, break as she spoke her name. It took her another second to realize that Laura was crying.

Beth sprang to her feet and went to her, only to find herself helplessly shy and unable to touch her. Until Laura lowered her hands and turned diamond-bright eyes up to her and reached for her.

They kissed each other with such tenderness, such perfect accord, such lovely waiting warmth, that Beth felt dizzy with it. Laura simply moved into her arms, giving herself to her with that whole-souled generosity that thrilled Beth almost to tears. They clung to each other, and still there were no words between them, there seemed to be nothing to say. Beth held her tight, feeling a flood of strength and sureness come into her arms, as she put her head down against Laura's and kissed her throat, her ears, the delicate expanse of shoulder that her negligee revealed. She could feel Laura trembling and it delighted her inexpressibly, this overpowering response they could feel for each other. It was as if Laura had known all along and was welcoming her home.

"I thought you might have changed," Beth whispered finally. "I thought you might never have forgiven me. Oh, Laura, Laura, oh my darling Laura."

But Laura, sensing better than Beth the futility of words at such a moment, pulled away, seeming to glide out of Beth's arms. Her eyes, her whole face glowed with a beguiling reticence that Beth remembered with a wrench of the heart, and she followed as Laura moved away from her, across the kitchen to a window.

"Laura, say something," Beth pleaded. "Say it's all right that I'm here. Say you're glad to see me."

Without looking at her Laura repeated softly, "It's all right, Beth. I'm glad to see you. Very glad," and her voice vibrated with amazed desire. When she felt Beth's kisses on the back of her neck she put her head back and let it rest against Beth's shoulder.

For Beth it was almost too much. There was so much to say, so much to excuse, and yet all she wanted was to touch Laura, to make love.

"I'm afraid to stop touching you!" Beth said. "I'm afraid you'll vanish, I'm afraid I'm dreaming. Oh, Laura, Laura...Just saying your name to you now, knowing you hear me...I can't bear it." She felt her own tears well up and she let them come. "I've said it so many times to myself, to the bare walls, to nobody and anybody. I feel as if I've spent my whole life trying to find you again, as if everything in my life that I've done without you doesn't count. Nothing matters but you. Laura, I was so afraid I wouldn't find you.

I've tried so hard, I've been so damn scared that you wouldn't want to see me, that you'd be different."

Laura turned around and put a finger on Beth's lips. "Don't talk," she said. "It's so hard to talk. You'll spoil everything." She took Beth's hand and led her into the bedroom. The scent of her pervaded the whole room and struck a whirling exhilaration into Beth. The beds were rumpled and welcoming and the clothes Laura must have worn the night before hung over a chair in the corner.

Laura pulled Beth down on the bed with tender graceful arms, slipping under her as she did so and letting her negligee fall away. For every feverish word Beth uttered Laura gave her a kiss until she had Beth helpless with desire, until all the words were stilled. Beth had not even the time to marvel at it, to be grateful; all that she saved for afterwards, succumbing to the sensual beauty of it now, while it was happening.

She had the feeling, whenever Laura touched her or moved with her, that no one, no living human being, had ever understood her so beautifully, so instinctively, and she felt too that Laura could not have been this way with anybody else. All Laura had to do was speak, and Beth would understand all. Their love was sacred to them. It made her feel that Laura had just been waiting for her all these years. Nothing of significance had happened to either of them since they parted. All their lives, all their actions, all their thoughts without each other lost meaning. It was as if nothing existed but the two of them, and they were more important than the rest of the world put together.

They lay in each other's arms throughout the rest of the morning, hardly speaking at first, just reaffirming a powerful attraction that had lain dormant for too long, thrilled to feel the remembered sweet response.

"It makes me think of the campus," Laura murmured. "Do you remember how it was in the spring? How it felt to walk under the huge old elms on the broadwalk and talk about classes and whisper about love? It's almost like being there, having you so close. I never thought I'd feel it again."

"Laura," Beth said, her hands full of Laura's hair. "I've been half dead all these years. I've needed you so terribly." There was a little pause. Laura looked away and Beth knew what she was thinking. "I—I know I could have had you in the beginning," she went on, hesitant but unable to stem the flood of feeling. "I know I should never have given you up. But you see, I didn't understand it then."

She paused, searching Laura's face for a light of sympathy, but Laura listened to her with her face averted. It made Beth feel, more than words could have, how profoundly she had hurt this exquisite girl. "I thought I had to have a man, then," she tried to explain. "But Laura, I was wrong. I've had to live with one and, believe me, I know. I've been sick—just sick with it."

"You'd have been sick with me too, Beth," Laura said with a wise smile, unexpectedly. "No matter which one of us you chose, it would have been the wrong choice. You would have spent the rest of your life wondering if you hadn't done wrong. It wouldn't have been so much different with me than with Charlie."

Beth sat up in bed, grasping Laura's face in her hands, her eyes hurt and shocked. "Laura, you're the only one who ever understood me, who ever cared so beautifully and completely for me. No man—certainly not Charlie—could ever measure up to you. No man can understand me when I can't understand myself. That's why I needed you so desperately."

"To be understood?" Laura interrupted. She smiled with a sad mouth. In the aftermath of shock and passion, her head was clearing.

"Not just that," Beth said, feeling somehow as if the ground were slipping out from under her, yet not knowing why. "I love you, Laura. I've loved you since we parted."

"When did you make that discovery?" Laura said. "On your wedding day?" And her smile was sharp now.

"Oh God, Laura, I don't know when I first realized it—what a mistake the marriage was."

"Probably the day you had your first quarrel," Laura said, and her expression hinted that she would have liked to have seen it. She looked suddenly like a minx—sly and taunting. Beth could tell just from her face, her smile, how much she had learned, how much she had changed. She would not be easy and yielding for long.

"Laura, don't laugh at me," Beth pleaded. "You don't know what I've been through, what I've given up, to find you."

"What, Beth? Tell me. Your reputation? Your fortune? Your rose-covered bungalow? Or just a little peace of mind?" She got up from the bed while she spoke and began to dress. The action was almost insolent, a soundless slap in the face that reverberated across nine years. Beth saw in her mind with stinging clarity the scene at the train, when she had sent Laura away. It had never seemed cruel to her until now because she had fooled herself into thinking she had done it for Laura's own good. But looking into Laura's haunting face she saw very clearly that it had been cruel after all. Laura remembered every word and gesture of it. She was remembering it at that moment while she looked at Beth with a smiling mouth.

"Laura, I'm speaking to you from my heart," Beth said, her voice straining. "I'm telling you the absolute truth the very best I can. Don't turn your back to me."

But Laura had kept her resentment in check too many years not to give herself the luxury of loosing it now. Just once. Just to let Beth know how it had been. That was all she wanted. "You turned your back on me often enough," she said, facing away from the bed and looking through her dresser drawers.

Beth looked down at her bare thighs in confusion and covered them with part of the sheet. "Never on purpose," she protested.

Laura laughed. She knew better. "Only for Charlie's sake," she said. "That it? He forced you. You never would have turned me out on your own. Where is Charlie now?" She pulled a gauzy slip from one of the drawers, and still her back was turned and her eyes ignored her lover.

And Beth knew from the toss of Laura's head, from the sweep of her smooth arm, that Laura meant to punish her.

"He's in California," Beth said darkly.

"How long has he been out there?"

"A long time. Years."

"Were you there with him?"

"No."

"He must be worried sick about you. Or does he know where you are?" And now, as from a great height, Laura's cornflower eyes swept over her curiously. Those eyes had lost their innocence through the years, but Beth loved them still.

"No, he doesn't know. I doubt if he's in any mood to give a damn, either. He thinks I'm in Chicago."

"Are you still married?" Laura said.

"No. Divorced. Oh, it was a long time ago, Laura. Don't ask me about it." She sped through the lie as if afraid of stumbling over it. But Laura's eyes, grown knowing and sharp, saw the shadow of uncertainty on Beth's face.

"Have you been looking for me all this time?" Laura said, and suddenly she was coy, teasing, needling Beth. "Was I so hard to find?"

"Not after I got to New York. I met Beebo Brinker in the Village. Beebo told me where you were."

"Oh." Laura pulled the slip over her head and her act of dressing defied Beth. Laura was so breathtaking without her clothes. The fact that she was covering herself up was almost depressing, as if she were putting an end to the tenderness, the caresses of a little while ago. She was telling Beth, subtly and wittily, to go to hell, and Beth was stung. Laura's whole graceful body told her impudently, *You took advantage of my surprise, my helpless love. Well, I'm not helpless any longer.*

"Did you have any children, Beth?" Laura asked. Her questions were slow, bold, rather hopeful of offending. And yet there was still restraint in her. She had once loved Beth utterly, and her first reaction to Beth's presence had been a quick unreasoning surrender.

184

Desire had made her weak. But desire was satisfied now; it remained to satisfy her wounded soul.

"No," Beth snapped. "No children." She was appalled at herself and at the same time angrily determined to deny that part of her life.

Laura gazed at her, aware from the tone and temper in Beth that she had touched an emotional sore. But then perhaps it was just Beth's disappointment in seeing Laura get dressed.

Beth, suddenly surly, got up and began to put her own clothes on. She stepped into her panties self-consciously and then, to her own surprise, broke down and began to cry. The chill between them was too much for her. She went to Laura humbly and embraced her.

"Laura, I want you," she whispered. "I love you. Nothing else matters. The rest of my life doesn't matter, it didn't even happen, if you'll just take me back. Be good to me. Help me, please, help me."

But Laura couldn't be had that easily. "Help you what?" she said. "You mean, help you now the way you helped me nine years ago? Put you on a train and send you to hell? One-way trip?"

"Please—dear God—don't be sarcastic!" Beth implored her.

"It's a very educational trip, Beth," Laura said softly.

For a moment it struck Beth as Nina's barbs had struck her. But she needed Laura's aid too much to risk antagonizing her. "I'm dead serious," she said through her tears. "Help me find myself. Help me know myself," she insisted, shaking Laura forcibly. "No one can help me but you."

And Laura, caught in Beth's strong urgent arms, began to understand, began to see through the clouds of passion and desperation that hung about Beth. She knew what Beth was there for. Not for love, not for Laura, not for nostalgia or passion or anything tender. She had come to find herself and was fanatically sure Laura could help. Laura was her tool, and, realizing it now, Laura smiled at her with pity.

"You're so lucky," Beth said. "So damn lucky!" And she couldn't keep the little green flash of envy from showing. "You've got it both ways. A husband and a child and a home. And at the same time, women. You worked your life out right, Laura darling. I made a complete mess of mine. God, isn't it ironical? When I said goodbye to you and watched you climb on that train and go out of my life, I felt sorry for you. I pitied you because I thought you were already starting out on the wrong foot. I thought nothing could set you right. You'd just bungle along and botch the whole thing. I thought you'd be hurt." She clung to Laura as she spoke, unconsciously rocking her as if the movement were a comfort.

"I thought you'd get lost, I thought you'd get taken, I thought the big city would devour you," Beth cried, almost wishing, out of spite, that it had. "I thought living like an outcast, a Lesbian, would destroy you. All this time I've worried and wondered about you. And now at last I find you and—and" she began to laugh a little hysterically—"and you're happy as a clam. You've got the world on a string. You're the one who did it right, who found the secret. Laura, let me in on it. I'm so damned miserable sometimes I feel like death. Like death." And she shook Laura with the angry demand for sympathy.

It was not a generous speech. It was not the declaration of love reborn or of gratitude that she had meant to make. It was an accusation. It said, "You have no right to be happier than I!" Laura had it all, Beth had nothing, and Beth showed her grudge in a sudden uncontrollable outpouring of envy and unhappiness. It was not what she had come all this way to discover and it was too much to bear.

Laura understood this while Beth did not. Beth thought she was speaking of love, and she was chagrined when Laura moved out of her arms with a laugh.

Laura walked across the room in her slip, one nylon stocking on, one in her hand, and her laugh burned Beth like salt in a cut. Laura turned and looked at her then, still smiling.

"Beth," she said, lingering over the name. "I still love you, Beth. God knows why. But now, for the first time in all these years, I can pity you too. It's a strange feeling. A little like being set free."

"No, Laura—"

"Don't talk. Listen! You need a little pity. You need a lot. You've spent so damn many years pitying me, Beth, don't begrudge me the same pleasure. It's my turn now."

Beth went over to the bed and collapsed on it. "How did you do it?" she begged. "Where did I go wrong? I never should have let you leave me."

"No? What would we have done together, you and I? Settled down in a vine-covered walk-up in the Village? Adopted a couple of kids?"

"I don't want kids, I never did!"

"You said you didn't have any."

"I don't!" Beth shrieked.

"Then don't get excited," Laura said curiously. "You could have lived with me once, Beth. Don't forget that."

"Anything would have been better than Charlie!"

"Even me?" Laura couldn't help laughing again.

"No! No! Good God, Laura, Laura, please don't laugh like that. Don't laugh at me!" She sounded quite frantic and Laura took pity on her. She was not malicious, only human, and she needed to hurt Beth a little. It was healthy for her. It would clear away the murky, pent-up bitterness and misunderstanding.

"If you don't want me to laugh at you, don't be such a fool," she said.

"Charlie was insufferable," Beth gasped, clutching at her self-control.

"Charlie loved you, Beth," Laura retorted. "I don't know what the situation is now, but you dismissed his love much too lightly a few minutes ago. It was a wonderful love, very deep and strong. If there were blind spots in it, they weren't weaknesses. He had enough love to smooth them over. I hated him but I respected him always. I knew how much he loved you."

"Are you saying that whatever happened between us must have been my fault? That I didn't love him enough?" Beth cried. And the frustrations of the last months colored her voice.

"No. I'm saying you couldn't have made a better choice than Charlie, if you wanted to get married. And Beth, you did want to. You were cocksure of yourself."

"Then why didn't it work? Why wasn't I happy?" Beth had lost control, even the desire for control. She wept noisy furious sobs like a child, her hands covering her face.

Laura watched her from across the room for a moment and then she went into the bathroom. She came back in a moment with a glass of cold water, walked up to Beth, and threw it in her face. She accomplished this quietly, experimentally, but with a certain satisfaction. She had never thought, in all her daydreams of Beth, that she would have the courage to treat her like another mere human being.

"I don't know why it didn't work, Beth," she said. "Maybe you'll be happy now. I hope so."

With an outraged splutter, Beth stopped crying. There was a moment of palpable tension between them. The water clung to Beth's hair and dripped from her face and for a moment she thought she would explode with rage. But it came to her slowly that she could not get any angrier than she had just been. She hadn't the strength and there was no way to express it without behaving like a madwoman. She was not that kind.

Beth turned her wet, violet eyes and open mouth up to Laura, struggling to find words, composure. But Laura, still smiling, spared her the necessity.

"Maybe the one thing you learned from living with a man is that you can't live with a man," she told her. "It's a sad, common little lesson. But sometimes those are the hardest to learn."

After a full minute of wet humiliation Beth brought herself to say, "What if it had been somebody different?" Her voice was unsure of itself, rough. "What if it had been somebody like Jack, maybe, who understood?"

"You said you didn't understand yourself," Laura reminded her, putting the empty glass down casually on the bed table.

"Do you want to marry a psychiatrist who'll spend all his time explaining you to yourself?"

"No." Laura's words made Beth vaguely aware of her own unreasonable thinking. "No, I wanted that from you. You grasp things others miss. I wanted you to tell me." And she wanted Laura to apologize for that glass of water; it was obvious in every inflection of her voice. *Redeem yourself; say you're sorry. Damn you!*

But Laura was on top of the situation now. She could play it her way.

"Tell you what, Beth?" Laura said suggestively, and brushed cold water from Beth's breasts. Beth shied away from her and stood up.

"Tell me what to do," she said through clenched teeth. "Who I *am*." She gave a tortured little laugh through her sobs and said, "God it's funny. It's so funny. I thought I'd know just by looking at you. I thought all you'd have to do was walk through that door and I'd suddenly understand everything. Just the sight of you would make it all clear."

"You were always a great one for oversimplifying things," Laura said. "I'm not the fortune teller who can read your palm. I'm not so easy to hurt anymore either, or so easy to teach. I've learned to protect myself. You gave me my first lessons years ago. Tell me something, Beth. Why did you think you had to find me to find yourself?"

"I don't know," Beth said and shook her head. Laura handed her some face tissue to wipe the last of the water off with and Beth snatched it from her, haughtily. She blew her nose. "It sounds—crazy, now. Irrational, even. But a few hours ago it seemed like the most natural thing in the world."

"And now I've disappointed you, haven't I?" Laura said. She seemed privately pleased at the idea; it might show Beth the folly of oversimplifying things, of hurting other people to spare herself. "Poor Beth. Poor silly Beth. It was all going to be so easy, wasn't it?" she said sympathetically.

Beth was without dignity, without resources. She could only mumble, "I guess I expected too much."

"You expected the impossible," Laura chided her. "And I thought at first you really wanted me. Really desired me again."

"I—I did."

"No, it was something completely different. Oh, not that you minded that part in bed a little while ago. But that was supposed to be the frosting on the cake. You could have done without that if you'd had to."

"Laura, don't persecute me," she whimpered, sitting down in a stuffed chair by the window. "If I had only found a guy like Jack!" she said, pounding her legs harshly with her fists. "If *only*—"

"You aren't going to make things better by copying my life," Laura said. "Even if you could, that's no answer."

"It was the answer for you," Beth snapped.

"But you're not me," Laura said. "Come on, Beth, you know that much."

"We're a lot alike," Beth persisted.

"We're entirely different. We always were."

Beth stood up again, turning her back to Laura. She stood tall and angry, hurt and bewildered, but recovering her pride. "Are you telling me you won't help me?" she demanded. "You refuse? I'm not worth the trouble? Or am I just a hopeless case?"

"Not yet, but you're trying awfully damned hard to make yourself hopeless," Laura exclaimed. "What right have you to get on your high horse with me? When you need help, Beth, you ask for it. You don't order it, like a meal. At least not from the people who don't owe you anything." There was another blazing silence. The air between them seemed very heavy.

"Is there anything I can do?" Laura said finally, placatingly. "I doubt it. But if there is, tell me."

"I want you to tell me!" Beth cried, turning on her in near despair. "Why do you think I'm here? Why do you think I've given up everything just to find you? What do you think I've been saying to you all morning?" And to emphasize her anger, to avenge herself for that shameful glass of water, she picked up Laura's bed pillow and swung it hard against the table. It broke. Together, silent, they watched the feathers snow down. Beth was too mad to feel sorry. She was entitled to ruin something, after all Laura had put her through.

Laura nodded distantly at the mess. "That's right, Beth," she said, and her composure infuriated Beth the more. "When things go wrong, throw a tantrum. When they aren't right, break them. You've always thought that way, haven't you? You're still a child. I guess that's the real cause of all your troubles."

"I'm a woman!" Beth cried. "A grown woman!"

"A grown woman would know herself, control herself. She'd know breaking a pillow wouldn't solve her problems. She'd know I couldn't change her whole life."

"You did once."

"I hardly touched it." Laura bent over and picked up a goose feather, and Beth watched her, fascinated and angry. "I passed through your life, I loved you. And it didn't work out because you didn't love me. We parted, as we should have, and it was over. I yearned for you for a long time. And what did you do? Got married to a handsome, intelligent, affectionate s.o.b. you were in love with. Was it so godawful, Beth? Was it really as bad as all that? Or did you just begin to be bored with housewifery? Did you just want to play around again, the way you played around with me?"

"I loved you, Laura," Beth said helplessly and suddenly went to her knees among the feathers. "I loved you, how can you think anything else?"

Abruptly, Laura's understanding, that wonderful understanding that Beth had needed and demanded and had traveled out of her life and over a continent to find, was unwelcome. It was painful and embarrassing, because it exposed the truth. Beth, on her knees, recoiled from it at the same time that she pleaded for it. It was a question which was worse: the endless wondering about herself, about her true sexuality, or knowing the truth and having the truth be ugly and selfish and pitiful.

"You loved what you couldn't have, Beth," Laura "You still do."

"But I could have had you! I know that, we both know that!" Beth shouted passionately.

"The minute you found out you could have me, you didn't want me anymore," Laura said. She turned her back on Beth, who was still kneeling, and began to comb her marvelous hair. "I wonder if that isn't what happened between you and Charlie. Once he married you he was hooked. He was yours. It was all sewed up, legitimate and approved of, and maybe that's why it bored you."

Beth felt a terrible rage rising in her. She wanted to scream, "Look at me!" Instead she said in a shaking voice, "I'm on my knees to you, begging for help, Laura. Give it to me. I'm not a dog."

"Then get off the floor," Laura said without turning around.

"You stand there and comb your goddamn hair!" Beth shouted.

"My hair needs combing."

Beth wondered if she could stand it or if her brains would boil in her head. Laura controlled the situation by controlling herself. Every shriek that escaped Beth made her own position weaker and sillier. With a supreme effort she held herself in check. "Charlie said once that I could only love when love was forbidden," she said. The admission gave her a little dignity; it was very adult.

"Then he sees what I see," Laura said.

"But you're wrong," Beth whispered. "You're both wrong. I can love without that. It doesn't have to be wrong to be desirable. That's so—so childish."

"Yes, it is. But that isn't what you came all this way to tell me," Laura said. "You didn't really come to see me at all. I think you're running away."

"No, I'm not. I'm facing things, Laura! For the first time I'm facing the things I should have faced years ago, but didn't have the guts to. I love women. I love you. And if you think it was the easy thing for me to run away and leave my—" She broke off, afraid to mention her children now that she had denied their existence. "It took all my courage, everything I had," she said, and her voice twisted with the enormity of it, the remembered pain.

"Beth, how long have you been divorced?" Laura stopped combing long enough to look at her.

"That's none of your business!" Beth shot back.

"You're making it my business. You're throwing your whole messed-up unhappy life in my lap. Listen, Beth," she continued kindly, "no matter how fast you run you can't catch up with the past. You've found me, all right, but you haven't found our college days. You haven't found a dead romance and brought it back to life. We're two different people now; we can't capture the past and live in it as if it were the present. I tried to run away, too. For years. Believe me, it's the one sure way to get trouble to follow you." Her voice was gentle; she meant what she said. Maybe it would help. She could see Beth had been pushed pretty far. But to Beth it was like being a naughty child again and getting lectured for misbehaving. She listened in pale anger.

"You're in love with all the things you can't have, Beth, with all the things you've never seen and never tasted. Once you do see them they lose their fascination for you. If *had* to live with a woman, don't you think pretty soon you'd be hollering for a man?"

"You mean—" Beth gaped at her. "You mean it has nothing to do with sexuality? It has nothing to do with love and desire? It's just a compulsion for something new? Oh, Laura. Now you're the one who's oversimplifying."

"It has a lot to do with love and desire, but that's only part of it. You were never cut out to settle down and put out roots anywhere."

"Laura, for God's sake, are you telling me no matter what I do or where I turn I'll never be happy? I'll always make myself unhappy?" It was a cry of desolation and protest.

"I'm telling you what you're like now," Laura said. "I'm not saying you can't change. Nobody has a right to say that to you but yourself."

"How do you know you're right about me? What makes you so sure?" Beth said brokenly.

"I don't know for sure. You brought me your troubles and said, 'Here, help me. Straighten me out.' Well, I'm trying." There was impatience in her voice, but also sincerity.

"Laura, darling Laura, don't you love me anymore? Did you ever really love me?"

"You know better than to ask. All the years that you and Charlie were getting along and still happy, I was dreaming of you. It's just that—" She glanced down at the tortoise shell comb in her hand.

"Just that what?" Beth demanded.

"Just that my love for you is different now."

Beth stood up, anger and triumph all over her face. "Then why did you make love to me the way you did? An hour ago we were making love, Laura! Or have you forgotten? Why?"

Laura gazed at her again, matching her own composure against Beth's hot, breathless emotion.

"I had no warning—" she began.

"Exactly! So you reacted naturally!" Beth exclaimed, her face flushed and excited. "That's what I wanted, that's exactly what I wanted!" She walked toward Laura, talking and gesticulating. "If you had known I was there you would have put me off, you would have behaved like a friend, nothing more. But you didn't know. It all took you by surprise and you gave yourself to me without a fight, without resisting me at all. The most natural thing in the world."

Laura looked into her feverish face, standing her ground royally as Beth approached. "Beth, if you're going to think of it that way, I can't do a damn thing to help you. You love your own delusions too much."

"Well, how in hell am I supposed to think of it?" Beth flashed. And in a sudden hopeless surrender to her misery, in the need to be right with Laura just *once*, Beth threw herself on Laura like a cat gone mad. She snapped the straps of Laura's slip with one hard desperate pull and caught the tender breasts beneath with angry rough hands. With a small startled scream, Laura lost her self-control. She struggled wildly against Beth but Beth had worked up a reserve of hysterical strength and tore the slip from her.

"Let me look at you!" Beth cried, throwing Laura to the floor and falling on her. Laura tried to scream again but Beth kissed her savagely and bit her neck and shook her shoulders till her head hit the floor painfully.

"Stop! God!" Laura moaned. "Beth, stop!"

"An hour ago you weren't too good for me," Beth sobbed. "Now all of a sudden you don't want to be touched."

"I don't want to be hurt. I can't stand to be hurt," Laura said, tears on her face.

"I'm not welcome, I'm not loved, I'm not understood," Beth went on in a strangling voice. "And you—you don't give a damn, do you? You stand there and comb your hair and turn your back on me and throw cold water in my face and tell me to go to hell—" Her face was scarlet and Laura, terrified, threw her hands up to protect herself.

But Beth didn't know how to hurt her. She was lost. All she had was her thoughtless fury, her shapeless unhappiness. It all came together inside her and exploded in bitter kisses, sharp bites, and sudden agonized passion. She vented it all on Laura and it gave her only a sour sort of satisfaction to know that Laura couldn't resist it, that Laura had succumbed to the animal fury of it and let herself go.

Beth lay beside her on the scratchy wool rug and sobbed when it was over. And then, slowly, she was overcome with a deep lassitude, a suspension of mind and emotions that would finally let her come back to normal.

Laura sat up beside her and stroked her back and after a while she said in a low voice, a voice that let Beth know she was forgiven, "Have you any idea what a shock it was? Do you suppose I didn't dream of making love to you every day and every night for over a year after I left you? Do you think I hadn't imagined every detail of it? I'd have given my soul for that experience once. Only, Beth, it came too late. It was beautiful, it was so beautiful this morning. I can't pretend I'm sorry, I can't pretend I would have done it a different way. But that's just it, you see. It's as if my reaction were planned years ago. As if the whole thing went according to plan in spite of me. I saw you, suddenly, with no warning, the way I always dreamed I'd see you. And we were alone, the way I always dreamed we'd be. And we made love."

Beth rolled over to look at her; at her lovely body with the fresh marks of teeth and nails in vulnerable spots. Beth touched the bruises and wept. "I'm sorry. I had to—"

"I know, I know. Just like I had to be nasty. It's over now. We can be friends now. Can you understand that, Beth?"

Beth heard, clear and genuine, the pity in her voice and she said, "I understand that you made love to me, that you wanted me, that it wasn't any different than it ever was, this morning." Then she paused, hovering between defiance and adoration. "That's all I understand."

"That's not enough," Laura said gently. "Grow up, Beth. Your problems aren't hopeless, you can solve them. You don't need me, you need yourself."

"If I hadn't started talking, if I'd just kept my damned mouth shut and stayed in bed with you, it would have been all right."

"Do you know how many times you've said 'if' this morning?" Laura said. "If only this, if only that—everything would have been all right. That's a child talking."

They remained a moment in silence and then, as if with one accord, got painfully to their feet. Beth couldn't look Laura in the face.

"I hope I didn't hurt you!" she said. "I'd rather die than hurt you."

"No. I'm all right."

"Do you want me to leave?"

"No, of course not," Laura said. Beth's eyes climbed only as high as Laura's breasts, faltered, and fell again.

"Are you in love with that girl? Betsy's piano teacher?" she said.

"I was."

"No more?"

"Not so much. But I wouldn't do anything to hurt her."

"Not till Betsy can play the 'Minute Waltz,' at least."

"You didn't hurt me till you learned how to play at love from me," Laura reminded her. "You were no fool You didn't get rid of me till you were sure you didn't need me anymore."

Beth deserved the dig. She finished dressing silently, with ferocious concentration, still ashamed of the hungry love and revenge she'd forced on Laura.

Laura slipped a negligee over her torn slip and watched Beth without speaking.

"Stay and have lunch with me," she said when Beth had finished, but Beth wanted to get away from her.

"I thought once I'd found you I'd hang on for dear life," Beth said. "But I'm so full of feeling, so damned mixed up, I don't think I could bear to sit here and let you watch me puzzle it out. I just want to be alone."

"Whatever you say," Laura said. "How about dinner?"

"I don't know." Beth looked at her and the corners of her mouth trembled. "You never find what you set out looking for, do you?" she whispered. "Damn. It's queer. Life is so queer."

Laura could see the bitter disappointment on her face and she put her hands tentatively on Beth's waist.

"I want you to come back, Beth," she said softly. "I've been hard on you, but I had a right to be. You got even. So we're square."

Beth still couldn't face her. "Do you love me still?" she asked again.

"I've already said it."

"Say it just once more. I'll think of it before I think of the other things. The things that hurt."

"I love you," Laura told her simply.

And Beth turned around and walked out of her bedroom and across the living room. She stopped a moment, remembering Jack's messages. "Call McCracken and cancel the order," she called back to Laura in an unsteady voice. "And send a check to Dr. Byrd." Then she went out the front door.

Chapter Eighteen

SHE WALKED. SHE SPENT MOST OF THE DAY WALKING, AND WHEN she got tired she went to the library and sat at a table in a corner of the Social Sciences room and stared ahead of her. She didn't consciously try to understand everything. She just let her mind wander from one peak of recollection to another, too worn out to steer her thoughts or make sense of them.

When it began to darken outside she got up and left, stopping by the post office on her way back to the Beaton Hotel. There was nothing for her, nor did anything come for the next several days. She didn't know what to do with herself. She felt desperately scared most of the time, lost between those two worlds, one renounced, the other closed to her. One was normal, ordinary, reassuring, with a home and a husband and children. And it had failed her. The other was gay and strange, exotic and dangerous, painful and, possibly, wonderful. But it was still untried, inaccessible somehow. And Beth, caught dead center between the two, was afraid she had lost both forever and would wander in limbo the rest of her life.

She couldn't go back to Charlie, even if he would have her. Her pride, her shame, her very nature, forbade that. And, having taken Laura's words as a rebuff, she felt almost as unwelcome in the gay world as the straight.

So she spent nearly a week in a fog of confusion and fear. She refused to take any phone calls, though there were several. *All from Laura*, she thought, and it gave her a bitter satisfaction not to answer, to keep Laura worrying and anxious.

Whenever she thought of her children her heart contracted. Something in her character prevented her from loving them openly, easily, naturally, like other women. Did a woman like her have a right to any children? She could hardly bear to think of it. At the worst moments she tried instead to think of what it would be like living with a desirable woman, with someone affectionate and understanding, someone who was all she had hoped to rediscover in Laura. Then it seemed like the only life for her. She was sure she wanted it, whatever it cost in pain and regret.

She remained shut up in a cocoon of private suffering and wondering for nearly seven days, meandering around New York in the afternoons and lying on her bed at night, sleepless. She drank quite a bit of whiskey. It seemed to ease her.

Every day she stopped at the post office, until at last there was a letter waiting. It was from Cleve, but she hadn't the heart or the interest to open it right away. She was curiously without feeling, as if she had lost her capacity to care.

Her feet were stiff and aching in their heeled shoes when she finally reached the hotel. She started to walk past the desk but the clerk called to her and held up a letter to catch her eye. For some reason it alarmed her and brought her back to life. A letter from Cleve was all right, but not two.

It was from Merrill Landon, of course. He had her hotel address; there had seemed no reason to hide it from him. The odd feeling of foreboding, of distress at the sight of the letters, stayed with her and settled in her stomach. She threw them on the dresser in her small stuffy room, placed a newly purchased bottle of whiskey beside them, threw off her clothes and showered, before she tried to read.

She opened the letter from Landon first. He was a reserved man, a cautious man, and he expressed himself carefully, but his pleasure was evident even in the controlled phrases that thanked her for having found his daughter.

"I owe you any joy there may be left in my life," he said, and the admission touched her. His note was brief. But at the end he added a shocker, in his terse sensible prose. "By the way, your husband is in Chicago. I found out through my 'spies' on the paper. Sorry I can't tell you more."

Beth sat on the bed with a stiff drink in one hand and the note in the other. Charlie in Chicago! Why? What in God's name for? He knew then, from her aunt and uncle, that she had run away. What else did he know?

She jumped up and grabbed Cleve's letter with quivering hands. Maybe it would explain, maybe it was a letter of warning about Charlie.

It was.

"Dear Beth," he wrote. "I just found out about this—hope it's not too late to tell you. There's been a detective following you ever since you left Chicago. Your uncle John and Charlie have gotten together. John told Charlie everything he got from the detective so all our little precautions have been for nothing. Charlie has known all along where you are and what you are doing—more than I know by a long shot. He left yesterday for Chicago. I don't know what will happen now. He has the kids with him—they're both fine."

The little domestic interjection almost threw her for some reason she couldn't fathom and she had to stop reading to clear her mind of guilty thoughts of her children.

"One last thing," Cleve wrote. "Just to make everything perfect. Vega has disappeared. She had been spending the weekends with us and seemed so much better. Sunday night I was going to drive her back to the hospital, but Mother called in a panic and said she was gone. Went out in back to help Gramp feed the cats and when his back was turned she got out somehow. Strangely enough, P.K.—that lessie Vega was always hollering about—has disappeared too. Romance? God, I hope not. Anyway, don't worry. I'm sure we'll find her. Will keep you posted. Cleve."

But he had only told her to make her worry, she knew that. She knew it was the one small revenge he had for the sick sister Beth had foisted on him, and she didn't blame him. She looked at the letter, with the written lines uneven and shaky, and she wondered if he had written it with a glass of booze in one hand, which was just the way she had read it.

God, we're all so weak, she thought dismally. *I'm no better than the Purvises. We can't even face the crises in our lives without this.* She made a face at the drink, and then she shut her eyes and finished it.

And suddenly she remembered something, hazily at first. Just a figure, small and dumpy, male and tired-looking. Then a face, round, heavy-eyed, high-crowned and balding. A short, heavy man. Who was he? She had seen him around the Village. She had seen him going far uptown on a bus, the same bus she was on.

"He was no damn John," she said aloud. "He was the detective. He's been following me all this time." For a moment she swayed a little and her stomach turned. And then she straightened up and stared at her empty glass. The bitterness she expected to feel, the resentment, the injury, were dissipated.

Everything seemed suddenly ridiculous. Love was senseless, life was hopeless. She didn't know what she was doing there in that stuffy room in a hotel in a city that was foreign to her. She didn't know what she had come to find or whether she had found it. Nothing was simple, nothing was clear, and she felt dangerously as if she didn't give a damn.

She had another drink. And another. And then she put her clothes back on and went out.

"You had another call, Mrs. Ayers," the hotel clerk told her, but she didn't even look at him and when she was out of earshot he told the elevator boy, "Snippy bitch."

She went to the Village. She went to all the bars she could remember having been in and drank in all of them. She went to some she had never seen before with girls she didn't know, and by early morning it seemed as if she knew all of them, as if they had all grown up together.

In the afternoon (who knew what afternoon?—the clock merely said two-thirty and the sun shone) she woke up in an apartment that stank of cats and orange juice. The girl in the bed beside her was still sleeping, her back to Beth. She was naked. Beth knew with a shudder, as she saw her, that they had made love. But she couldn't remember her name. She couldn't remember her face. She didn't know where they had met or what they saw in each other.

At first her physical pains were sharp enough to engross her mind, and she didn't worry about the girl. She got out of bed, holding her head, found the bathroom and tried to wash and dress herself. In the mirror her face looked tired and she felt a little dizzy. When she leaned over to brush her teeth a wave of nausea clutched her and she threw up precipitately into the washbasin. When she straightened up she discovered a number of curious bruises scattered over her limbs and body, as if she had fallen down. But she had no recollection of falling.

She opened the bathroom door to find the girl she slept with standing there, evidently waiting for her. She seemed fairly cheerful and she tweaked one of Beth's breasts familiarly, as though she had the right.

"Hungover?" she said, and went past her into the bathroom.

Beth had raised a quick angry hand to stop the tweaking but it was too late. The girl laughed at her and said, "Bad-tempered Beth," in a singsong voice.

And suddenly Beth was frightened. What in hell was her name? Why had she picked *this* girl? She found her purse and opened it, almost surprised to find her money still there. She ran a comb through her tangled hair and then she bolted for the front door like a prisoner on the run, buttoning her dress as she went.

"What's the matter, honey? Don't you want breakfast?"

Beth looked up to find her leaning in the open bathroom door, smiling suggestively. She was still undressed and laughing at Beth's confusion.

Beth gave her one last look, wild and accusing, and then went out.

"Come and see me again sometime," the girl called after her and her voice rang down the narrow hall. "When you can stay a little while."

Beth found her way out of the labyrinthine apartment house and down a couple of very crooked streets full of homogeneous brown houses. She burst upon Seventh Avenue abruptly, without recognizing it, and found a restaurant.

It was small and not overly clean, in keeping with the nightmare atmosphere she was in, but it had food for sale, cooked. She ordered breakfast, but after letting her enumerate the items and tell him how she wanted her eggs, the waiter said, "What's the matter, sister, can't you tell time? It's three in the afternoon. We got no eggs after ten, in the morning."

She gave him a baleful look and settled for pastrami on rye. As an afterthought she ordered a beer. Unexpectedly it went down well and she ordered another.

When she left there seemed to be nothing to do but wander again, lost and looking, through the Village streets. The hotel depressed her unutterably; she couldn't go to Laura, she wouldn't go to Nina. And somehow, without exactly understanding where it started or how, she wound up in a bar again, drinking too much, talking too much, forgetting names and faces.

Late in the evening she found Franny's telephone number in her pocket—Franny, the girl Nina had in bed with her one morning, and who had been taken with Beth. On an impulse Beth called her.

It was almost worse to wake up in bed the next day and know who she was sleeping with than it had been to wake up with a stranger. At least that other way it had been impersonal. But now, feeling sick and full of hate for herself, she had to get up and talk to Franny, apologize, make an effort to explain. It only alarmed her when Franny responded with all the exaggerated understanding and sympathy of a crush aborning. Beth wanted to grab her hands and say, "No, don't fall for me, Franny, don't even like me. I'll hurt you. I hurt anybody, everybody, who gets in my way, anybody who tries to stop me from going—" From going where? She didn't know.

She spent a couple of days with Franny and she kept on drinking and crying and trying to explain all the things she couldn't understand about herself. And Franny, a good-natured girl with a shock of innocent blonde hair and a smile reminiscent of Jean Purvis's, listened in passionate silence, her eyes riveted on Beth. Her heroine worship upset Beth, who didn't want it and couldn't return it and so responded to it with a twinge of guilt. She asked Franny about Nina but Franny only shrugged and stuck her tongue out, giving Beth to understand that that affair was dead.

Beth finally escaped, leaving during the day when Franny was at work. She couldn't face her hotel room. Her clothes were getting raggedy and quite plainly dirty, and still she couldn't return. Not yet. Tomorrow, maybe. Tomorrow she would go back, set her affairs in order, clean herself up, contact her family and confess what they already knew in a pitiful effort to salvage her self-respect. She would collect her small courage and get it over with.

Tomorrow, that is. Not today.

She went drinking again. Somewhere along the way she saw Nina. They were both quite drunk at the time and it was a curiously friendly meeting, though brief. Nina sat down, putting an arm around Beth's waist, and said, "Guess who's gay?" And she began to call out names like a drill sergeant, names of movie stars, names of Broadway luminaries, names of writers, names of generals, names of celebrated female social workers and adventurers and courtesans.

"All gay," she said, pausing for breath, while Beth listened in a sort of mesmerized silence, wondering what possessed Nina to rattle these names off in her face, both interested and ashamed of her interest.

"If they're all gay, what're you worried about?" Nina said. Beth said nothing and Nina went on, "Did I ever tell you you listen beautifully? You make a beautiful listener, Beth. That's what you ought to do. Just go out and listen. To hell with sex. Forget about it. Just sit around and listen, honey, you do it so well. It's a shame you're such an independent bitch." She kissed her, lightly and briefly, and Beth remembered with a drunken ache why she had been so fascinated with the girl in the first place.

It was the only encounter she recalled over a period of several days. The next time she woke up she was sick. Really rotten from top to bottom and too trembly to make it out of bed. She didn't know where she was and she didn't care. There was a period, after her first wakening, of four or five hours when she slept again, fitfully and in spite of rhythmic pains in her head.

At the second wakening she got her bearings. She was in a small, gently worn but comfortable bedroom on a familiar bed. Lifting her unwieldy head cautiously, she looked around. And then she sat up and surprise eased her throbbing pain for a moment. She was in Beebo's apartment.

Very slowly, gingerly, she lifted the covers and got up, stumbled into the bathroom which opened directly off the bedroom, and took a shower. She stood in it for fifteen minutes, just letting the water rain on her, warm and soothing. At first she thought she would never feel clean again. At least not inside. But the shower relaxed her, cleared her head a little.

She was startled to hear the bathroom door open and Beebo step in. Beth looked at her from around the shower curtain, inexplicably frightened of her. Just a little, but still frightened.

"You aren't drowning are you?" Beebo said with a smile. "You've been in there a while."

"No." Beth turned the water off and then stood uncertainly behind the frail shelter of the curtain while Beebo faced her, arms folded over her chest, smiling

"Towel?" she said at last, handing one over leisurely.

"Thanks." Beth grabbed it and dried herself behind the curtain. "Where did you—find me?" she asked diffidently.

"I doubt if you've ever heard of the place," Beebo said. "And you probably wouldn't recognize it again if they threw it at you."

"Just the same, I'd like to know," she said.

"It's called The Gorgon's Head," Beebo said.

"God." Beth made a face, stepping carefully out of the tub. One foot slid a little and Beebo caught her, steadying her, and helped her out the rest of the way. The towel had come loose and Beebo handed it back to her before Beth even realized that a long sweet curve of flesh was open to view. She snatched the towel gratefully from Beebo with a sudden shyness, and irritation and pleasure were scrambled up inside her, momentarily aggravating her headache.

"Here," Beebo said, opening the medicine chest over the washbowl. She took a couple of pills resembling aspirin from an unmarked plastic drugstore container and handed them to Beth, along with a glass of water.

"What are they?" Beth said, looking at them as if they were capsules of arsenic.

"What the hell do you care? You couldn't feel any worse, could you?" Beebo grinned.

Beth took them, and Beebo said when she saw them disappear, "They're hangover pills. Aspirin, codeine, caffeine, and God knows what else. Should bring you back to life." She stepped out of the way when Beth moved toward the bathroom door, letting her find the way back into the bedroom.

"Beebo, I—would you mind telling me where my clothes are?" Beth faltered.

"I was just ironing them. Everything but the undies, and they don't show," Beebo said. She pulled Beth's things from a drawer in her dresser. "Never iron what doesn't show," she said, holding them out. "Life's too damn short."

Beth took them, gazing at her. "You mean you cleaned them up? You washed them all out? All my clothes?"

"Didn't take much figuring to see they were dirty," Beebo said. "How long do you ordinarily wear a thing before you wash it?" She was smiling, a warm, even and compelling smile of amusement that both pleased and disconcerted Beth.

"I—I haven't been back to my room for a few days," Beth admitted, ashamed and exasperated to feel her face color.

"I would have guessed as much," Beebo said, sitting down on her bed and crossing her long legs at the ankles. "Only, I didn't have to guess. You told me."

"I told you? When? Last night when I was drunk?"

"Last night and the night before that. I didn't realize how far gone you were, baby, or I'd have rescued you sooner. My friendly enemy, Nina Spicer, called me finally. Said she'd have taken you home with her but she already had company, and she thought somebody'd better get you out of sight before the cops got interested."

Beth, struggling to get into her brassiere without exposing any of herself to those sharp and interested eyes of Beebo's, said mournfully, "The cops already know."

"Know what?" Beebo exclaimed, suddenly concerned. "The bastards," she added under her breath.

"There's been one following me for days. Weeks, I mean. God, months, for all I know." She lost her towel suddenly and pulled the panties up the rest of the way with a movement that betrayed her self-consciousness.

"Do you mean a cop or a lousy detective?" Beebo said. "There's a difference."

"Is there? Which is best? Or worst?" Beth said, standing on the towel and wiggling into her brassiere.

Beebo watched her, but not critically, not suggestively. "Depends," she said laconically. "Have you done anything wicked lately?"

Beth pulled her slip over her head before answering, as if the extra covering might increase her dignity a little. Then she sat down at the foot of the bed, turned half away from Beebo, wondering what to tell her, whether to tell her anything. It would feel so good, it would help so much, the way it had helped to spill some of it to Nina before. But how far, how much, could she trust this strange man-nish woman who had taken her in and out of harm's way?

"Afraid to tell me?" Beebo said. "You don't have to. But if it's bad, maybe I can help. I've been in every conceivable scrape in my time, baby. I know the ropes."

Beth lowered her head. "I—I ran away," she said, her voice only slightly above a whisper.

"That's nothing new."

"From my husband. I'm not divorced, Beebo. I just ducked out."

"Well, I never had a husband, thank God, but I've done some running away."

Beth turned her face to Beebo's and searched her for hidden laughter, for the sort of veiled scorn Nina showed her, for the hint of future betrayal. But Beebo's face was frank and open and Beth found, being so near her again, so close to that face, that she liked it inordinately. There was wisdom in it and the trace of pain lived through and learned from, and a very special personal beauty that almost no one else would have called by that gentle name.

"I ran away and left Charlie. And my children," she said. "I have two, a boy and a girl. I abandoned them, Beebo. There was no excuse for it, no warning, no preparation for the kids. They just woke up the next morning and I was gone. I had no right to do it. I had no right to have children. Oh, God..." She stopped a minute to steady her voice. "If I'd only known years ago, if I'd only realized...."

They simply gazed at each other for a moment and then, as naturally as a mother and child coming together, they embraced.

Beebo took Beth in her arms and comforted her and let her cry. She never asked her if she loved her children. She knew.

"I failed them," Beth sobbed. "They were so young, just five and six, and they needed me so. But I was beastly to them; I hurt them. It was worse being there with them—worse for them, I mean."

"Worse for you, too, baby," Beebo told her gently. "Don't lie to yourself."

"And now Charlie, or Uncle John, or *somebody*, has a goddamn detective following me around New York. He must know everything, he must have seen everything."

"Well, he can't see this," Beebo reassured her, and Beth felt Beebo's lips against her forehead. It sent a curious thrill through her that pierced even her melancholy and made her cling the tighter. "How do you know he's found you yet?" Beebo said.

"Because I know who he is. I didn't realize it; I just thought he was somebody from the Village at first, but I've seen him uptown too and I swear it's the same guy. A dumpy little guy with bags under his eyes and a wrinkled suit. He looks tired all the time. And he's bald. I'm sure he's the one. Anyway, it doesn't matter, he's all over the damn place, everywhere I go. He's probably downstairs right now, picking his nails and waiting for me to leave."

"I'll break his head," Beebo murmured.

"And now Charlie's in Chicago and he'll probably come to New York and give me hell. And my family will disown me. Charlie at least had some idea of why I left him. He knew about Laura. We were all in school together nine years ago. I was in love with both of them at the same time. But Uncle John! And Aunt Elsa! They'll never speak to me again." Her voice cracked under the load of emotion it carried.

"And the kids?"

"Oh, the kids," she wept. "They'd be better off if they'd never been born. I guess Charlie will keep it from them, if it only doesn't get out back there and ruin their lives."

Beebo held her and comforted her for a long time, her arms warm and strong and profoundly welcome to Beth. She didn't laugh like Nina, she didn't shriek hysterically like Vega, she didn't analyze, with devastating truth and painful love, like Laura. She said nothing, she judged nothing. But, oh, how good she felt, how sure and how reassuring.

"Beebo," Beth whispered after a while, the urge for catharsis still in her. "Did you ever fall for a woman, a very lovely desirable woman, and then discover that she wasn't at all what she'd made you think she was? Maybe she was sick, or deformed, or something. Something awful that shocked you badly and sort of—knocked the passion out of you. And you tried to go on like before until the whole thing made you sick and she got desperately jealous and finally you just ran away, without even saying goodbye, just to get rid of her?"

"Sounds like the story of my life," Beebo said.

"Really?" Beth twisted in her arms, half sitting up to look at her. "Just like that?"

"Not *just* like that. But I've done some rotten things, baby. I've treated some girls like dirt. I could have been great friends with them, but I couldn't be a lover. You can choose your friends but not your lovers. They just happen to you."

"Did Laura just happen to you?" Beth asked.

Beebo smiled privately at the past. She released Beth and got up to light a cigarette, offering one to Beth from the pack. Beth took it. "I guess she did," Beebo said, lighting them both. "She was so different from the others—to me, at least—that it's hard to think of it happening the way any other affair happens. But I guess it did."

"Beebo, do you think Laura was right about me?" Beth asked anxiously. "Do you think I'm just running away, looking for romance and all that?"

"I don't know, baby. I don't know you that well."

"Laura says I only want what I can't have. Once I've got it I don't want it. And Charlie thinks so, too."

Beebo grinned and scratched an ear. "They should get a license and set up practice," she said. "Laura always did like to figure people out. Not maliciously, though, not for fun, like Nina. Just interested in people."

"Is she right? Am I just chasing rainbows because they can't be had?"

"I don't know, Beth. I'd guess you just want to belong somewhere. Most of us do. When you find out where you belong the pieces seem to fall into place by themselves. The puzzle works itself out."

There was silence for a few minutes while they smoked and thought and Beth felt a sort of calm, a near peace, that came close to being what she had sought so long and unsuccessfully. She didn't want to move, to change things or spoil the mood.

But Beebo said, "You'd better get back. I called the hotel, they were on the verge of closing you out. You've been gone six days."

"Six days!" Beth whispered, appalled. *Six?*"

"That's what they told me," Beebo said. "Have you ever done that before?"

Beth shook her head. She dressed, putting on her freshly ironed clothes and eating some breakfast with Beebo. "What'll I do if that miserable detective is out there?" she said when she was ready to leave.

"What can you do?" Beebo said. "It's too late now. Just get a cab and go back to the hotel. And don't flirt with any women."

Beth gave her a hesitant smile. "Okay," she said. And still she stood in the door as though reluctant to leave, even a little bit scared.

"What's the matter?" Beebo said, running a finger softly over Beth's cheek. "Got you down, sweetheart?"

"I don't know," Beth said.

"There isn't anybody waiting for you, is there? I mean, besides the detective?"

"No. Unless—unless Charlie has gotten here already. Or my uncle."

"Do you want me to go back with you?" Beebo asked.

Beth considered. What would it be like to walk into her room with Beebo and find Charlie there? He would decide at once that this was her new lover, that Beebo was what she had traveled across the continent to find, and no amount of talking would argue him out of it. But did it matter anymore? For she felt sure now that no matter what he said to her she couldn't go back to him. She had burned that bridge behind her. Even if he wanted her she had gone too far. She had deserted her children, and when a woman has done that there is no atoning, no going back, no starting over. It's final.

"Would you, Beebo? You don't need to stay, just drive over with me. I'd feel better."

"What if he's there?" Beebo said.

"I've made my choice," Beth said.

"Okay, baby." Beebo picked up another pack of cigarettes from a table by her sofa and followed Beth out the door, pulling it to and locking it behind her.

Chapter Nineteen

OUTSIDE IT WAS MUGGY AND HOT, WITH AN OVERCAST SKY. "Rain," Beebo said. "In an hour. It can't miss."

They walked over to Sixth Avenue and hailed a taxi, and all the while Beth was looking around her, behind and on all sides for the little man she was so sure was the detective. Now, when she was aware of him, when she knew who he was and what he was up to, she couldn't find him anywhere. And yet she was convinced that his eyes were on her, peering around some shadowy corner.

"Do you see him?" said Beebo, noticing her nervousness.

"No. I'll tell you if I do."

At the Beaton she checked at the desk for a note from Merrill Landon. Or her family, she thought suddenly, with rancor. There was no reason why they couldn't write to her now if they wanted to. They certainly knew where she was.

But there was nothing, nothing but the curious stares of the clerk and the elevator boy. Beth didn't know if they were for her or Beebo, or both. For Beebo cut rather a startling figure, even in her own milieu in the Village. Uptown, where everybody looked or tried to look perfectly conventional and ordinary, she was painfully obvious. Beth guessed that she didn't often come uptown, if only to spare herself embarrassment. There wasn't much Beebo could do about her looks, and rather than hide them she had finally surrendered to nature and even exaggerated them. It was a question which would have made her stand out the more—trying to hide her looks or playing them up. At least playing them up didn't expose her to the condescending pity that hiding them would have.

Beebo went with Beth up to her room. "It's a miracle I still have the key," Beth said, opening her purse. "And a little money. I thought people were supposed to rob you in the big city."

"They are," Beebo said as Beth pushed the door open. "Keep trying, they will."

Beth hesitated a moment before going in, feeling her heart give a tight squeeze and half expecting Charlie's handsome disillusioned face to rise up from the chair or the bed and stare at the two women with a look of evil suspicion confirmed. But the room was empty.

"Will you come in?" Beth asked, turning to Beebo, but Beebo shook her head.

"You rest, baby," she said. "You don't need me. You're beat. It shows all over you. I'll call you later, maybe tonight."

"Thanks," Beth said, "for coming home with me. I was so afraid he'd be here."

"I don't know what I could have done if he was," Beebo grinned. "Except get the hell out and let the sparks fly. He probably will show up, by the way, if your detective is worth his pay."

"I know. But I'm glad it's not now," Beth said. "I couldn't face anything just now."

"Okay, baby, get some sleep," Beebo said and turned to go.

"You will call, won't you?" Beth called after her, and immediately wished she had kept her mouth shut. It made her sound so eager.

"Yes, I'll call." Beebo smiled, and then Beth shut the door after her, leaning on it until she heard the elevator stop, open, and start up again, carrying Beebo down with it.

For the first time since she had met Beebo, it caused her real pain to leave her. Beebo seemed like a protection to her, a gentle strength and a certainty to lean on. Was it only because Beebo was good to her? Patient with her? Was it because she knew so much about the strange and special world of Lesbianism and was willing to share her knowledge without making it painful for Beth?

Or was it something compelling, something ineffably attractive in Beebo herself?

I'm just grateful to her, that's all, Beth tried to tell herself. *She saved me from a lot of extra suffering. She's been good and generous. But then, why is it—why—?* Why did she tremble when Beebo touched her? It was not the quake of fear but rather the lovely shivering of pleasure. Beebo stirred her physically. At first Beebo had appealed to Beth's mind, her need for help and understanding. And then, subtly and softly, like an enveloping cloud, the appeal had broadened and deepened, assumed an erotic glow.

Now, at last, thinking of her and afraid to think of her, wanting her and afraid to want her, Beth found herself absorbed in this unique, rather frightening, rather wonderful human being.

Coming back to reality, Beth turned and pulled down the bed, taking off her shoes and dress and tossing them carelessly into the chair beside the bed. Then she opened both windows partway, letting in a breeze and a few drops of rain. She lay down, half falling because it felt so good to let go, and she lay with her eyes open for a little while, fixed on the ceiling but seeing Beebo. She did not try to puzzle out the glow she felt. Instead she simply relaxed and let herself be drawn to this odd human being who was like no one else she had ever seen or known.

Her limbs began to feel warm and soft, and gradually, in spite of herself, her eyes closed. They fluttered open once or twice but shut again almost immediately. Her thoughts reached that state of confusion and haphazardness that resembles dreams, and she was very near to sleep when the door opened.

Which door? Beth never afterward was sure. The closet door and the door to the hall were the only two in the room, and she could not recall whether she had locked the hall door after Beebo or not.

It seemed to her, later, when she tried to reconstruct it all in her mind, that it must have been the closet door, that Beth and Beebo had surprised Vega when they first entered the room and she had taken refuge in the closet, like a spy in a bad thriller, and waited until everything was quiet again.

Beth opened her eyes at the small sound of the door squeaking and looked about a little, unalarmed. There was still a breeze in the room from the two half-open windows. It could have moved the door. But it hadn't. She realized, with a sudden horrified shudder of fear, that she was not alone. And when she raised herself up partway on the bed she saw Vega standing at the foot of it.

"Just stay there, don't get up," Vega said, and her words, the look of her, her tragic eyes, terrified Beth. "Who was that other one? The one that was just here with you?" Vega said.

"Beebo?" Beth said. "Do you know her?" she added inanely, her fear distorting her sense.

"No." Vega smiled sadly.

"Vega, what are you doing here? How did you find me?" Beth stammered. "How long have you been here?"

"Since yesterday. The whole family knows where you are now, Beth. I only wish I'd known sooner." There was a flat controlled quality about her, as if she was hanging on tightly to herself, her feelings, that was new and ominous in Vega.

Beth made a move to get up, but Vega motioned her back on the bed with a swift movement of her hand, and Beth saw then for the first time that she held a gun. It was small and black, shiny and almost dainty for the deadly thing it was. It gleamed softly with reflected light in Vega's hand and for a long time Beth stared at it incredulously. The knowledge that she was in mortal danger gave her a grip on herself, a sort of eerie calm that floated on top of her panic.

"Vega, you aren't going to use that thing," she said, her voice low and coaxing. "Whatever I did to you, it wasn't that bad. I don't deserve it."

"It didn't seem that bad to you because you weren't the one who was hurt," Vega said.

"It was a lot of things that hurt you, not just me," Beth urged.

"You were all that mattered."

She was so beautiful, so pale, so alarmingly thin, thinner even than Beth had remembered her. Beth felt a start of compassion for her, but the weapon in Vega's hand restrained her.

"Vega, can't we talk?" she pleaded. "Can't we talk about it? Don't do something you'll regret for the rest of your life."

"I wish somebody had been there to tell you the same thing before you left me," she said.

"I—I'm desperately sorry, Vega," Beth murmured. "I was a coward. I'm ashamed of it. God knows I've suffered too. I've thought of you so often, I—"

"I know, I saw your letter to Cleve. You must have asked about me at least once."

"I was afraid it would upset him to ask more."

"You just didn't care."

"I cared, Vega," she said urgently. "I loved you once."

"Is that what you call it?" Vega said and her eyes widened and her hand began to tremble. "Is that what you call the hell you put me through, never knowing if I'd see you or hear from you from one day to the next? Dying of love for you and need of you, and having to beg to see you? You loathed me, Beth, you were just looking for a way to get rid of me." Her voice rose steadily through her words, though she tried to stop it.

"No, Vega. That's not why I ran away. That had nothing to do with it."

"Don't lie to me, Beth!" Vega cried, and Beth could almost feel, like a tightening wire, her nerves stretching and the electric feeling of hysteria in the air. She mustn't let Vega get hysterical.

"Vega, whatever happened, it was all a mistake. It was all my fault, too, I should never have done the things I did, but I did them anyway. I did what I felt compelled to do. I wasn't happy hurting you. I never wanted to see you suffer."

"You left in time to miss most of it," Vega told her acidly. "Maybe you know about that part. I was in Camarillo for a while. Did Cleve tell you?"

"Yes, he told me," Beth said, humble before this catalog of torments.

"Did he also tell you that he knows everything about us?"

"No!" Beth cried, chagrin plain in her open mouth and startled eyes.

"I told him," Vega said with quiet desperation. "I was out of my mind. I couldn't help it, but I think I would have anyway. It couldn't hurt me anymore and I had to hurt you somehow. It festered in me like a cancer, Beth. It's been eating me alive all this time." The feverish flush in her thin cheeks bore out her words.

Beth tried to sit up again but Vega threatened her with a swift movement of the gun and Beth stayed where she was, propped on one elbow. "Vega," she pleaded, beginning to lose faith in her powers of persuasion. "I know it's been bad, I know it's been terrible for you. Do you think that's the only reason I ran away? Didn't Cleve tell you anything? I told him to explain about Charlie, and the rest of it. Do you think it was easy for me to leave my children?"

"I don't know. I only know I'm the one who suffered most from your going. Aside from that I don't think anything anymore. And I know just one other thing, Beth, I want to see you suffer. I want to see you scared and shaking and miserable the way I've been ever since you left."

She sat down in a chair facing the bed, as though she meant to stay a while.

"Will you—have a drink?" Beth asked. *God, if I could just get her drunk!* she thought.

"Cleve's been doing all the family drinking lately," Vega said. "I dried out in the hospital." Her voice was so cold, her attitude so rare and strange in one given to hysterics, that Beth shivered involuntarily.

"Cigarette?" Beth said. If only she could get things on a talking basis, instead of this sharp bitter exchange that cut and frightened her; if only Vega would break down and cry and wail and let herself be comforted.

"I don't feel like it," Vega said, waving the pack away. Her voice, her eyes, left no doubt that she spoke the truth.

They stayed like that for a little while, neither one speaking or moving. Beth found Vega's desperate eyes, the only part of her that seemed alive, more than she could bear, and she looked away.

"How long are you going to stay there like that?" she said at last.

"As long as I need to," Vega said cryptically.

"Vega, I know what I did was crazy. I know you've been miserable."

"My life was wrecked, Beth."

"I—I know—"

"You have no idea."

"I only meant—"

"Nothing you can say means anything."

And Beth, for the first time, thought that her life might end that very day in the face of that very gun, sitting idle and quiet in the hands of a madwoman. For it was clear that Vega blamed her whole life on Beth. All the sorrows and errors and accidents somehow had been Beth's fault and Vega, feeling as she did, could kill her with a clear conscience. It made Beth's flesh creep.

Death. She had never thought about it much before, except to wonder how it felt, *if* it felt, and to think it could never happen to her. It was as unreal as old age, as a hydrogen war, as blindness, as any tragedy that had never happened to her. How could you face death when you knew nothing about it? How could you die all unprepared like this, terrified and ugly and foolish in your underwear? Didn't she have a right to dignity, a right to respect and to a decent end with some warning? Didn't she have a right to a long life before that happened, a life that would end slowly and gradually and gracefully—not in one sickening crack of doom?

When would Vega pull the trigger? Beth began to watch the gun as if it were an animal with a life of its own, a third presence in the room. She couldn't drag her eyes from it. She looked at the sleek short barrel and the small black hole at the end, wondering when it would erupt in flashing death.

Maybe the bullet will miss me, she thought, feeling the pounding of her constricted heart. *Maybe she'll just wound me. And I'll leap at her and grab the thing before she realizes what's happened. No, maybe it would be better to pretend I'm dead, just fall back and lie on the bed as if I'm stone dead. But what if she comes over and looks at me and sees it's just a flesh wound? Or what if she empties the damned gun into me?* She almost whimpered aloud with terror. Her fear was a thing alive, a separate living creature in that haunted room, and Vega could feel it. But her face was stony and dreadful.

Beth lay back on the bed at last. *If she wants to shoot me dead she'll have to stand up to do it now,* she thought. *At least that'll give me some warning.* And almost in the next instant she wondered if she wanted any warning. If it had to be, wouldn't it be better to die abruptly and without the agony of seeing it come and being helpless to stop it?

The day ended little by little to the tune of rain and wind and the room grew dark. Small drops pattered in at the windows. Beth reached over with utmost caution and turned the light on beside the bed, and immediately cursed herself for it. It only made her a better target. But Vega would have done it herself anyway, sooner or later, and maybe the mere fact of having to move would have stirred her to fire.

Beth watched her, her mad, despairing eyes, and the horror of it was almost unbearable. "Vega, do something," she cried, and her own voice shocked her into stillness again. "It couldn't have been that bad," she cried again, later, supplicating, unwittingly using the same words to Vega that Charlie had used to her.

"If you scream I'll do it now," Vega said, and with a sick gasp Beth clamped her mouth shut.

They sat in tortured silence for a while longer. Beth looked at her watch. It was past ten. Her stomach stirred and she knew it was empty, but there was no desire for food in her. She thought with urgent envy of the careless, casual people below her in the streets, eating in the bright, cheerful restaurants, seeing the movies and shows, crossing the streets and chatting with each other. And life, so mundane and full of anxieties, seemed achingly beautiful to her. It didn't matter who she was, it didn't matter where she belonged. It only mattered to keep on living, to keep life strong and safe and have a second chance at it.

"Vega," she tried again in a raspy voice at close to midnight, "you'll never get away with it. You know that, don't you?"

"What makes you think I care?" Vega said. "Do you think I could possibly give a damn anymore what happens to me?"

"But your mother. And Gramp. And Cleve and Jean!" Beth said, hoping with the force of panic to hit a sensitive chord.

"I spit on them all," Vega said. "Do you wonder why I'm not screaming, Beth?" she added in her voice that was calm with the serenity of madness. "I've done all my screaming, that's why. I did it all at Cleve and Mother. And the doctors, the first few weeks I was in the hospital. There isn't any left in me. Gramp is dead, Beth. And Mother is dying, just like all those neglected cats. Cleve doesn't count, he never amounted to anything. I have only you now. I have your whole future in my hand, here. And it's going to pay for my whole past." She shook the gun back and forth. "I have your life and your death, I have infinite power over you, and nothing, not tears or begging or hypocritical love or fancy excuses, is going to save you. Nothing."

"Then do it now!" Beth cried in a cracking voice. "Do it now!" But every inch of her was tense with prayers for mercy.

"When I'm ready," Vega said. "When I'm good and ready."

And so they sat on in the small pool of light in the little hotel room with the instrument of death a wall between them and an everlasting tie. Beth thought of Gramp, Vega's grandfather, small and dry, coming into the overheated house with his arms full of cats. He was only a vague image in her mind, yet she mourned him with a sort of stricken sympathy.

She wondered if Vega was trying to drive her mad, too, and she felt so near to abandoned shrieking, so near to violent shudders and agonized pleas for help, that she thought her heart and bones would crack from the pressure. If that was what Vega was after, it wouldn't be long before she had it.

And still they sat on and on and on. And Beth thought of her children. Perhaps now, at long last, they'd be happy. She couldn't shame them anymore. No rotten little detective was going to follow her around New York or any other town, taking notes on the girls she met and the food she ate and the money she spent, and then sell his pitiful information to her rich uncle.

And Charlie. Would he care? How would it strike him? Would he mourn her? In her deepest heart she knew he would, and that made her more frightened, more miserable.

The phone rang with a shattering clamor that drew a small scream of suppressed hysteria from Beth. She looked at Vega with wide eyes, and Vega said, "Answer it."

It was Beebo. "I meant to call earlier," she said. "I know it's late." Beth looked at her watch. It was past two. "I got stuck at a party, baby, you know how it is. Am I forgiven?"

"Of course," Beth said. *God, what can I say, how can I warn her?* She looked slyly at Vega, but the look on Vega's face told her the gun would speak instantly if Beth spoke too much.

"Well, that was easy," Beebo laughed. How warm her voice was! Close and relaxed. Beth yearned for her. "I expected to get a lecture. Or hurt feelings at the very least. How about coming down for dinner tomorrow? We could take in a movie or something."

"Tomorrow? I don't think I'll be able to," Beth said, putting all her hope into the *double entendre,* but if it was innocent enough to get past Vega it was obviously too vague to alarm Beebo.

"Okay, the day after," Beebo said, unperturbed.

"I don't think I'm going to be around," Beth said and Vega sat up in her seat and aimed the gun at her and Beth nearly fainted with fear. She would have laughed at their histrionics if she had seen them in a movie, but this was actually happening and just the terror of it nearly squeezed the life out of her.

"You're not going out of town, are you?" Beebo said.

"No." Her voice was little more than a whisper.

"You are mad at me," Beebo said.

"No! No, I swear!" Beth protested with such vehemence that Vega motioned her to hang up and she did, abruptly, without so much as a goodbye. She hoped her strangeness on the phone, if nothing else, would alert Beebo somehow. If only Beebo didn't suppose she'd been drinking and was acting silly. And she experienced a flash of truly passionate yearning for Beebo, her physical presence, the strength and safety of her arms.

The hours went past with ponderous slowness and Beth tried to value them, to treasure each moment that she was still alive. And yet each moment struck such fear into her that she found herself crawling with it.

Every ten or fifteen minutes she would say Vega's name, or ask her to leave, or offer her a cigarette. It didn't matter that her words were useless. It mattered that she was still able to speak and understand herself. Every leaden moment made life dearer to her. Her thoughts skipped sporadically from Laura to Nina to Beebo, to the others she had met in the swift passage through the enormous city. They ranged over her college days, over the exotic greenery of California and the face Charlie showed her when she left him, standing alone at the end of the drive. And the Scootch, and Skipper with a skinned knee. And her aunt and uncle. And Vega. Vega herself, chic and smooth and so desirable when Beth first knew her. And in between the fragmented pictures of her past, the people she knew, came moments when her heart froze and her mouth went desert dry.

She was still lying on the bed in a bath of sweat and anguish when she heard Vega rise at last. The first tired light of dawn was showing in the windows. The rain had stopped. Beth noted this with surprise, for she had not heard it steal off. She stiffened all over, seeing Vega approach her.

Vega turned off the bedside lamp that had shown them to each other throughout the dark hours and they appeared to each other then as silvery shadows.

"No, Vega, no, Vega, no-no-no-no-no," Beth said in a sort of singsong, nearly hypnotized with fear.

"I want to know how you'll take it."

"You'll wake everyone up. They'll catch you."

"I want it that way."

They gazed at each other. Communication was no longer possible between them and Beth finally shut her eyes, unable to look at the gun any longer. She wept, "I want to live. That's all I want in the world. Just give me that and I can work out the rest."

"I wonder," Vega said. "I'd like to see you try."

After what seemed an age to her warped sense of time, Beth reopened her eyes. Vega stood stock still where she was, at the side of the bed. The light from the windows was brightening around her.

"Have you suffered tonight, Beth?" she asked.

"Horribly." Beth choked a little trying to answer.

"Will you ever regret what you did?"

"I do, I *have,* since the day it was done."

"Did you ever love me, I wonder?" But she held up her hand to Beth and said, "Don't answer, I don't want any more lies from you."

There was another dreadful silence and now the minutes were flying, the sun was coming up with awful haste, and Beth's heart was in her throat.

Vega lifted the gun, and the power of speech failed Beth. Nothing was real but the thunder of her pulse in her ears and the stout hard barrel two feet from her.

Vega lifted the gun higher. "I do this for you, Beth," she said. "All for you."

Then she shot herself, very suddenly and awkwardly, in the right temple, grimacing like a child expecting a tanning. Her features collapsed and her body relaxed onto the floor before Beth's eyes.

Chapter Twenty

IN THE SILENCE THAT FOLLOWED BETH LAY WHERE SHE WAS, nailed to the bed. She had neither the courage nor the physical strength nor the desire to sit up and look at Vega. What happened afterward remained forever in her memory as a weird and warped nightmare.

Moments later an elevator boy and two maids rushed into the room, with a couple of guests following them, and found the two women—one dead, the other in a state of near-shock. At first glimpse they took Beth for dead too, and one of the maids gave a little scream when she stirred.

"This one's alive!" she cried.

They helped her to sit up and besieged her with questions, and though she heard them and understood them she was unable to answer coherently. She began to giggle morbidly when one of the guests referred to Vega as "the poor stiff" and her awful uncontrollable choking laughter struck them all aghast. It changed, as suddenly as it had started, into sobs. Someone forced her back down on the bed and put a cold cloth on her head and she heard a coarse hearty female voice somewhere in the room remark, "Don't know why we're taking such fine care of her. She probably did it!"

Very shortly the room was crowded and everyone in the crowd was firing questions at Beth, who had not even the small comfort of her clothes in which to face them. No one touched the body. It was grotesquely dead.

There was much murmurous comment about the arrival of the police, mingled with pleas from hotel officials for clearing the room. Beth struggled to her feet, climbing off the bed on the side opposite that where Vega lay. She collected her clothes from the chair where she had thrown them the night before and went into the bathroom. They made way for her as if none of them wanted to touch her, though they continued to ask her, "Why'd you do it, sister?" "Hey, you did it, didn't you?" "Look at her face. You can tell she did it."

In the bathroom she was momentarily alone, and desperately sick for the first few minutes. She wept sobs that were torn from the depths of her. She mourned Vega. Vega had anticipated her curses, her fury, her despair, everything but her pity. And yet pity was all Beth had to give, all she could feel.

When she emerged, washed and dressed, the police were there. Methodically and quickly they emptied the room. Notes were made on the disposition of the body and it was photographed from several sides. The gun had been tenderly separated from Vega's index finger which had curled around the trigger guard, and rested in a handkerchief on the bed table.

Beth looked high and haughty into the face of the Law. She was not able to look down at the floor. They led her to a chair—the one where Vega had sat all night—and asked her what happened. She was quaking with exhaustion but not with fear. It seemed she had felt all the fear she would ever feel for the rest of her life in the night just past. She answered them with the confidence of truth. She only hesitated once, and that was when a Lieutenant Scopa, who was doing most of the questioning, asked her why Vega would want to kill her.

"Well—she—she was a mental patient. She had gotten it into her head that I hurt her, that I hated her. She thought I was responsible for all her troubles, and she wanted revenge. That's all I can tell you."

They held her for two days and she sat in a bare orderly cell with another, fortunately taciturn, woman, and cried most of the time, except when they were interrogating her. Then she made it a point of pride to maintain her composure. She was prepared to have them disbelieve her, finally. At first she thought they would let her go at once, just because she was truthful as far as she went with her story. When they continued to hold her she began to realize that they doubted her. They didn't understand, they wouldn't accept her words. The thing looked odd to them. She expected to be told outright that she shot Vega in the head and then wiped the gun clean and put it in the hand of the corpse. They had even intimated this.

"We know she was a mental patient," Lieutenant Scopa told her. "We've checked up on her. Now if you want to plead self-defense and tell us what really happened it'll easier on you, Mrs. Ayers. Nobody'll blame you for saving your own life. Vega had threatened other people with the same gun."

"What?" Beth cried, startled.

"A couple of people," he said briefly. "We know it was her gun. It's registered in her name in South Pasadena. Of course, she didn't shoot the other people. But she might have scared you into thinking she *would* shoot you. If I had been you and I had a chance to grab that thing, I would have done it myself."

"If I'd had a chance to grab it, Lieutenant, don't you think I would have done something with it, too? I could have scared her at least. But I couldn't have killed her. It's true, she did threaten my life, and I had to wait there all night thinking she was going to kill me—"

"Without doing anything about it?"

"Doing *what?*" Beth said. "Every time I moved she aimed that damned gun at me and told me to stay still."

"Okay, okay," he said.

"And finally, at dawn, she got up and came to the bed and told me what she did she was doing 'all for me.' And I waited to die. But she shot herself instead." She could never talk about it without breaking up at that point and they had to hold off the questions for a while to let her recover herself.

They allowed her one phone call when they took her in and she made it to Beebo. She didn't think about this or weigh the sense of it. She simply called. Beebo would understand and she'd do the right things. Beth didn't feel that way about anybody else.

"You've been in every scrape there is," she said brokenly into the receiver. "Help me out of this, Beebo."

"God, Beth. I—I couldn't believe it when I read—" Beebo began, but Beth interrupted her.

"Call my uncle in Chicago," she said and gave her the number. "He'll get me a lawyer. And, Beebo, I didn't do it."

"I know, baby, I believe you. Who was she?"

"She was the one I ran off and left."

"Jesus," Beebo breathed. "She took it pretty hard, didn't she?"

"Will you help me?" Beth said.

"I'll do anything, everything I can," Beebo said. "Don't worry, sweetheart, if you're innocent you'll get off."

"I'm not so sure. Nobody saw it. I can't prove a damn thing."

"Worrying won't change things, Beth," Beebo said, and Beth hung up somewhat reassured.

But after two nights in a jail cell she was almost unstrung with anxiety, nerves, even the fear she thought had been exhausted in her. The truth, unsubstantiated, simply wasn't enough. They were going to hold her. They thought she did it, and it was her word against the word of a dead woman. She wondered miserably what Cleve and Mrs. Purvis thought of her now, who had liked her so well in the past. Cleve was probably dead drunk and cursing the both of them, and Mrs. Purvis, majestic in her infirmities, was probably dying quietly of the knowledge that her daughter was a Lesbian.

Abruptly, the morning after the second night in jail, they released her. A matron came and opened her door and said, "You're free, Mrs. Ayers."

Beth sat up on her cot, struck dumb for a moment with surprise. Her cell mate grunted at her, gave her one envious glance, and went back to sleep.

"On bail?" Beth asked at last through a dry throat, staring incredulously at the woman. "Do I have a lawyer? My uncle—"

"No bail. You're free. No strings attached. Except we'd like you to stay in town until the last details of the case are straightened out."

"How did it happen? Why?" she cried, collecting her things with hasty hands, almost afraid to believe in her luck.

"They'll explain it to you up front," the woman told her and Beth followed her down the clanging corridor and out the barred doors to the elevator. The matron took her to an office on the first floor and returned her coat and purse. They made her sign some release papers and then they led her into a waiting room.

Charlie stood up to greet her.

Beth stopped in her tracks, speechless at the sight of him. His presence struck her in the heart like a physical blow.

"Hello, Beth," he said softly, his face heavy and serious.

"Charlie," she whispered. And then she went to him put her arms around him and cried. "I never thought I'd see you again," she said, "Least of all here."

"I wouldn't desert you, Beth," he said, holding her. "You're still my wife. I love you." It was awkward but determined, stubborn and proud and hopeless.

"Oh, no, please don't say it," she pleaded. "Please. I can't take it." After all she had been through to escape him she was wary even of the words that might entangle her again. She was glad, grateful, infinitely relieved to see him there. But she was not in love with him and her gratitude did not extend to a reconciliation.

"The children?" she asked before he let her go, and he nodded.

"Fine. Both fine. But they miss you." She started to ask him more but he interrupted, "I've got a room at the Blackwell. Let's get out of here, we can't talk here."

Beth clutched his sleeve. "Am I free?" she begged. "Am I really free? Did she tell me the truth?"

"Yes," he said.

"But how—"

"Come on, I'll explain."

He hailed a cab outside and as soon as they were in it Beth asked, "Are Uncle John and Aunt Elsa here?"

"No," he said. "They were going to come but I talked them out of it. There wasn't any need, and it would only have been painful."

"It must have been a terrible shock for them."

"Yes. It was pretty rough."

They sat side by side, Charlie in his lightweight blue summer suit, solemn and handsome and preoccupied, Beth in her rumpled clothes, the same she had worn on her Village spree. They seemed by now to be the only clothes she had ever worn. She sensed that be wanted to take her hand, even to kiss her, but also that he had a stern lecture saved up, a couple of months worth of grievances and loneliness and resentment to get off his chest. But still, he was not harsh with her or short-tempered, and she knew without his having to say it that he wanted her back. That he could, after what had just happened, warmed her heart and touched her, even though she understood that he was using her troubles to suit his own ends. He was taking advantage of her fear and confusion, using them as a lever to prod her out of New York. But she could not go back and start over with him, however she might have botched her efforts to find a new life here. She dreaded hurting him with her decision.

"My things," she said. "They're all at the Beaton."

"They were. I picked them up," he said.

"There wasn't much."

"No."

Between their short exchanges hung a thousand things unsaid, a thousand things not for the ears of cabbies, things better left unsaid even to each other. But they would say them anyway, Beth thought with a shudder.

Chapter Twenty-one

HE CLOSED THE DOOR OF THE ROOM HE HAD TAKEN IN THE Blackwell and turned to face her. Beth couldn't look at him. She sat down on the bed—a spacious double bed that unnerved her slightly—and kicked off her shoes. Slowly she glanced up at him.

"I'll order us a drink if you like," he said.

"I'd love one," she said thankfully, and he called room service and ordered two vodka collinses. Beth was burning to know by what miracle she had been released, but she didn't want to drag it out of him. Let him tell her in his own good time. He understood how anxious she was. She supposed he was waiting for the drinks to come and lighten the atmosphere a little.

"I'm going to take a bath and change my clothes," she said.

"Good idea." He showed her where he had put her things and she took a change of underwear and a dressing gown into the bathroom with her and bathed herself, weeping softly with relief in her first privacy in forty-eight hours. Warm water, a leisurely bath, a refreshing drink on the way—all the foolish little symbols of a serious and necessary condition to her life: Freedom.

Only Charlie disturbed her. She had been so glad to see him that she had run to his arms and wept. And now she sat in her tub suddenly full of misgivings about him again. She knew enough now to know she loved him, in a way. Only it was the wrong way; it was not sufficient for him or for a marriage. It was enough to make her want him forever as a friend, too little to make her want him back as a lover. If only he could understand that. If only he could accept it. She tried, while she bathed, to clear her mind and think of a way to tell him her feelings which would not offend him.

When she came out, clean and fresh and powdered, the drinks had arrived. He lighted a cigarette for her and handed her a glass.

"How did it happen?" she said, sitting down again on the bed. She couldn't hold it back any longer. She wondered why he was so reluctant to get started with it. The whole thing seemed slightly fantastic. A little less than an hour ago she had been a prisoner in jail, a murder suspect; now she was free.

"Well…" He turned his back to her and gazed out the window. "Heinrich saved you—" he began.

"Heinrich?" She broke in. "Who's he?"

"He's a—well, a sort of detective we hired—"

"Who hired?" she demanded.

"Your Uncle John and I. Are you going to let me tell you this, Beth, or are you going to keep interrupting me?"

"I'm sorry," she said, but she felt the flush of indignation on her cheek.

"Beth, we hired him because we were so damned scared," Charlie said suddenly, turning to face her. His voice, his gestures, pleaded for her understanding. "He was supposed to be the best and we wanted only the best. He did a couple of jobs for Uncle John once, long ago. John trusts the guy and I went along. I was out of my mind worried about you the first couple of weeks. When John phoned to say you'd run away from him, too, I told him to go ahead and hire Heinrich."

"I see." She looked down into her glass, humiliated.

"We never meant to—to spy on you, darling," Charlie said. "But when he found you, in New York, we were—well, anything but reassured by what he told us. We told him to stay with it, and he took a room next to yours at the Beaton."

"He what?" she cried. "Oh, Charlie, that was going too far." *My God, we even shared the same bathroom!* she thought.

"It was going pretty far, maybe, but he was doing his job, Beth."

"Well, I guess there's nothing I can tell you about my stay in New York that he hasn't already told you!" she exclaimed.

"Not much," Charlie said quietly, as if embarrassed.

"I suppose he was peeking through the keyhole when Vega showed up," Beth said, near to tears with indignation. The fact that it might have saved her life was lost momentarily in the shame of the situation.

"Not exactly. He had the room wired," Charlie said. "He recorded everything. He just gave the tapes to the police and explained to them that Vega was in love with you. The whole thing became clear as a bell. She damn near killed a kid in Pasadena named P.K. Schaefer. With that same gun. P.K. took a chance and ran for it. Vega fired and missed her." He shrugged. "Well, Heinrich's testimony and P.K.'s and the doctor's Vega was seeing— they were too much for the police. It was plain that she was unhinged. And that you didn't do it."

There was a silence then while they were both absorbed in their thoughts.

"My children," Beth said. "My poor kids."

"They don't know anything about it," Charlie said quickly. "They've been in Chicago all this time. I'm going to keep them there till it blows over. You've been exonerated, Beth."

"But Vega was a Lesbian. That part of it you can never wipe out. That part will haunt me. I guess that's what she meant by killing herself to make me suffer."

"I guess it is," he said. "I heard the tapes," he added diffidently. "She sounded pretty desperate."

Another pause. Beth finished her drink and Charlie ordered two more.

"How can you take those children back to Pasadena to live?" she asked.

"It doesn't need to be Pasadena," he said. "California's a big state."

"But the business is in Pasadena. It's all established. You can't just pick up and move out."

"For something like this I could. And I would." He gazed directly at her as he said it, wanting her to see all the hurt and determination and love in his face.

"But, Charlie," she protested, feeling caught and flustered, "it would mean dragging everybody with you, all the office staff, the craftsmen, the machinists. Cleve and Jean—"

"Cleve and Jean don't need to worry about it any longer," he said, and he was gazing down at his drink now, lines of concern on his forehead.

"Why not? What does that mean?"

"Cleve isn't with the company now. It's just—Ayers Toys."

Beth's mouth dropped open a little. "What happened?" she breathed at last.

"He climbed into that damn bottle and stayed," Charlie said. "He was coming to work drunk all the time. It was getting bad when you left, Beth; you must have heard in me mention it a couple of times....Well, it just got worse. It got intolerable, to tell the truth. He wasn't doing anything, he wasn't contributing anything. He just sat in his office and tipped the bottle. I did all the work. And goddamn it, I didn't feel like sharing the credit and the money with a souse who didn't raise a finger for either one."

"Oh, but Charlie," she said, and there were tears in her voice, "it was his business, his idea. You were the newcomer not so long ago. You were the one he took in, and taught the ropes, and made an equal partner." She was hurt for a moment, as Cleve must have been hurt when it happened.

"Well, damn it!" he cried defensively. "It didn't have to happen that way, Beth. I begged him to quit drinking. I dragged him around to a couple of specialists. I got Jean to help me, and Mrs. Purvis. And Cleve tried. When it got too bad, he felt the same way I did.

"Honey, you don't think I went in there and fired the guy, do you?" he said, flinging out his hands in a plea for sympathy. "No! Hell, no. Cleve brought it up himself. I couldn't do a thing like that. He just came in one morning about a month ago and told me he thought it would be better for the business and for himself if he quit."

"Who's going to hire him now if he's been drinking?"

"Beth, it's rough, I know. It's a rough life, nobody needs to tell me that."

"Maybe Jean will get a job and support them for a while," she said.

"He's leaving her!"

"What?" It was impossible. "They were always so happy!" she exclaimed. They had seemed so stable as a partnership.

"It's a trial separation," Charlie said. "I think they love each other, all right, but they just can't stand each other, if you know what I mean."

"I always thought Jean took everything in her stride. I thought there was nothing that girl couldn't face with a smile. I even used to resent that smile of hers, because I thought it meant inner peace. I thought she had learned to cope with life, and because I was jealous I used to tell myself it was only because she was so stupid. I thought anybody as smart as me could never be happy. Only the nice, jolly, stupid people like Jean."

"She isn't stupid, honey," Charlie said, sitting down on the bed beside her. "Her only answer to her problems was to smile. She and Cleve have been just—roommates for years. Not husband and wife. I think that's why he drinks. It had something to do with Vega, too. He never did explain it all to me. Just little hints and remarks when he was tight. I guess he and Vega were too close or something. When they were younger, I mean. He even made me think, one time, that it went as far as—" He stopped.

"As far as what?" she prompted with unhappy curiosity. "Well, as a sort of affair," he said, obviously embarrassed to talk about it. "Anyway, they were abnormally close. For a long time. And suddenly there was an awful fight. I guess they both got scared and ashamed when they got a little older and realized it wasn't very healthy for a brother and sister, and all that. And they both turned on each other. Vega blamed Cleve because he was a man and men are always responsible for these things. And Cleve blamed Vega because she was the oldest and she showed him the way and encouraged it. And all of a sudden, where there had been so much love, there was hate. They hated each other with real dedication. I guess to hide the fact that they would always love each other anyway, no matter how they tried not to.

"Well, it was too much for both of them. Vega turned to women for relief and affection. And Cleve tried to find a substitute in Jean for Vega. But Jean was the wrong girl entirely. They were different as night and day—the two women. I guess that's why Cleve chose her. He didn't want to be eternally reminded of his sister. But it didn't work, for either of them."

After a pause Beth said softly, "Explains a lot of things, doesn't it? God, it makes you wonder, though. It just makes you wonder if Cleve and Vega wouldn't both have been better off to stay with each other and let the world go to hell."

"You know it wouldn't," he said, and though his voice was even she could feel the sudden rise in his emotional temperature.

"At least Vega wouldn't have ended up horribly dead on the floor of a hotel room."

"I wouldn't count on it. It's never better to prolong a sick relationship. She might have ended up dead even sooner."

"If prolonging a sick relationship will keep you alive, it's worth it."

"Things would have been much worse for them if they lived together," he said positively. Anything abnormal he automatically loathed, without understanding it, without questioning himself.

And rather than fight him in an area where his will and his emotions could not be moved, she simply said, "He always managed to write and tell me how you and the kids were. No matter how drunk he was. And sometimes those letters looked like he had palsy when he wrote them. But I was so grateful for them."

"He was writing to you?" Charlie said, turning where he sat to look at her, surprised.

She nodded, her eyes on the floor. "I asked him to," she said. "I knew you wouldn't write, and I had to know how you were."

He seemed touched. After a moment he reached for her hand and she let him have it, dreading to argue with him.

"Beth," he said quietly. "Have you had enough now? Enough of this running around and trying to 'find yourself,' or whatever it is you think you're doing?"

He meant to be kind but he sounded condescending, and it wounded her. "You mustn't laugh at me, Charlie," she said.

"No, darling, I'm not laughing. I know it's serious. God knows I have nothing to laugh about," he said quickly.

Beth made herself look at him and for a brief moment she saw him the way he had been nine years ago in college when she had loved him so romantically. Or thought she had. The tenderness was reflected on her face and he brightened a little to see it. "Charlie, darling, I'm so grateful to you for so much," she said. "I owe you a lot and I wish there were some way to repay it."

"There is. Come home with me."

She almost bit her lip. She hadn't meant to give him an opening like that. She wanted to steer him out of the idea without inflicting pain on him. He had come a long way and put up with a lot.

"I—I wish to God I could," she said.

"You can. Oh, Beth, I've been so damned miserably lonesome—"

"I know, so have I," she broke in swiftly, afraid to let him start telling her what he had been through. It would be very bad, it would hurt them both, and it would make her feel more obligated than ever to him.

She stood up, walking away from him a few steps, as if that would help her to think clearly. "I'll never be proud of what I've done to you, Charlie," she said. "I've failed as a wife to you and as a mother to my children. For a woman that's the ultimate disgrace. I suppose it sounds pretty hollow to say that I couldn't help it. But I was as much a failure to myself as a human being as I was to you. When you fail yourself how can you be any good to anyone else?"

She turned a supplicating face to him.

"I don't understand it," he said. "You were all I ever wanted. The only thing wrong with my life now is that you're not in it."

"The only thing wrong with your life when I *am* in it is me. I had to leave," she said, feeling that old needling desperation that plagued her when she tried to explain her private self to Charlie. He felt it too, as he tried to grasp it all, and came away with a head full of her words and no meanings to hang them on.

"I thought when I found Laura it would all come clear, all be explained to me," she said, speaking as though explaining it to a child. "But when I found her, it was more like the beginning of the search than the end of it. I guess I'll never know the answer to who I am. Or why. I guess the answer is that there is no answer." She gave a shy hopeless little laugh. "Does that make things any clearer?"

"No," he said and shook his head, an earnest sweat of concentration on his face. "I hope you aren't telling me you won't come back with me. That's the only thing that matters."

"But Charlie, darling, we're right back where we started. That isn't enough. Not for me. If we could only be friends and—"

"Friends!" he flared, and she knew she was in for it now. "How can a husband and wife be just friends? Do you want to live like Cleve and Jean lived all these years? A pitiful farce of a marriage? It may fool their friends but it doesn't fool them."

"Charlie, let's face it, ours wasn't much better."

"It was till you got a bunch of goddamn half-baked ideas in your head!"

"I don't think I could go back to you now, even loving you," she said.

"You mean you don't love me enough? Beth, Beth, I've always known that. In a marriage, one always loves more than the other. I'm willing to be that one." He had risen and come toward her and now he stood behind her with his big warm hands on her shoulders, feeling her sobs and aching to stop them with kisses.

"Oh, don't!" she cried, shaking him away from her. "Don't talk that way. You'll break my heart."

"Come home with me then."

"I can't!" she cried, moving still further away from him.

"I need you."

"I can't, Charlie."

"The children need you. Think of them if you can't think of me, for God's sake."

"I have, I have, I've almost lost my mind over them. I wish somebody had cared that much about me when I was a child! I can't go home!"

"You can, goddamn you! You will!" he exclaimed.

She whirled and faced him and shrieked with desperate determination, "No!"

There was a trembling silence for several moments while they stared at each other, both shaking with the intensity of their love, their hate, their helplessness.

"Beth, not once since I found you and got you out of that jail and brought you here have I said anything about what you've done to me. I was hoping I wouldn't have to. I haven't told you about the nights I've spent alone and the restaurant dinners I've eaten and the stories I've had to make up for the kids about you and the things I've had to tell the neighbors. I haven't told you—"

"Don't!" she cried in anguish. "Don't tell me unless you want to kill me."

"I want you to know what I've been through!" he said fiercely.

"Charlie, I'm telling you now and forever, once and for all, I can't come home with you. I can't go back to you. I—"

"You said you loved me." He had turned quite pale and was staring at her.

"I want a divorce," she said, and crumbled into a chair at the foot of the bed.

They sat in utter silence then for ten minutes, neither of them moving, neither speaking. At last he said, "I could have killed you when you left. I felt that way for a long time. But when I heard about Vega, all the mess in the papers, everything changed. I was so worried about you. I knew you couldn't have done it and I wanted to forgive you. I don't know why, I guess I'm just a glutton for punishment. I just wanted you back, no questions asked."

"You didn't need to ask. Mr. Heinrich had all the answers," she said sharply.

"I came here to forgive you, to rescue you and start over."

"I can't be rescued," she said firmly.

"You're not worth it," he said grimly. "I didn't know that till now. Or rather, I couldn't face it. I guess because I loved you so much."

She covered her face with her hands, refusing to look at him or answer. At last he rose.

"I'll take another room," he said. "I'll be leaving tomorrow, I guess. There isn't much point in staying on."

She listened to him moving about the room, taking his things from the drawers where he had put them the night before, and her heart contracted. But still she didn't move, didn't try to stop him. It was better that he go off mad. It would give him strength and reassure him in the future that he had done the right thing. It would help him give her up.

He stopped at the door and she looked up then, aware that he was leaving. His chin was set and his eyes were hard. He was very handsome and straight.

"Charlie, I wish—with all my heart, I wish—"

"I know. So do I," he said.

"I'll never know, all the rest of my life, if what I'm doing is a brave thing or a cowardly thing, Charlie. A right thing or a wrong one. I only know I have to do it."

He listened, quiet and uncomprehending, and then he said, almost gently, "Goodbye, Beth."

"Goodbye," she whispered.

He shut the door softly after him.

241

Chapter Twenty-two

THERE WAS ONLY ONE THING LEFT THAT SHE KNEW SHE HAD TO do, and that was see Laura and tell her the truths she had withheld before. She wrote to her aunt and uncle first and explained why she could not, and never would, come home, and thanked them for the hospitality. She was honest, although she was brief.

If she had to start a new life, and there was no question anymore about that, she was going to start it without the lies and self-deceptions that had marred the other. She was going to pare away the fibs and selfish miseries, as many of them as she could, even if it meant hurting herself, hurting others. It would be a clean, honest pain and it would heal.

She hadn't the guts to face Laura that day; to face anyone, for that matter. She waited until the next morning and then slipped out early, afraid of running into Charlie in the hotel lobby. But she was spared that.

She took a cab over to Laura's apartment. It was only eight-thirty. It seemed like an odd hour for confession and atonement, an odd time of day to be making your apologies and refashioning your life. But we don't pick our own times for these things; they happen when they are ready. The tangled strands of Beth's life were smoothing out a little. This was the last task. Until it was done she was not free. The rest would have to wait. When Laura herself knew the whole truth, Beth would be liberated at last from her self-contempt, from her obsessive need for Laura.

She rang the elevator buzzer after the clerk had phoned the Manns and told her she could see them. She rode up with her spine tingling and all the delicate nerves of her face taut. It wouldn't be so bad; it couldn't be worse than what she had been through with Charlie or with Vega, she told herself. It had to be done. And still she trembled.

She tried to think of herself riding back down in that same elevator in half an hour with her lies behind her, her selfishness exposed and, in part, atoned for, and her heart lighter. Even if Laura was angry and disillusioned with her, even if her idealization of Beth was rudely shattered, even if there was no friendship left to salvage. It was Laura she had come to find and Laura was her last bridge to cross before she could begin her life over again somewhere and try to do better with it this time.

She knocked quickly on Laura's front door, as if by hesitating she would squander her courage. Jack opened it for her. She stared at him.

"Good morning," he said. "It's all right, I live here," he added, seeing the look of faint dismay on her face.

"I thought you'd be at work," she said clumsily.

"I'm on my way, sweetheart," he said, smiling. "She's all yours." He thumbed over his shoulder and Beth saw Laura behind him in the living room, tying Betsy's hair ribbons. "Come on in," he said and Beth walked in behind him. "We're relieved to see you," he told her seriously.

Laura stood up, her face a picture of pale consternation. "Beth," she said. The name was almost a question. "Are you all right?"

"Yes," Beth said, and the relief Laura showed touched her.

"We saw in the papers that it was all over. They released you and everything."

Beth sat down in a chair and Laura busied herself with goodbyes until Jack and Betsy had gone out. She understood intuitively that Beth had to talk to her, only her, to set things right with herself.

When they were alone she came and sat on a hassock beside Beth's chair—the leather chair that Jack liked so well.

"I came to tell you the truth about a few things, Laura," Beth said softly. "I won't take much time."

"Have some breakfast with me," Laura said, but Beth shook her head. "Some coffee then?" and without waiting for an answer Laura sprang up and went into the kitchen. Beth didn't want her hospitality. She didn't want to watch Laura's warm concern turn slowly to disdain when she found out that Beth had deserted two children and her husband. The children, mercifully, had been kept out of the papers. It was up to Beth to confess their existence to Laura.

Beth came over to the stove where Laura was arranging two cups and saucers.

"Laura, please," she said, touching her, hand gently. "Don't do this. You may not want to look at me after I tell you—tell you—"

"You don't have to tell me anything, Beth. I trust you," Laura said. "I love you. Friends don't need to apologize to each other."

"Yes, they do. Sometimes it's the only way."

"We've said too much to each other already. The less we say to each other, the happier we are together." And she smiled intimately.

"I can't help it," Beth said miserably. "There's one thing more."

"Have your coffee first, then," Laura said with a sigh, pouring it and carrying the cups to the sunny breakfast table. She sat down and looked up at Beth expectantly.

"I'm still married," Beth blurted fearfully after a tight little pause. She stood rigidly by the stove, forcing out the words with an effort of will. "I have—I have two children." She stopped to steady her breath, to quell the shakes, shutting her eyes for a second. "I lied to you. I had made love to other women when I saw you before. Not just you. Vega—Vega—" She broke down and had to turn away.

"I know," Laura said softly. "I know it all. You don't need to tell me, Beth. Come sit down."

After a stunned pause, a hiatus of disbelief and relief both, Beth cried, "You know! You know—all that—about the kids, about—"

"Yes. All of it." Laura held out her hands and Beth came toward her, trembling, and suddenly sank to her knees and put her head in Laura's lap and wept. "How?" she said. "How did you know?" She looked up with a quick premonition. "Charlie didn't try to see you, did he?"

Laura shook her head. "My father," she said, stroking Beth's hair. "My bastard of a father, who still loves me in spite of everything. I wonder why I still love him?" She looked away, perplexed.

"Your father?" Beth felt a stab of regret go through her. She should never have trusted him.

"He wrote to me," Laura said. "He told me about you. Just a couple of days ago, after all that stuff in the papers. He said he wouldn't have written even then, but you were in such desperate trouble and he thought I ought to know. And you know something? I'm glad he did." She was really surprised at herself. "I never thought I could care about him again, when we quarreled years ago. Not after what he tried to do to me. I would never have broken down and written him myself. But I worried about him. I've thought a lot about him these past years, now that my life is so much happier. So in a way it was a load off my mind to hear from him."

"He promised me he wouldn't write," Beth whispered. "He promised me he wouldn't interfere with your life again. I should never have told him about you behind your back."

"Maybe not, but it all turned out all right," Laura said. "Now I'm glad. No, really, honey. If you had asked me first I would have said no. So maybe it's for the best, because I would have been a stubborn fool if I'd refused. He was so curious about Betsy. I guess the idea of being a grandfather really tickles him. He didn't know he was until you wrote him about it."

"And all these days you've known about me," Beth said, raising her head a little to look up at Laura. "You knew what I was, what I'd done, and you didn't despise me for it."

"Oh, but I did. At first," Laura admitted. "I was good and mad at first. But I think I've gotten over it. What good is it to stay mad?

It doesn't help things at all. Besides, everything you've done these past few weeks you've done in a fog. I know that."

"I did some terrible things to you, Laura," Beth said. "I've lied to you and betrayed you to your father and accused you of bad faith and—"

But Laura put a restraining finger on her mouth, and then, to Beth's surprise, she kissed her. It was a pardon for all the sorrows, big and little, Beth had caused her. It was an end to pity and a start to love without illusions, the tender love of friends.

"Please," Laura said. "It's over now. You told me everything. I wouldn't have asked that of you. I gave you a chance to get out of it, and you had the guts to go ahead and tell me on your own. That's enough for anybody, Beth."

And Beth understood, looking at her, that she really meant it. She was not angry or hurt. She had had her moments of temper when she heard from her father, but they were past and Beth had missed them. And Beth knew, too, that if Laura still loved her the way she had loved her once, long ago, she would be furious now with jealousy and disappointment. There could be no more eloquent testimony to the change in Laura's feelings than the gentleness and affection Laura showed her now.

"I came so far to find you, Laura," Beth murmured. "I thought it was terribly important to revive your love for me; I thought that that by itself could save me. I wanted you to think of me the way you did when we were roommates in school." She gave a small self-deprecating laugh. "You know, I wonder if it isn't true after all."

"If what isn't true?"

Beth walked slowly to the breakfast table and sat down opposite Laura, fingering her coffee cup cautiously. "I wonder if I didn't need to find you in order to define myself. It's wiped away a lot of my delusions about myself—just knowing what your delusions about me used to be. It's taught me a lot, too. More what I am not, and can't be, than what I am. But even so, that helps."

"You've been through a lot of hell to find what you were looking for, Beth," Laura said. "If I helped in any way, I'm glad."

"So am I." Beth smiled at her warmly and finally took a sip of fragrant coffee. She felt much better, though she couldn't have said why. She should have been thoroughly ashamed of her deceptions. But she felt more hopeful than shamed, closer to happiness than despair.

"I want to thank you for the crystal candlesticks," Laura told her. "I keep forgetting. They're lovely."

"I got them the same day I saw Charlie's Scootch in the toy window. Lord, I was so afraid to come and see you. So excited. It seems like a million years ago already, and it's been only a week or two."

Laura studied her over the rim of her cup. Her eyes were smiling. "Do you still think you're in love with me, Beth?" she asked.

Beth shook her head, feeling a little sheepish. "I've been in love with my daydreams. My past. My hopes. Everything but reality. I never knew you, Laura, until now. I guess I never was in love with you—the real you. I was in love with what I thought you were."

"With what you thought I could do for you," Laura grinned. "And I tried so hard to live up to it, years ago. I tried so hard to be what you thought I was, for fear of losing you. God, I loved you, Beth."

They gazed at each other quietly for a moment.

"Loved? Past tense? It's all over, then?" Beth said, almost wistfully. *You aren't loved like that very often in one lifetime,* she thought. It was a wrench, even now, to see it end.

"All over but the good part," Laura said. "The part about being friends. Only the pain and the romance are missing, and we've both had too much of them. Feels good, doesn't it? To have somebody who knows everything about you, and still be able to love them. To get rid of the damned misunderstandings."

"Yes," Beth murmured. "It feels good." Impulsively she reached across the table and grasped Laura's hands. "I don't need you now, Laura. I'm not desperate anymore. I can make it on my own. And I have you to thank for opening my eyes."

"I wasn't very nice about it," Laura said.

"You couldn't afford to be. I wouldn't have seen the truth if you'd been nice about it. You did it right." And in a spasm of gratitude she pulled Laura's hands up to her lips and covered them with kisses. "Thanks," she whispered. "Thanks, Laura darling."

The phone rang and startled them both into a laughing fit. Laura got up and answered it from a small table around the corner in the dining room. "Yes," she said. "Hi. No, she's here. That's what I said." And she swung around to smile at Beth who returned the look, mystified. "Do you want to talk?" She held the phone out, chuckling.

Beth was seized with alarm. She half-rose from her chair. "It's not Charlie, is it? Does he know where you are?"

Laura shook her head. "It's Beebo."

Surprised and pleased, Beth took the receiver from Laura and answered. A sudden fluttery feeling grabbed at her stomach and she felt curiously like a teenager talking to her prom date.

"How are you?" Beebo said. "It's all over, I see by the papers. I would have called you or come down to see you, but I was afraid there was already too much going on. They would have done a double-take if I'd showed up. Might have kept you over a day just to explain me."

Beth laughed with her. "Thanks, Beebo," she said. "I don't know why I called you from jail. I just thought you'd understand." She knew very well why she'd called Beebo, and she was trying too hard to keep their talk casual, the way she had when she'd fallen in love once or twice before in her life. She recognized the symptom with a shock.

"I'm flattered," Beebo said and she wasn't kidding. "Well, what's next? Where do you go from here? Back to Charlie?"

"No. We talked it all out when he came to get me. I'm going to stay in New York a while, I guess. Maybe I can find a job."

Laura took the phone back and asked Beebo over. Beth felt a sweet shiver of anticipation at the idea of seeing her once more. All at once it was important that her hair be combed right, her lipstick smooth.

Chapter Twenty-three

WHEN SHE CAME SHE HAD COFFEE WITH THEM—THEY WERE ON their third cups—and she listened quietly while Beth explained what she had been through with Vega—and what Vega had been through with her, for she didn't spare herself or her faults.

She felt a slow, lovely enchantment going through her at the sight of Beebo; just the sight of her tired, handsome face pleased her oddly in a new and special way. She could not even fib to herself that it was simple gratitude anymore. It was too strong for that.

When Beebo asked her later if she could take her home Beth agreed without thinking. But suddenly she had to admit, "I don't really know where I'm going. I don't have a home."

"Back to the hotel?" Beebo said.

"I guess so."

"That's no place for you at a time like this," Beebo told her. "Come home with me. It's not luxurious but it's a hell of a lot friendlier."

"Thank you," Beth said quietly, without even arguing. "I'd like to."

They said goodbye to Laura with promises to call her soon and went down together in the elevator. "It's funny," Beth said. "I was coming up in this same elevator a couple of hours ago and wondering how I'd feel when I went down again. Scared and ashamed, or just glad it was all over."

"Which is it?" Beebo said, leaning against the wall of the elevator and looking down at her.

"Neither," Beth admitted, smiling.

"What, then?"

"I guess it's closest to...a sort of happiness," she confessed shyly. "Or hopefulness, maybe."

Beebo touched her face gently with her hand, a gesture she had used once before and that delighted Beth. "You've been through enough to whip anybody," Beebo said. "I don't know if it'll help to think of this, but you know, a lot of strange things have been done in the name of love. In the search for love. And for the love of women. Crazy, silly, unreasonable things, some of them. You've just made a journey across the continent to find yourself. But the real journey was into your own heart. Isn't that so?"

Beth nodded as the sliding doors opened, and they walked into the lobby. Beebo pulled her aside and talked to her. "Let me finish," she said. "I want you to understand this. For the love of women I've made a fool of myself, just like most of the men I know. And a lot of the girls. I've suffered like an idiot. At least what you suffered had purpose and reason to it. You've learned from it. I'll tell you one thing," she added with twinkling eyes, "the silliest goddamn thing I ever did was fall for a girl I hated for years."

"Who was that?" Beth said.

"You."

Beth dropped her gaze and a warm thrill suffused her. She could feel her face turning pink and she didn't mind at all. Perhaps it was real or perhaps it was all a dream. She didn't know or care. All she knew was that Beebo was offering her a chance at happiness and she asked only that chance. It might work out, it might not. But she had life and youth and even courage now, and looking into Beebo's fine, worn face she felt a solid reassurance. Beebo's eyes promised shelter, they promised love, they promised that glorious undeserved chance at contentment that Beth had no right to expect from fate. But there it was.

Beebo's strong hands held her shoulders. "I understand, baby," she said softly. "I understand. If that makes any difference to you."

"It does. All the difference in the world."

They walked out of the lobby together, hand in hand.

THE END